The Shepherd's Walk

The Shepherd's Walk

from the manger to the cross and beyond

a novel

MARIAN RIZZO

WordCrafts Press

To my Neighborhood Church Group: Pastor Wayne and Lynda King, who provide the lesson; Paul and Kay Blake, who host the location; and members Peggy, Betty, Joanna and Vicki.

"Day by day continuing with one mind in the temple, and breaking bread from house to house, they were taking their meals together with gladness and sincerity of heart, praising God and having favor with all the people.
~Acts 2:46–47a

Chapter One

The Lord is my Shepherd; I shall not want.

~Psalm 23:1

4 BC, Judea

I was 15 years old the night the angels came.

My brothers and I were tending our father's sheep on the plains of Judea, a Sabbath day's journey from our farm in Beit Sahour. I was the fourth son of Osiah ben Shallum and his wife, Marita. Our sister, Sophina, entered the world two years after I did.

My parents named me Jesse after the father of King David, who once grazed his sheep on the very land where I now stood. My main goal in life was to one day have my own sheep farm. I loved my work as a shepherd, and though it was among the least favored of occupations in the land, it offered me the freedom of being outdoors and doing the kind of work I loved. Like my ancestors, I carried a sling to ward off predators, a rod to confront attackers, and a staff to nudge wayward sheep back to the fold.

My attire was simple. A linen tunic with a wide belt cut with pockets to hold my earnings, a woolen cloak for protection from the chill of night, and a sheepskin blanket to raise as a shield against snow or rain. I was quite content and did not mourn for the ornate attire of the rich. On that memorable night, I'd come to the field with a sheepskin bag filled with enough food for the next two or three days. I carried a ram's horn of goat's milk, and nearby was a well where I could refill it with fresh water.

Night was falling. I drew in a breath of the crisp evening air and turned my attention to the rumble of activity on the western road. The caravans had been coming for three days. Some of the travelers rode on camels or horses. Others came on foot, their hunched shadowy forms rippling against the horizon. The glint of the setting sun fell upon their raiment. The jingle of their harnesses wafted across the plain, as they moved closer to the Holy City.

A footstep sounded on the stony ground behind me. I turned to see my eldest brother, Bartimaeus, approaching. The big man thundered close, like a lumbering ape, half man, half beast, with a full, tangled beard and a head of billowing hair. His broad forehead was lined with annoyance. His dark eyes flashed with irritation.

"Look at them," Bartimaeus boomed. "They come from afar, obeying Caesar's decree to register in their native towns and pay his required taxes." He shook his head in disgust. "Will the oppression of the Romans ever end?"

"Be at ease, Bartimaeus." The soft reprimand came from our brother Eli, who'd suddenly joined us. "The travelers will be hungry. They'll buy our sheep for their supper, and with Pesach and the Week of Unleavened Bread upon us, we will sell most of our lambs for the daily sacrifices. Our pockets will be full, our barns will be empty, and we'll be able to retire at home."

Eli's lip curled with arrogance. Slowly, the curl stretched into a smile, but the haughty light in his eyes remained.

Bartimaeus grunted. "As you say, Eli." Our big brother could have won every disagreement with his fists, but for some reason he often backed down when Eli confronted him.

Breaking into laughter, Bartimaeus poked my arm. "And

you, little brother, will have money to spend in the marketplace. Perhaps you will buy a gift for some young girl you have yet to tell us about."

A surge of heat rushed to my face. I shook my head. There *was* a girl, but I did not want Bartimaeus to know. Ignoring the twinkle in his eye, I attempted to turn my brothers' attention back to the approaching caravans.

"Do you think they'll find lodging?" I said.

"The inns might take a few," Eli reasoned. "The people in nearby villages might offer their stables—for a price." He tossed his head and snickered. "Be thankful our father has already paid our family tax near our home in Beit Sahour. Unlike those weary travelers, we have no need to go anywhere else."

I studied my brothers with amusement. Bartimaeus and Eli were as different as night and day. One a big, overgrown ape who said whatever came into his head no matter how insulting, but who also brought much laughter into our home. The other more reserved in nature and rarely concerned with anyone else's needs. Only his own. Suntanned and muscular, Eli had won the envy of the young men in the village, and he'd attracted the attention of the young girls.

I eyed him with a mix of envy and concern. At 19, he was four years older and a head taller than I was. Eli would have no trouble choosing a wife when the time came, but I was troubled about his lack of care for others. I'd seen him walk past beggars without giving them so much as a piece of bread. Once, he stood laughing at a woman who had dropped a basket of vegetables in the marketplace, never bothering to help her retrieve them. And another time, he nudged aside a blind man who'd stumbled across his path. I wondered that one so handsome on the outside could be so dark on the inside.

In contrast, my eldest brother had no outer beauty, but the big ox spent much time in the village mingling with people of low estate. I sometimes followed the sound of his boisterous howling, only to find him reveling with some of his drinking friends or squatting on the ground, sharing his lunch with a beggar.

I would have been content to have Eli's good looks and Bartimaeus' kind heart. But the truth was, I didn't match either one of them. I resembled my third brother, Andrew. We both had curly brown hair and dark eyes, and we were of average height and weight—a little too lean, but strong. We could have been twins had Andrew not been eleven months older.

One big difference between us was that I was content with my life as a shepherd, but Andrew complained almost constantly. Many times he said he wanted to leave Beit Sahour and find his fortune somewhere else.

Even now, Andrew joined us there on the field and immediately began to complain about his lot in life.

"Look at them." He gestured toward an approaching caravan. "They come from afar with their riches, and they look down their noses at us shepherds. They compare us to the hated tax collectors and to the slaves who sweep human waste from the streets of the Lower City. We smell like sheep dung. Our clothes hang on us like rags. While those strangers sit in palaces and at the city gates, we labor day and night in the lowest profession of all."

Of course, I took offense. "You forget, my brother, in the days of our patriarchs, shepherding was a noble occupation. Abraham, Isaac, and Jacob had large herds, and they prospered. David was a shepherd before he became king. And didn't the Almighty prefer Abel's sacrifice over that of Cain?"

Andrew raised his eyebrows at me. "I see you've memorized many of Father's recitations," he said with a hint of disdain. "His ancient scrolls have turned you into a helpless little lamb. No mind of your own, simply follow the shepherd wherever he goes. Well, my brother, you can remain in this humble life, if you wish. But I have other plans." He raised his chin and announced, "I will be leaving soon."

Eli snickered. "You are a dreamer, Andrew. Father will never allow you to leave."

"I won't ask his permission," Andrew snorted.

Having heard enough, I turned away from him and collected an armload of kindling to help our father build a campfire. I carried it to the knoll where he'd already kindled a pile of moss. I set the bundle at his feet and started to walk away when he raised his hand, a signal that he had something important to say to me. I stood before him, suspecting another piece of scripture was about to pour from his feeble lips.

"Trust the Lord to guide you through life, my son. Count your blessings, and seek his guidance," he said as, piece by piece, he added my kindling to the pile of smoldering moss. Then he straightened and looked me in the eye. "As I told your brothers when they were your age, it is time for me to give you a portion of my sheep as your own. Separate those you choose and notch their ears with your letter."

"Thank you, Abba," I said, thrilled that he'd brought me one step closer to owning my own sheep business. I reached for my rod and left him to tend his fire.

Eager to claim my flock, I entered the enclosure my brothers and I had erected only that morning. The circle of rocks and branches spanned a large area, enclosing our father's entire herd of animals. I strolled past the clusters of ewes, and passing my rod over the backs of those I had claimed, I numbered them. Twenty-seven in all, with more lambs expected within the next few days. I paused by each one to make a cut on the ear, making them my own. There was Abigail, my favorite, staggering under the weight of her bulging abdomen. I drew close, gave her a pat, and carved the letter "J" into her ear.

Only three years ago Abigail herself was a tiny lamb, struggling to stand on four spindly legs. Her dark face and soft brown eyes had won my heart. Now she was about to deliver her first. Abigail had been laboring for the past five hours. She swayed with each birth pang, and her cries grew louder and more pitiful. I feared she might drop to the ground and roll onto her back, a dangerous foundering we shepherds called being cast down.

Cast down, I mused. *My favorite ewe will not be able to breathe or right herself. If that should happen, I could lose Abigail and her offspring as well.*

I stayed close by her side and waited for the little one to show. The hours passed. Then without warning, Abigail wretched, gave a piercing cry, and bent low to the ground. A lamb slid from her in a pool of blood. The little one let out his first cry, the most precious sound of the night.

"He's a good one," Eli said over my shoulder. "Unblemished, to be sure." He nodded his head. "I am rarely wrong, Jesse. Trust me. It won't be long before he's ready for the altar."

I choked on Eli's presumption. I could never sacrifice Abigail's firstborn. Nor did I want to prepare him for someone's supper table.

"I will call him Reuben," I said, claiming him as a favorite. "He'll be used for breeding and nothing else."

I proceeded to notch his ear with my letter.

Eli shrugged and let out a grunt. "Whatever you say, Jesse. He's your lamb."

Abigail settled on the ground and began to clean her babe with flicks of her tongue. She nuzzled him and purred into his neck.

There, on a spread of grass on the plains of Judea, I breathed in the earthy scent of mother and newborn child. A new life had come into the world, and it belonged to me. Eager to share the news, I left the lamb to its mother's care and joined my father by the campfire.

"I have a newborn," I boasted. "My Abigail has delivered a fine male."

My father smiled, nodded in acknowledgement, and leaned back against his mat. Expecting him to be asleep soon, I pulled my lyre from my pack, squatted on the ground beside him, and began to strum a favorite melody. My brothers joined us there. Our hired workers unrolled their bedding and settled on the plain. Except for the one who had drawn the lot for the first watch at the gate of our sheep enclosure, they could rest until it was their turn to stand guard. Neighboring shepherds also caged their flocks and began to lay out their own sleeping mats. Peace settled on the Judean wilderness.

Breathing in the still night air, I was about to begin another song, when I was startled by a bright light breaking through the darkness. Wonderful, soul-stirring music filled the air. I set down my lyre and stared into the blinding mist. A lone figure hovered there. He wore a white robe, bound at the waist with a golden girdle, and his face shone like the sun. I trembled at the overwhelming sight of him.

My brothers began to stir. Other shepherds left their places on the field and drew close. They froze like pillars of stone, their upturned faces bathed with wonder in the brilliant light.

"Do not be afraid," the visitor said. "I bring you good news of great joy that will be for all people."

I leaped to my feet and offered a hand to my father to help him stand. My brothers gathered around us, their faces radiant. Even Bartimaeus' stony features softened in the light of the heavenly aura.

"Caesar has sent an emissary," Eli concluded. "We are being called into service."

Andrew shook his head. "Roman officials can't hover above the earth in such a manner. Besides, why would Caesar consider us poor shepherds for any kind of service?"

"This is no emissary of Caesar," Bartimaeus decided. "It has to be an angel." He raised a hand. "Be still now and let us hear what he has to say."

I pondered the visitor's words. "*Good news ... for all people ...*" Did "all people" mean the message was for everyone, not only us shepherds, not only the Jews, but also the Gentiles? The Greeks? Even the Romans who had overrun Palestine? I held my breath.

"Today, in the town of David, a Savior has been born to you," the angel sang out. "He is Christ the Lord."

The Christ? The anointed one? The long-awaited Messiah? I

shook my head as though sorting through a jumble of uncertainties. *Could this really be happening? Had the Almighty chosen this moment to reveal himself? Had he selected a group of humble shepherds to receive a message our people had been awaiting for centuries?*

From the time I was a small boy I had learned about the Messiah who promised to come and deliver us. But deliver us from what? Like most of my countrymen, I'd been praying for deliverance from the Romans.

"The angel mentioned the town of David," I said, looking toward my father. "Bethlehem Ephrathah was King David's city, wasn't it?"

My father rested a hand on my shoulder. "You speak the truth, my son. The prophet Micah declared that out of Bethlehem Ephrathah was to come one who would be ruler of Israel. It appears that prophecy has been fulfilled."

There it was again, another of my father's recitations from those ancient scrolls he kept in a dried up water jar in Mother's kitchen. He'd filled my head with messages from the prophets. Was it all for this moment?

His eyes sparkled, and he threw back his shoulders. "We can be in Bethlehem within the hour," he said, excitement in his voice. "Perhaps the Messiah is already there, reclining on a ledge, beckoning people to come and sit at his feet."

The angel was speaking again, and what he said next dispelled the image my father had conceived. "This will be a sign to you. You will find a babe wrapped in cloths and lying in a manger."

"A babe?" I said aloud. It was easier to think of him as a grown man sitting on a ledge.

The gathering of shepherds mumbled their puzzlement as well.

"Impossible," Bartimaeus insisted. "The Messiah is supposed to come on horseback, wielding a sword—a brave warrior with his teeth set against the enemy. He is not coming as a tiny babe—helpless and dependant on the nurturing of a *woman*."

He'd said the word, "woman" with such revulsion, it was no wonder he had not yet married.

Our father held up his hand. "Yes, it could be a babe," he said. "The Almighty's ways are not like man's ways. His thoughts are greater than man's thoughts." He looked around at the gathering of shepherds. "Who among us can know the mind of God?"

He no sooner finished speaking when the angel was surrounded by a great company of glorious beings. Their magnificent voices blended as they sang out heavenly praises. The glow surrounding them grew brighter.

"Glory to God in the highest, and on earth peace to men," they sang out. "Good will toward all."

Then as quickly as they had appeared, the company of angels vanished into the night sky, leaving a sparkling trail of mist in their wake. The stardust glistened briefly, then also vanished, and except for the glow of campfires on the plain and a scattering of stars in the sky the place where we stood fell into darkness.

At first, no one spoke. I also stood transfixed, my eyes fastened on the place in the sky where the angels had briefly appeared. I couldn't move. My brothers also had gone silent, even Bartimaeus, who stood there with his mouth open, his eyes filled with wonder. I laughed to myself. My boisterous brother had nothing to say.

Suddenly, a great commotion rose up all around us. The shepherd leaders started shouting orders. They hurried about and hollered commands at their hired men. They selected those who should stay behind to guard their flocks and those who could travel to Bethlehem.

My father also ordered our hirelings to remain with our sheep. Then, his face aglow, he waved an arm at me and my brothers.

"We've received a command from Yahweh," he said. "Let us go now to Bethlehem."

Chapter Two

He maketh me to lie down in green pastures.
~Psalm 23:2a

Without hesitation, my father grabbed his staff and started up the hill toward the town of Bethlehem. I grabbed my own staff and fell in step behind him. I thought about Abigail and her newborn lamb. A few of my other ewes also were heavy with child. Reluctantly, I set aside my work as a shepherd for an even greater calling. I was on my way to Bethlehem to welcome the Messiah.

I hadn't traveled far when I recalled my one adversary had been on the plain earlier that day. Abijah and his father often grazed their sheep close to the same area we chose. Now I wondered if they also had seen the vision. I secretly hoped they had missed it.

From the time we were little children Abijah became my greatest adversary. He competed with me in the marketplace and in selling of our lambs to the priests. We competed in every level of a young Hebrew's life, from scripture memorizations before the village rabbi to staff throwing contests in the village. Sometimes Abijah won, sometimes I did. I could hardly call him a friend, for an intense rivalry had grown between us.

His father troubled me too. I had seen the way he mishandled his ewes, often punishing them for straying from the flock, unaware that those who strayed were likely trying to find a safe birthing place. His treatment of his rams, however, was quite different. They thrived under Jedediah's care. He provided the best grazing areas for his rams, and he took care to bathe their faces in olive oil and herbs to ward off the pesky flies, but he allowed those insects to swarm about his ewes, nearly driving them mad.

I wondered if the two of them also had seen the vision and were already on their way to Bethlehem. What if they arrived there before us and received the Messiah's blessing? I stopped and looked back toward the plain where I'd last seen them. They were nowhere to be seen. Another thought struck me. Perhaps they had moved their flock closer to the Jordan and had missed seeing the angels. A smirk crept onto my lips. It could be I had been chosen to witness the heavenly vision and Abijah had not.

"Jesse, get moving!" My brother Bartimaeus broke into my thoughts. "Our father has almost reached the ridge and you are lagging behind," he called out from close behind me.

Shaking off my concern about Abijah, I turned my attention to the road ahead. Eli and Andrew had already joined our father and they were about to move beyond the limestone ridge. Bartimaeus stomped close to my heels and then passed me. Other shepherds stood out like dark shadows all around us. Like the swell of a river, they advanced farther up the hill, leaving me behind. Quickening my step, I moved upward on the stony path and passed the villages in the foothills, among them Beit Sahour. I envisioned my mother and sister attending to their sewing and baking, unaware of the frenzy that was taking place outside our cottage. I climbed faster in pursuit of my father and brothers.

I moved beyond the inns where people from the caravans had found rooms for the night. Those who'd been turned away had settled on the hillside, some in tents, others on blankets they'd spread on the open ground. Weary travelers sat hunched around campfires. Then there were the caves where innkeepers sheltered the animals of their guests. This was the lowliest kind of shelter of them all.

As I trudged up the hill, I leaned against the staff I had carved from a branch of a sycamore tree. It was a sturdy piece of hard wood. I'd made the top smooth and had included a little hook for lifting wayward lambs from a pit or a cluster of brambles. The sharp end was meant to serve as a weapon against an attacking wolf or wild boar, though I hadn't yet had to use it for such a purpose. To prove the staff belonged to me, I'd carved my initial in the top—a prominent "J," like the one I notched in the ears of the sheep my father had entrusted to me. Now that staff was aiding me in my climb up the hill.

Leading the way, my father turned toward the village of Bethlehem. I was amazed at the old man's sudden burst of energy. It was as if the angel's message had instilled new life into him.

Exhausted from the climb, Bartimaeus had fallen behind again. Panting and grumbling, he stumbled up the slope in my footsteps. I drew close to Eli and nudged his arm.

"My heart has not stopped pounding," I admitted. "Nothing like this has ever happened to us. Look at my hands, how they tremble."

I thrust an open palm at my brother. My hand shook like a dry leaf in the wind.

Eli snorted and put his own hand out. It was rigid. I looked at his face. There was no sign of anxiety. He raised his chin. His silver blue eyes flashed with confidence. He had no need to speak. His lip curled with determination. Puffing out his chest, he wielded his staff and moved on, leaving me to stumble along behind him.

I often thought my brother foolish and even dangerous, at times, for he tended to follow his impulses instead of relying on our father's direction. Many times he listened to our father's commands and then went and did whatever he wanted. That was Eli. A man with far too much confidence in himself and nearing disaster with every turn.

Keeping close to his heels, I marched on in silence. The hillside overflowed with travelers. They'd brought much activity to the sleepy little villages with their blazing campfires, loud singing, the playing of flutes and tambourines, and laughter rising from tired but happy people who had at last reached their destination. A gentle breeze carried the aromas of singed lamb and roasting vegetables, along with the sharp odor of animal droppings and the disgusting scent of travelers who hadn't bathed in days.

I hurried past them and went through the village gate to Bethlehem Ephrathah with its spread of one-story, white-washed dwellings, their flat roofs separated by walls and stairways. The tiny village had about 300 residents. Visitors had nearly tripled the number in the last few days.

Our father and the other leaders began to search the rock-hewn caves where people housed their donkeys and goats.

I was perplexed. "Why are they searching the stables, Eli?"

He smirked at me. "Have you already forgotten what the angel said? The child will be found in a manger. Where else do you think a manger might be?" Shaking his head at my ignorance, he strode on ahead.

"A manger," I mused. "Yes. The angel didn't say an inn or a house or even a tent. He said a manger."

We passed the first few caves, and, finding no babe and no manger, we moved on. The leaders scanned the rooftops, looked inside tents, even peeked in the doorways of homes. But, none of them announced the discovery of a newborn babe, nor did I hear a baby crying.

Some of the shepherds began to mumble amongst themselves.

"Perhaps we were mistaken," one said.

"Yes, we may have misjudged what was told us," added another.

"Maybe it was a trick of the eyes," a third suggested.

"Or a mistake of the ears," said someone else.

Two of them expressed concern for the well-being of their sheep. They chose to return to the field. They stumbled down the hillside, their shoulders slumped in disappointment.

"We should leave with them," Andrew said, scowling.

But our father stood firm. "No. We will search one more

house. One more inn. One more stable." And he thrust back his shoulders and moved ahead with the others.

Puffing with annoyance, Andrew turned away and started down the hill behind the two who had left. "One of us has to look after our sheep," he mumbled. "We can't depend on our hirelings to tend them all night."

I considered joining him, but only for a moment. My father, Eli, and Bartimaeus, had moved on. I looked at Andrew, now growing smaller in the distance. Then I looked at the others moving farther into the town with confidence. I pondered the angel's message for a moment, and I chose to stay. Pressing ahead, I caught up with my family. My father continued to check stable after stable, cave after cave, and every cleft in the rock wall. Deep into the village we went and finally approached an inn that was bursting with activity. A crude shelter was carved out of the rock wall beneath the inn. A soft glow emanated from its opening.

The shepherds moved toward it. I followed and found it to be a typical stable where travelers could shelter their beasts. But there were no animals in that place. No donkeys or camels. No sheep for the sacrificial altar. Straw was strewn about the ground. In the center of the room stood a rock-hewn feeding trough. On one side of it knelt a young man. He was dressed in a poor man's traveling clothes. He gazed at us with welcoming eyes. On the other side of the trough lay a young woman, shrouded in veils and blankets and looking tired and worn. Yet, instead of sadness, the woman's face glowed with joy, and her eyes shone like stars.

I stepped cautiously inside and drew closer to the trough, stunned to find a babe inside, exactly as the angel had foretold. The child was bound with strips of cloth, again as the angel had described.

The shepherds swarmed around the manger. My father drew close, sank to his knees, and bowed his head. His display of obeisance sent a shudder through me.

"Woe is me!" he said, his voice breaking. "I am undone, a

man of unclean lips and I dwell in the midst of a people of unclean lips; for my eyes have seen the King, the Lord of hosts."

The words were familiar. My father had drawn them from the scroll of the prophet Isaiah, one of his favorites. I shook my head in wonder. Nearly everything that came out of that man's mouth had been written by a prophet long ago. Yet he knew what to recite at the appropriate time.

I dared to move closer, my eyes on the child. The babe stared back at me, and I gazed trembling into those knowing eyes. Eyes that unveiled my very soul—the good and the bad— exposed before the Holy One who lay there. My heart in my throat, I couldn't speak, could only stare in wonder. I dropped to my knees and bowed my head, humbled beyond belief. And I knew my life would never be the same.

Chapter Three

He leadeth me beside the still waters

~Psalm 23:2b

Though filled with awe, I pulled my eyes away from the child and turned my attention to the young couple. The father, whose name turned out to be Joseph, beamed with pride. He said his wife's name was Mary and that they had traveled there from their home in Nazareth. They'd come to Bethlehem in compliance with the census. Shortly after they arrived, Mary's labor began. Joseph immediately sought out comfortable lodging, but the only shelter available was the stable where we had found them.

I knew immediately this was the fulfillment of the angel's message. Then I recalled the scripture my father had recited by the prophet Micah that *Out of Bethlehem Ephrathah would come one who would be ruler of Israel.* I stood frozen, astounded that the scriptures were unfolding before my very eyes.

My musing was shattered when, suddenly, my brother Eli pushed past me and boldly rested his hand on the edge of the manger.

"The babe's name?" he asked the man named Joseph.

"Jesus."

I knew several people who bore the name Jesus. Some preferred the longer form, *Yehoshua.* Some favored Joshua. The truth was, they all meant "Savior." Then another name came to mind, one mentioned in my father's scroll of Isaiah. The prophet had named Emmanuel as the one who would deliver the nation of Israel. "God with us," I mused. And I knew without a doubt. This child had to be the Messiah, Israel's long-awaited promise. A lump rose to my throat and tears rushed to my eyes. If this truly *was* the Messiah, then we humble shepherds had been given a wonderful gift.

Humbled beyond words, I lingered by the manger. The child's shining eyes continued to peer back at me. Unable to move or speak, I held his gaze, and my heart surged with joy. Everything around me began to fade. In that moment, there was no rock wall, no straw on the floor, no remnants of animal waste, no fire warming the room, and no other people. Only the babe and me. The other shepherds' excited whispers diminished. So did the outside noises—the campers' conversations, the braying of donkeys, the raucous laughter pouring from the inn, and all the other sounds of life—they all receded into nothingness. All that remained was the babe, staring back at me, and I sensed a bond unlike anything I'd ever known.

Then, for reasons I could not explain, I was overcome by the sins of my past. The intense hatred I'd held for Abijah now troubled me. I thought about the fist fight we'd had over nothing important, just two boys vying for dominance in front of our friends. I sometimes cut in front of him to sell my lambs to the waiting priests. And I resented when he cut in front of me. I hated him for it. Then there was the time I cheated in the throwing of our staffs. No one noticed when I took a step forward, crossing the line of restriction.

Other wrongs surfaced, hurtful accusations I'd made against my brothers. The piece of jewelry I stole from the merchant's stall as a gift for my mother. The lies I told, and the chores I had left undone though I'd promised to complete them before the day was over.

Before the innocent babe in the manger I crumbled under the guilt of my sins and could hardly bear the weight of them.

I knew the Ten Commandments of Moses. I had recited them often enough. Now they returned to plague me with accusations. If this truly was the Messiah then he knew all about me. I could hide nothing from his knowing eyes.

Slowly, I backed away from the manger and left the stable.

Once outside, I breathed deeply of the night air, but I found no relief. Uncertain about what I should do, I waited there for my father and the others to join me on the street. I was tempted to follow Andrew back to the field. But he'd already disappeared down the hillside, and I didn't want to travel the hills alone in the darkness. Nor did I want to go back inside the stable and face the child again.

I paced from one end of the street to the other, crossed the doorway several times. Still there was no sign of my father and brothers. I dropped to my knees, bowed my head, and begged the Almighty to take away my guilt. Why, after so much time had passed, was I thinking about the wrongs I had committed years ago? Most of my transgressions had seemed so small at the time I had brushed them away as meaningless mistakes. Now I admitted what they were. Sins of pride. Sins of greed. Sins of selfishness. And all of them committed against the Almighty God of Heaven. I wondered, was the same thing happening to my brothers? Were they also facing a moment of truth?

I knelt there for a long time before my father and brothers joined me. The other shepherds who were with us poured out of the stable, filled with excitement.

"We must spread the news," one of them shouted. "Deliverance has come to Judea."

Armed with a powerful message that the Messiah had finally arrived, they swarmed over the hillside and spread out in all directions. As they departed, singing and praising God, I was humbled by their fervor. I looked to my father and brothers for direction. Eli and Bartimaeus had begun to argue. Bartimaeus wanted to return to the field and tell the good news to those who had remained behind, including the Edomite hirelings.

Eli wanted to follow the other shepherds into Bethany and Jerusalem. There was that curl of his upper lip again.

"We have a message to deliver," Eli insisted. "I can hardly wait to see the surprised faces of those we tell. Our words will travel far. We will be known throughout the land."

It was my father who ultimately made the decision for us. He frowned at Eli, a silent reprimand against my brother's arrogance.

"We will return to the plain, tend to our sheep, and bring the message of deliverance to our neighbors in Beit Sahour," he said, his tone final.

I was grateful for his decision, for I had no confidence in myself. I couldn't run around declaring that the Messiah had come. People might treat me the way they had treated other self-proclaimed prophets. They would mock me as a foolish boy. They might even throw stones at me. I did as my father had said. I went back to the plain, but I didn't know how I might tell anyone beyond my own household.

On our way back to the field, we stopped by the house to relate the news to my mother and sister. They responded with such elation, they even had their servant girl leaping about and shouting for joy. A celebration had erupted under our roof. But what did the angels expect us to do next? Should we carry the message beyond our household? Who else could we tell? The hirelings? The neighboring shepherds? Jedediah and his worthless son?

When the excitement settled down, Andrew stepped to the middle of the room, demanding our attention. "I'm leaving home one of these days," he declared. "I will no longer tend sheep. I will make my own way. I will travel great distances, and wherever I go I will spread the news about the Messiah coming to Judea."

Our father stood rigid, his face like stone. "What are you saying, Andrew?"

"Don't worry, Father," Andrew said, his tone imploring. "My travels will open doors for me to tell about the miracle of the angels. None of the other shepherds will be able to take this message to the ends of the earth. But I can."

He said this with a prideful sparkle in his eye.

Bartimaeus shook his head. "You are a fool to think the Almighty has chosen you alone," he said with a huff. "As for me, I will remain in Beit Sahour. The people in our village also need to know about the miracle that has happened. I will tell them, and I will leave it to them to take the message to places beyond."

Eli was nodding in agreement. "I know exactly what we should do," he said with an air of confidence. "We can spread the news in Bethlehem and Bethany and throughout all of the villages, and then we can go to Jerusalem. We can begin here. In time we can go a little farther and then a little farther, perhaps even to Galilee."

Unlike my brothers, I trembled at the thought of having to tell people about the vision. Who would listen to a young shepherd boy? People might call me a simpleton and claim I was telling stories. They would laugh me to scorn.

Still, I knew something special had happened. A part of me wanted to do as the other shepherds had done, run off and declare to others what I had seen and heard. I recalled with clarity the angel who hovered above me on the plain, his entire being aglow, and then more angels surrounding him and singing a heavenly song. I wanted to be a messenger, like the angels, but with a much easier calling.

Then the truth struck me. Even if I could mend my tattered robe, scrape the sheep dung off my sandals, and wash myself free of the filth of the field, I was still a lowly shepherd.

Downcast, I left our home with my father and brothers and hurried back to the field, the one place where I belonged. I slipped past the hireling at the gate and searched for Abigail and her newborn lamb, found them curled up in a ball of wool, and smiled down on them with the kind of love a father might have for his children.

Contented that I had found them well, I retreated to my

mat on the grassy knoll by my father's campfire. I rekindled the embers. Then I settled down, and pulled my wool cloak over me to ward off the chill of night. Aside from my mother and sister, I had not yet told a single soul about the visitation. What was worse, our women got most of the message from my father and brothers. I fell asleep believing I had failed the angel's edict.

I awoke to a sliver of morning light on the eastern horizon, grabbed my rod, and went to check on my sheep. The hireling greeted me at the gate, eager to be relieved of his watch.

I pulled away the bramble barrier and the sheep dropped in line for their release onto the plain. I extended my rod over their backs and counted them as they escaped from the pen into the field. My own flock now numbered twenty-eight with the newborn that had arrived last night. Then, along with a dozen goats under my care, they spread out to enjoy the dew-laden blades of early morning grass. I sat on a rock and kept an eye on them as they gathered in clusters, my newborn lamb frolicking around them, happy with his newfound freedom.

My brothers also released the sheep our father had entrusted in their care. Except for Andrew. As usual, he paid little attention to his flock, but set them off and found a place to relax apart from them. Like always, he got our two dogs chasing a stick. Those scruffy dogs preferred Andrew to the rest of us, probably because he tossed them scraps from his lunch bag and ran his hands playfully over their furry bodies. With a snap of his fingers, he could get them following him wherever he went. If only he paid as much attention to his sheep.

I stared after him for a moment and, despite our similarities in appearance, I had to admit our differences. He loved those two spirited dogs, while I preferred the quiet gentleness of my sheep. He anxiously awaited the day he could leave our humble home. I was content with our life in the field.

I turned away from the sight of him romping with his two dogs and went to bathe myself at the well. I returned to the knoll, and squatting on a slope near my sheep, I opened the lunch my mother had packed, then savored the sweetness of the berries and figs, the sharpness of the goat cheese and olives, and I thought myself fortunate, aware that some shepherds had little to eat when out on the plain. I quenched my thirst with the goat's milk, then went to refill the horn with fresh water from the well. All the while I kept a protective eye on my flock.

As the sun crept skyward, Bartimaeus went to our farm and returned with our donkey and dray in preparation for a journey to the Holy City. The dray could easily carry ten of our unblemished lambs for the sacrificial altar. With Pesach upon us and the Week of Unleavened Bread to follow, a continuous wisp of smoke rose from the temple.

After preparing several ewes for the marketplace, Eli turned to look at me and raised an eyebrow as if to say, *Well, are you coming?* Then he spun away and overtook Bartimaeus who had started out, pulling behind him our donkey and the dray filled with our lambs.

I tied a rope to one of my ewes, tossed a lamb across my shoulders, and hurried after my brothers. As expected, Andrew remained behind. He'd altogether lost interest in the sales. The angels' vision had made little difference in him except to fuel his desire to leave home. He'd said he wanted to deliver the heavenly message beyond the borders of Judea. But I saw his desire for what it really was. A chance to leave home and never look back.

I compared Andrew's fervor with the way Bartimaeus and Eli had reacted to our experience on the plain that night. They also wanted to spread the word the angels had bestowed upon us. And they each had devised a different plan. At the end of each day, after our work was done, Bartimaeus spent every evening in Beit Sahour and came home late at night raving about the great number of people who had surrounded him in the village, eager to hear about the heavenly vision. Because of Bartimaeus, I was certain the entire village believed the Messiah had finally come.

And Eli? He performed the story like an actor on a stage. Starry-eyed young women flocked around him, urging him on.

He responded with arrogance and added so many embellish-ments the original story was lost amidst his boasting.

Even Mother and Sophina said they couldn't wait to tell other women about the amazing miracle their men had wit-nessed. Father went to the farms of nearby shepherds and shared the good news. I was most likely the only member of my family who was afraid to approach my friends and tell them what I had witnessed.

Many questions pestered me about the night the angels came. Was it a dream? But how could all of us have had the same dream? Was it a miracle? And why had we lowly shepherds been worthy of such an honor?

I struggled to bring back every detail—the brilliant light, the angel's voices, the music, the singing, the journey up the hillside to Bethlehem, and the encounter with the babe in the manger. I couldn't deny something wonderful had happened that night.

The vision, I conceded, must have occurred, for I was fully awake. The angel gave us specific directions. There *was* a family in a stable in the town of Bethlehem. The babe was *real*. But was he the Messiah?

Whether anyone believed my brothers' stories remained an unanswered question, until several fathers came knocking on our door seeking to offer their daughters in marriage to Eli.

My father's answer was always the same.

"I must first marry off Bartimaeus, for he is the eldest," he told the hopeful petitioners. They departed disappointed, because no one thought Bartimaeus would ever marry, which meant Eli might never marry, and perhaps Andrew and me as well. Unless we could challenge that ridiculous rule, the rest of us boys were doomed to a wifeless existence.

Though our father had imposed several rules upon us, he was a fair and just man under most circumstances. My appre-ciation for my father grew one day when I walked to the edge of our property that joined our neighbor's land. I watched in horror as Jedediah prodded one of his ewes with the pointed end of his staff and drew blood. Then he complained loudly and beat the animal about the head with his rod because her pelt had been ruined by the bloody stain—a stain he himself had caused.

Without concern for my own safety, I stepped across the barrier between our farms and confronted the man, who was raising his rod a second time. "Do you want to harm her?" I said, blocking the blow. "She's a helpless animal, Jedediah. And look, she's heavy with child."

"She attempted to wander off," was his only defense.

"Look at her. She's about to deliver a lamb." I gestured toward the sagging bulge of her abdomen. "Or lambs," I added, aware that she may have been carrying twins. "If she needs to wander, it's because she's trying to put distance between herself and the others. She needs a private birthing place."

Jedediah stepped back, an embarrassed grin tugging at his lips. He lowered his rod and shrugged with noticeable unease.

"You're supposed to be their shepherd, not their jailer," I said. "My father would never stand for such harsh treatment of a helpless animal."

My words appeared to have touched him, because the next thing he did was lead the struggling ewe into a private pen and shut the gate. With renewed confidence, I stomped away and went straight to our barn. I located my brother Bartimaeus cleaning the enclosure, and I told him what I had seen at Jedediah's field.

He shook his head in disgust. "You have to understand, Jesse, Jedediah doesn't know much about the sheep business. He inherited his farm from a wealthy uncle. His ewes are of the Egyptian breed—poor quality, long legged, slight of wool, and with little meat on their tails. Jedediah eliminates the blemished males when they are young. He slaughters them shortly after they are born or removes their male parts and overfeeds them to increase the meat they will provide. None of the other shepherds in Judea use the knife in such a cruel manner."

I grew quiet then and allowed my gaze to stray to the neighboring farm. Abijah was out in the field tormenting his sheep. He waved his rod like a club, prodding them away from the brush, forcing them back to the field. I narrowed my eyes at him knowing the stupid boy was following the path of his father.

I nudged Bartimaeus. "Last week, that boy bolted in front of me in the marketplace while I was about to make a sale." I grabbed a rake and began to help my brother clean the enclosure. "Not only does he interfere with my sales, he lowers his price on sacrificial lambs and wins the approval of the temple priests. He beats me in the marketplace *and* in the temple."

Bartimaeus shrugged. "Do your work, Jesse. Ignore him and he will go away in time."

"I can't ignore him. One day I caught him sneaking around our pen. The next morning two of Andrew's newborn lambs were missing. I was certain Abijah had stolen them, but I had no proof. And Andrew wasn't aware they were gone."

"The notches in our animals' ears are sufficient proof," my brother reminded me. "All we need to do is search them out in Jedediah's herd."

I shook my head. "The mark is easily altered," I insisted. "Think about it, Bartimaeus. Jedediah's mark is similar to mine. His worthless son keeps his knife ready to make the extra cut."

"Relax, Jesse," Bartimaeus said, sniffing. "For a long time we've been in competition with that family. The war started when I was your age, and that was more than ten years ago."

I bowed my head. "There's something else," I mumbled.

Bartimaeus stopped raking and tilted his ear in my direction.

"There's Ariel," I admitted, a hot flush racing to my face.

"Oh, yes, the physician's daughter," he said, tossing his head and laughing. "So, your competition with Abijah goes beyond selling sheep and throwing staffs. You have set your eyes on the same girl. That should prove interesting."

I struggled to remain calm. It was difficult enough to admit I had feelings for the girl, now my brother was making light of it.

Bartimaeus pressed his forefinger to his lips and with a twinkle in his eye he said, "Don't worry, Jesse. Your secret is safe with me."

I puffed out an exasperated sigh. "It won't be a secret much longer," I said, setting my rake aside. "I am planning to ask Father to arrange a contract."

The concerned wrinkle on my brother's brow disturbed me.

"I plan to approach him tomorrow," I said with a little less confidence.

Bartimaeus shook his head. "You forget, I'm the eldest and I've not been pledged to anyone. Father has failed to get the Beit Sahour fathers to agree on my behalf. I'm afraid, my brothers will have to wait."

"Then hurry up and choose someone. Surely you have set your eye on one of the village girls."

Bartimaeus snickered. "Not possible. But go ahead, approach our father. Who knows? Perhaps he will forget this senseless rule and agree to your request."

Chapter Four

He restoreth my soul

~Psalm 23:3a

Bartimaeus left me standing there, pondering his urging to approach our father. The big ape sauntered off to the field and strolled among his flock, stroking this one and patting that one on the head. He ran his hand over their wooly backs and smiled with contentment. He bent to lift a baby lamb and drew it against his chest. Though gruff with nearly everyone else, Bartimaeus took quiet pleasure in his animals. He cared for them with a gentle hand and a soft-spoken word. In a sense, Bartimaeus was a little like one of his sheep—gentle and dependent on the shepherd, a heavenly one who cared for him. Watching my brother I was more aware of our relationship with the Almighty than I'd ever been before. It was what my father had pounded in my head since I was a child. "Yahweh is our shepherd, and we are his sheep," he'd said multiple times.

Though my brothers and I had come from the same strain, we were each one different from the others. While outwardly appearing gentle and kind, Eli had a hidden meanness that surfaced at unexpected times. He was handsome and charming on the outside, but plotting on the inside. Few people looked past his outer appearance. But I knew the truth. I'd seen that curl of his upper lip when other men challenged him. He strode into town with his shoulders back and his fists balled up, ready for a fight. The village girls flocked around him, their faces turned up at him, their eyelashes fluttering in his direction. I shook my head at their ignorance.

Then there was Andrew, who'd ungratefully refused his share of our father's flock. Though he consented to tend the sheep for a while, he never wanted to own them. He handled the birthing and the sales, pocketed a good portion of the money, and gave what was left to our father. Andrew worked like a hireling, and like the hirelings, he cared little for the sheep but expected just rewards for his labors. He didn't draw close to the animals as Bartimaeus and I had, didn't mingle with the other shepherds, the way Eli did, but simply lingered in the field looking forward to the day he could depart.

When I asked Andrew about his future plans, he responded with a wink of his eye, and a simple, "Someday."

For now, the four of us worked the sheep farm, tilled our mother's garden, and prepared grain and seed for the next year's crop. We made it through the spring plantings and the shearing of wool. The summer growth filled our cupboards, then autumn was upon us. We pulled in the remaining harvest, and it was time for another trip to the Holy City. Bartimaeus set about preparing our dray. In addition to seven full-grown sheep for the marketplace, we gathered a dozen unblemished lambs for the temple sacrifices. It was the month of Tisri, the onset of Sukkoth, time for the making of booths and more sacrifices for the temple.

The Holy City again was overrun with Jewish families on a pilgrimage from afar. We needed to get our animals to the marketplace ahead of the other shepherds. In the past, Abijah and his father, Jedediah, often sold all of their animals before we stepped foot inside the temple court. Stirred by a desire to beat them, I helped Bartimaeus load the remaining lambs, bound them with cords, and readied several ewes for the hike up the mountain. Eli and Andrew cut a few lambs from the flock and mounted them on their shoulders or tucked them under an arm.

I was about to help Bartimaeus finish tying off the load of sheep when I happened to turn around and spot Eli bending to pick up my Reuben. I gasped in shock. Then, dropping the cord from my hand, I stumbled over my own feet running to stop him.

"Not this one," I shouted in a panic. I pulled Reuben from my brother's grasp. "This one stays."

I returned Rueben to the field and sent him off with a pat on the backside and a whispered, "Be good."

Eli's brow quirked in surprise. He opened his mouth to speak. Then, shaking his head, he backed off.

"That lamb is my favorite," I snapped. "He will never go to the temple. He will never be sacrificed."

I stomped past Eli and joined Bartimaeus for the trek up the hill.

In recent months, our father had ceased joining us in the tedious climb. These days, the aging man directed us in our work, and that was the end of his participation. As we departed, he shuffled inside the house, most likely to take a nap. His health was failing, but he had four sons to tend to the family business, plus the hirelings we brought in from time to time.

Bartimaeus moved ahead—the biggest and strongest of us, driving our load up the hill like it was made of feathers. I tied a rope to three ewes that were fit for sale, and I flung a prize lamb over my shoulders for the priests. Using my staff for support, I followed Bartimaeus up the long, difficult hill, confident that we could sell them all.

The Holy City marketplace had come alive with visitors. The Sukkoth celebration had begun. Celebrants marched by, shaking palm, myrtle, and willow branches in remembrance of the Israelites' forty years in the wilderness. The outer court resounded with the strains of pipes and lyres, tambourines and bells. People milled about the stalls, searching through bright colored fabrics, dazzling gemstones, and elegant pottery. Pockets and purses jingled with coins ready to be spent. I was struck with the aroma of lamb roasting on a spit over a fire, unleavened bread pulled fresh from an oven, olive oil burning in the temple lamp stands. Children ran through the crowds, shrieking and laughing. Merchants shouted their prices and beckoned shoppers to their tables. Roman soldiers stomped along the pavement, keeping order of the crowd, their burnished swords flashing in the sunlight. Several priests stood guarding the waste-high wall that separated the Gentiles' court from the place of the Jews. They crossed their arms in pious resistance and narrowed their eyes at the Greeks who ventured too close.

After disposing of our sheep in the marketplace, my brothers mingled with the shoppers, while I went to the temple area with the sacrificial lamb. I approached the priests and was about to offer my animal when someone shoved me aside. I stumbled, nearly dropped my lamb, and struggled to regain my balance. Irritated, I turned to look at my assailant.

"Abijah," I snarled. "I should have known it was you."

He charged past me with two lambs, one under each arm. I scrambled to my feet, but before I could cut him off, one of the priests was already dropping a handful of coins into his palm. Abijah cast a sneer in my direction and strode away counting his coins.

Two of the priests left with my adversary's lambs. One priest remained by the wall. He took one look at my lamb, shook his head, and departed after the other two. Anger rose within me like a raging fire. Abijah looked back, snickered, then melted into the crowd.

I stood helpless and sought for another priest to buy my remaining lamb. If none came, I'd have to sell it in the marketplace for a much lower price. I heaved a sigh and began to look for a buyer.

In the end, I settled for less than the lamb was worth. Thankfully, Bartimaeus had sold every animal on his dray. We returned home at the end of the day with a good part of our flock gone. Aside from the selling of our sheep, we came home to find our father waiting to direct us in additional labor. In honor of our ancestors' journey in the wilderness, the Jewish people constructed shelters similar to the huts they used in the desert. Everywhere makeshift enclosures popped up on the hillside outside the city and on the flat roofs of village homes. My brothers and I needed to build a similar structure for us to sleep under each night during the weeklong observance. As we did every year, we erected huts on our rooftop abode using palm fronds and willow branches. When finished, we went inside the cottage to count our wages.

"Supper is ready on the hearth," my mother greeted us. She smiled and began to ladle a hearty stew into a bowl.

Despite the long hours she must have spent laboring in her garden or washing clothes by the stream, she moved around the kitchen with the energy of a woman half her age. Her cheeks had a pink flush from having spent time over the fire pit. Her black hair was pulled into a knot behind her neck. Her dark eyes sparkled with the joy of a mother tending to her flock. Her sons had come home and were once again seated at her table.

Our mother kept a clean house. She labored long hours to make life comfortable for us, and though her hands became cracked and raw from her labors, she never complained. Meanwhile, our father stood tall and proud over his home. He ruled us with a gentle hand, often using the scriptures in support of his rules and admonishments. The two balanced each other well. One standing charge over us, the other assisting with love and care.

While Father paced the floor and spouted scriptures, Mother went on her knees to speak quietly with Yahweh. I wondered that Osiah ben Shallum had been able to find such an ideal helpmate. I thought about Ariel and wondered if we, too, might make such a match.

Though Ariel came from a wealthy home, she didn't flaunt her position. Like my mother, she behaved in a meek and quiet manner. The daughter of a physician in the village, she delivered medicines to the sick and sometimes accompanied her father when he visited his patients. She appeared to have a servant's heart. I imagined her as a wife, greeting me when I came in from the field and offering a meal, the way my mother did.

For the moment, we squatted on large pillows in our usual places. In the center of the table was a bowl of lamb stew, a platter piled high with unleavened bread, and several baskets of dried fruit and nuts. Around the perimeter of the room oil lamps cast a warm glow over our gathering, and I settled back in the comfort of home. Following my mother's blessing, my brothers and I scrambled to fill our stomachs, and our sister, Sophina, sat in a corner of the kitchen with a bowl on her lap. She ate her meals there, apart from the men, as was our custom. But she wasn't alone for long. Mother soon joined her.

As we ate, we passed our earnings to our father. He counted the money and divided the portions among us.

Then the usual argument erupted between my brothers. Ever since we witnessed the angels and visited the babe in the manger, Bartimaeus and Eli had been arguing about the significance of that special evening. This had become a nightly ritual.

Bartimaeus dipped a piece of bread in the stew, then raised it to his mouth. His eyes glowed with the memory.

"How could it be that we humble shepherds were chosen to see angels?" he said, reviving a conversation that had come up once too often. "We were unworthy of such a gift."

"Unworthy?" Eli snapped. "Who else but us shepherds received such an honor?"

Bartimaeus frowned at him, then turned back to the food on his plate. He tipped a bowl of stew to his lips, wiped his mouth with his hand and glared at Eli. "While you have repeatedly boasted about that night, as if you had something to do with it, I'm happy to simply share the good news. There is nothing special about us, my brother, only the message."

Eli shrugged. "So, why not boast a little?" he snarled.

"Only a little?"

"Who else can say they met the Messiah on his first day on earth?"

Bartimaeus was quick to answer. "The truth is, we had no real part in this miracle, except to have witnessed it. We're messengers, Eli, and nothing more." He tore off a piece of bread and was about to bite into it.

"Then we're fools!" Eli raised his voice. "We're nothing but puppets. Actors on a stage prepared by the Almighty."

Bartimaeus dropped the piece of bread. "We should not go around boasting. We're simple shepherds who have been given a great gift."

Eli leaned across the table and drew close to Bartimaeus. "Yes, and other shepherds were with us that night. They witnessed the miracle too. And they vowed to spread the word." He leaned back, a smug smile on his face. "Have you so soon forgotten, Bartimaeus? We told the news to the shepherds and hirelings who had remained behind that night. We took the message to people in the village and whenever we went to the marketplace. We did our part. We spread the word. There is no pride in that. Only honor."

Bartimaeus didn't back down. He straightened and lifted out of his seat. The big man towered over Eli. "You can deny the truth, my brother. But I have seen how you prance about the village, claiming glory for yourself. Instead of spreading a wonderful message to others, you want to prove how wonderful *you* are."

They were blood brothers, yet they were behaving like bitter enemies. Our mother hovered nearby, concerned wrinkles on her forehead. Our father stopped eating. He sat back and eyed my two brothers with displeasure.

"So many opinions," the old man said, his voice soft. "So much uncertainty. Only one thing is certain, my sons. The angel spoke to us, that much I know. He called us to witness a miracle. He said it was for all men. *All men.* All we did was follow the command to go to Bethlehem. After witnessing the miracle, we wanted to go and tell others. As the prophet Isaiah said, *"Here am I, Lord. Send me."* Our work is to do the will of Him who sent us.

He looked at each of my brothers, in turn. First Bartimaeus, then Eli, then Andrew. At the last, his eyes settled on me and remained. I was the youngest of his sons. He must have known I paid attention to his scripture readings, perhaps the only one among my brothers who memorized and vowed to obey them. Yet, despite what I had stored inside my head, I could not dispel the guilt in my heart. Surely, the message of the angels held a greater purpose for me than to be a humble messenger. I wanted to please Yahweh, to obey Him, and to serve Him. Thus far, I had failed.

Chapter Five

He leads me in the paths of righteousness for his name's sake.

~Psalm 23:3b

That night I settled on my mat and stared at the canopy of palm branches we had erected in honor of *Sukkoth*. My father's final words swarmed into my head. I didn't know why but I was certain he'd spoken them directly to me.

"Here am I, Lord. Send me," Father had recited. Those words kept repeating inside my head. As the youngest of the boys in our family, I didn't think myself worthy of being called into service. I wasn't even a man yet. So, why hadn't my father directed his words to Bartimaeus or Eli? Or even Andrew? Why did I feel like they'd been meant for me?

The clinking of metal drew my attention to Andrew's mat. He was sitting upright and was digging into his bag of coins. He'd been keeping an account of his earnings, as though his departure depended on how much money he had acquired. The most frugal of us brothers, he rarely spent his money in the marketplace, but hoarded away his earnings. I began to believe he truly would leave us one day.

Unable to fall asleep, I also pulled out my coins, but for a different purpose than Andrew's. I spread the pieces of metal across my mat. I had enough to purchase one or two flat-tailed rams from one of the shepherds who lived near the Jordan where the grass was lush and well-watered. Their flat tails provided a great amount of succulent meat and plenty of oil for cooking and for lighting lamps. Those rams promised to breed well with my healthy ewes.

I dropped my earnings inside my leather pouch and shoved it under my mat, fulfilling my plan to one day have my own thriving sheep business. For now, I remained content to labor under my father's rule.

The cottage at Beit Sahour had a long history. It was home to my ancestors since the Diaspora ended and my forefathers returned to Judea from captivity. The land was there for the taking. Because of the vast pastureland, they settled near Beit Sahour and took on the business of herding sheep. They passed the property and their methods from one generation to the next. I barely remembered my grandfather. The old man died when I was extremely young, and all I could recall was someone who looked a little like Bartimaeus—big and burly—but with a head of pure white hair.

Grandfather Shallum used to take me on his knee while he recited the scriptures. "Yahweh is watching over you," he said one day, and I trembled at the thought of the God of Heaven seeing everything I did. Then he added a comforting phrase. "When you turn to the right or to the left, He will direct you and guide you."

I suppose it should be no surprise that my father continued those teachings. Just as his own father had done, he recited scriptures to us boys and always included a lesson in life. Each of us responded in a different way. Bartimaeus listened intently and then made light of the message, bringing the rest of us to tears of laughter. Eli shrugged with indifference. Andrew was the most stubborn of us. He rarely listened to Father's recitations and insisted there was much more to learn from life's experiences. The true teachers of wisdom existed beyond the borders of Israel, he insisted. Now he was planning to leave home and find them.

I followed an entirely different path from my brothers.

Unlike Bartimaeus, I saw nothing humorous about the scriptures. Many of them were filled with judgment and condemnation. Still, I didn't ignore them, as Eli did. And I didn't know if Andrew was correct, for I'd never been outside the confines of Judea.

Our father encouraged us to memorize the holy verses. I did not put forth any effort to do so. You can imagine my surprise when some forgotten lesson rose to my aid at the exact time I needed it. I wasn't indifferent to the recitations, as Eli had been. Somewhere deep inside me, I knew they had value. And while Andrew wanted to go the world's way, I was content to remain on the farm, marry the girl of my dreams, and spend the rest of my days raising sheep. To some, that dream may have been senseless, but to me, it was heaven.

I had already learned the business of sheep raising according to the methods my father's ancestors had passed down to him. I knew how to ward off wild animals and robbers who came in the middle of the night. I could protect my sheep from the flies and mites that tormented the face and the nose. A smear of olive oil and herbs kept those vicious insects away. It was obvious when a ewe had been attacked. She stamped her feet, shook her head wildly, and scrambled away from the rest of the flock in search of a cool and restful place.

I often caught sight of Jedediah's animals frantically shaking their heads to rid themselves of the flies. I knew he had not bothered to treat them for the onslaught.

There were other dangers, such as poisonous weeds that sprang up in the grazing areas. Our father had insisted we prepare the ground well before setting our flock free to graze. We used hoes, rakes, and even our bare hands to remove the weeds and to stir up the good vegetation. This took hours of hard labor, often beginning early in the morning before the sun rose, and continuing into the night.

My brothers and I also sought out fresh water from the snow-fed streams that flowed down from the mountains, and we looked for wells that had been filled by a recent rainfall. Many an evening I fell on my mat exhausted, but satisfied that I had cared well for my sheep.

Jedediah and his lazy son did little to groom their pastures, and they allowed their animals to wander into stagnant pools and even wade into rivers, an added danger, because sheep cannot swim and could have been swept away.

In my opinion, the feeding and care of our sheep was a sign of the way we cared for ourselves and for our own young. I wouldn't eat poisonous plants or drink polluted water, so why would I allow my sheep to do so? The truth was, those ignorant animals didn't know the difference. They needed our guidance and protection.

"A man who takes good care of his sheep also takes good care of himself and his family," my father said more than once. Then he recited another scripture from the scrolls he kept in the water jar. The ritual was always the same. A life lesson followed by a supporting word from one of the prophets. Or the opposite. A reading from a scroll, followed by my father's message.

In a way I could understand why Andrew wanted to be free of all this. Not only did he complain about Father's unending "words of wisdom," he let us all know he did not enjoy the work of a sheep farmer.

"While I rub the oils on my sheeps' faces, those nasty flies attack *me*," he whined. "I hate working the soil. Let them eat the grass that grows on the farmer's land." And, "I'm tired," he'd moan, at the end of a long day. "There has to be easier labor."

It was no secret Andrew longed for a different life and a different job. I suppose I could have had a similar dream. But a hesitation rose up within me, whether it came from fear of the unknown, or from not wanting to disappoint my father, or from simply feeling comfortable where I was.

Only one thing concerned me more than the care of my own sheep, and that was the way other shepherds treated their flocks. I was particularly annoyed whenever I caught Jedediah mistreating his ewes. The man had no patience with them. One day, when I was laboring near Jedediah's property, I again caught him mistreating his ewes. Instead of leading them onto the field in the normal fashion, he poked and prodded them with the sharp end of his staff. Though I'd seen the man doting over his prized rams, he showed little patience with his ewes. I made my way over to the fence that separated our two farms and prepared myself for a confrontation.

Abijah stood nearby, his arms crossed, a smirk on his lips. I stepped in front of him, but before I could speak he shook his fist at me.

"Go home, Jesse. You have no business here."

"You and your father need a lesson in caring for sheep properly. Look at how he's prodding those ewes. A good shepherd never prods them into submission, he gently leads them. Why don't you and your father learn the proper work of sheep farming?"

He laughed scornfully. "Tend to your own worthless flock, and we'll see whose lambs sell in the marketplace next week."

I left Jedediah's field shaking my head in disgust. They had inherited the farm from a rich uncle. Neither one had grown up around sheep. The business fell into their laps, and they didn't know the first thing about it. Jedediah had a vile temper. What kind of legacy was that man leaving his only son?

Because of that man, my appreciation for my own father had grown. Osiah ben Shallum presented an example I wanted to follow for the rest of my life. His concern for his animals was but a sample of how he also treated other people, especially his family. He sometimes set aside his own work to help my mother with her household chores. Though he had four sons and one daughter, he never showed partiality to any of us, but treated all of us fairly, though differently, according to our own character traits.

Besides caring for his sheep, he had provided for us. Though our family was large and our cottage small, it was adequate. We four boys slept on the roof. Our parents and little sister stayed downstairs in sleeping quarters separated by a veil. Over the years, our father increased the size of the house his ancestors had passed down to him. He gave our mother a larger indoor kitchen with shelves carved into the rock wall and, in addition to the outdoor fire pit, he used river rocks to make an ample indoor hearth for cooking and baking. Our table stood a foot off the ground, surrounded by plush pillows for our comfort.

Though Sophina helped Mother as much as she could, Father hired a young girl from Beit Sahour to work as a servant in our home. She came to our cottage for a few hours every day and then returned home to her own family.

Very early in the morning, Mother and Sophina hauled water from a cistern in the center of town. I was surprised, one day, to see my father lifting the heavy jar off my mother's shoulder and walking home with her. My heart softened a little more toward him. I wanted to treat my own wife with the same kindness one day, proof that I was learning more than how to memorize scriptures from him. I was learning how to live what the scriptures said.

With winter coming, we led our sheep into the enclosures and barns where they could be protected from the harsh weather. Then, in late spring, we took a few at a time into the shearing pen, plucked the wool from their backs or cut it away with a sharp knife. We washed the wool in the stream and carried it inside where the women were ready with their hand-held spindles and loom. Mother and Sophina created cloaks and blankets to be sold in the marketplace. Our buyers preferred the white wool, which could be dyed any color of the rainbow.

Like most sheep herders, we kept our rams in a separate pen until the appropriate time for breeding. We paired the best ewes with the rams. We butchered a few for our own use and sold the rest in the marketplace. Every spring we proudly displayed unblemished lambs before the priests who purchased them for sacrifices. The need was especially great during observances, such as Pesach and the Day of Atonement. Though we could not claim to be wealthy, we lived a comfortable life.

For relaxation, my brothers and I played athletic games in the field behind our cottage. We competed to see who could hurl his staff the farthest. We wrestled, held foot races, hiked into the nearby hills, and, at the end of the day, we sat around a campfire and challenged each other to see who could tell the best story. At bedtime, our conversations turned to the females who lived in our village.

Eli had the most to say about the Beit Sahour women, for he was extremely popular among the girls. Bartimaeus remained quiet at such times. He'd rarely shown interest in any girl in particular. Andrew mentioned one or two names, but his interest in females paled beneath his desire for adventure. I had nothing to say. There was only one girl who'd caught my attention, and I didn't want to give my brothers something to tease me about. It was bad enough I'd confessed to Bartimaeus my interest in Ariel.

As for my sister, Sophina, she often begged to be allowed to join us. But, being so young and a female, our mother kept her at home, learning the ways of a homemaker.

"Sophina's place is with her mother," our father cited another rule. "Girls don't run and play the way you boys do. They could be injured, or worse."

The only thing worse than an injury was death. I certainly didn't want my little sister dead, so whenever she came around where we boys were playing, I sent her home.

And Father's recitations continued, mostly pointed in the direction of his four sons.

"The lips of an adulterous woman drip with honey," he said, and he looked directly at Eli. "Smoother than oil is her speech."

Then, he shifted his gaze from one to the other, until all of us boys had been addressed. "Listen to me," he concluded. "Keep far from her."

Even when he ended with that, I knew I had to stay away from the village girls. Only one had caught my interest, and that was Ariel.

To my happy surprise, Sophina developed a friendship with

Ariel and often invited her to our home. Though I was certain Ariel did not come there to see me, I caught an occasional glance in my direction.

The only child of the town's physician, she lived in a more affluent section of the village. Yet, she did not appear to be prideful. She brought gifts to my mother—a special bread from her mother's kitchen, a multi-colored veil she had woven on her loom. Surely, my father's warning was not about her. No such threat swam within those innocent blue-green eyes.

Nevertheless, my father's lessons from the scriptures kept coming. The day I bragged about having bred a greater number of unblemished lambs than my brothers had, Father's appraising stare had me bowing my head in shame. He concluded with, "Pride goes before destruction and a haughty spirit before the fall."

Even our mother could not escape the rebukes that came from our father's lips.

"Better is a dry morsel and quietness with it than a house full of feasting with strife," was the scripture he spouted the day she disagreed with a decision he had made.

My father's recitations stayed with me for weeks after. Try as I might, I couldn't shake them from my head. One verse nearly brought me to my knees, when he said, "A wise son accepts his father's discipline, but a scoffer does not listen to rebuke." I didn't know what I had done to deserve such a warning, but it left me examining my actions for the rest of the day. Even as I lay on my mat trying to sleep that night, I thought over my entire day and recalled every word I had spoken and every act I had committed, without ever knowing my fault.

In spite of all the lessons and reprimands, and maybe because of them, peace prevailed in the home of Osiah ben Shallum. Our father appeared content to have instructed us, and none of us had complained about it. Each of us boys simply accepted this was our father and this was how our life was going to be. What we did with those lessons was different for each one of us.

More than a year had passed since the angels' visit. It was close to the start of summer when the big argument erupted, stirring up a windstorm inside our little cottage. We had only moments ago sat to eat our evening meal when Andrew once again spoke of his discontent.

"Word is out that a caravan of merchants is preparing to leave for the coast," he said, reaching for a wedge of unleavened bread.

Our father didn't say a word, but kept on eating.

Andrew tore the bread in half. "I'd like to go with them."

Father still didn't say anything and kept eating.

My brother dipped the bread into his bowl of lentil stew, but his eyes were fastened to our father.

"There is a great fortune to be made buying and selling goods," he went on. "I want to try my hand at such work. I'm better with people than with sheep. I know I can succeed." He chewed and swallowed the bread, then added. "I seek your blessing, Father."

A dark silence fell upon our gathering. I stared at my brother, surprised that he was so bold to suggest a different life for himself. Our father also set his eyes on him, though he did not appear to be shocked as I was. Instead, a flaming red anger rose to his forehead.

"My blessing? *My blessing?*" Father slammed his fist on the table. "Why should I give a blessing so you can go against our family tradition? Our ancestors established this business of raising sheep." He shook his head. "What you ask is *impossible.*"

Andrew discarded the other half of his bread. "You don't understand, Father. I will not stay away forever. I will come back, and when I return, I will bring some of the most wonderful presents." He flashed a hopeful glance at our mother. "I want to travel across the sea to Alexandria. The city of the Greeks is rich in glassware, pottery, and special fabrics." He returned his gaze to our father. "And they produce the sharpest blades for shearing sheep, and tools for building enclosures and tilling the ground, and sandals that wear well when traveling great distances."

The old man's eyes sparked with interest, but only for a moment. Then, collecting his thoughts, he frowned and shook his head again.

"I will not give my blessing to this nonsense. You are not of age, 17 years old and still under my care. You cannot leave this house except to guide the sheep to the field and to tend to our needs in the village."

Bartimaeus and Eli had stopped eating. Their eyes traveled back and forth between our father and Andrew. I couldn't move, couldn't even breathe. Our mother stood frozen with a platter in her hand, and Sophina pressed her fingers to her ears and scrunched down on her cushion in the corner. It was like the air had been sucked out of the room.

The truth was, Father could blame himself for Andrew's restlessness. When Andrew was a youngster, Father took him to Alexandria to sell sheepskin blankets and to purchase a gift for our mother. The Phoenician goblets and jade-handled knife hardly made the trip worthwhile. Soon after they returned, Andrew began to whine about his boring life. He wanted to go back to Alexandria, to live there and learn a different trade, one that didn't subject him to bleating animals.

As time passed, Andrew became less interested in the care of our sheep and did his chores as part of a daily routine. He spent hours dreaming about a different future, though he never could say exactly what he wanted to do. On several occasions, he packed a sheepskin bag and left home, only to return a few hours later and set about unpacking. In time, Andrew's discontent grew into bitterness. Many evenings, after a long day of laboring in the sheep cote, he came into the house scowling and muttering curses under his breath.

"I need to breathe!" Andrew whined one evening. "I need to get out of this place. I'm dying here. Please, Father, if you want me to live, give me my inheritance and let me go. But first, give me your blessing. I *need* your blessing."

Our father's scowl melted into despair. Andrew had worn

him down. When the old man finally spoke, his voice trembled.

"Go, if you must," he said. "I am tired, Andrew. Tired of your complaining. Tired of your disrespect. I no longer have the strength to fight you." He pointed at the door. "Go out in the world. Find your way. I will give you your inheritance, but you will go without my blessing."

Father rose from the table and removed a sack of coins from its hiding place beneath the hearth. "This should equal the price of the sheep you have called your own," he said. He spilled a pile of coins on the table. Then he returned the bag of remaining coins to its hiding place, and he disappeared behind the curtain into his sleeping quarters. He didn't come out for the rest of the night.

The next morning, I awoke to find Andrew gone. I knew he wouldn't be back. I feared for his life and ached that I might never see him again. Yet, I knew he had to go.

I went downstairs to the main house and found my parents in a sad embrace. Mother was weeping uncontrollably. Father stroked her back, and uttered words of comfort.

Bartimaeus and Eli stood by the door like two statues, their faces stunned with grief. And poor little Sophina sat curled up in the corner, sobbing into her hands. At the sound of my footstep, my father stepped away from my mother and faced us.

"The name of Andrew will not be uttered again in this house," he said with a finality that sent a chill through me. "I no longer have a third son." And before turning away, he uttered three final words. "I have spoken."

Chapter Six

For weeks after, a troubling silence settled on our home. My brother's departure left me feeling like someone had died. I went into a period of quiet mourning, for I'd been forbidden to speak his name.

In the evenings I sensed an emptiness in our upper room where we brothers slept side-by-side. Andrew's mat was gone. There was a big space where it used to lie. At the table where the family shared a meal, his place was empty. In the pasture where the rest of us mixed games and contests with our daily work, the absence of his laughter left a sad void within the wind.

I think I suffered the loss of Andrew more than anyone else. We were little more than a year apart. To me, he was more like a best friend than a brother.

Days passed, Mother and Sophina milked the goats and sheep, used some of the liquid in their baking, then poured the rest into a bag made from the lining of a sheep's stomach and hung it from a rope around our donkey's neck. With every movement the animal shook the bag, eventually churning the milk inside to butter.

We boys got busy with the shearing ahead of the hottest days of summer. The plucking and cutting took hours. We piled the wool in a corner of the barn, cleaned the pelts, and pulled them apart. Mother and Sophina, with the aid of their servant girl, spent the next few weeks spinning the strands into garments and blankets. Each of us got his pick of the finished cloaks. The rest were set aside for market.

During the summer, we moved our animals from pasture to pasture. It didn't take long for them to strip a field clean. By the end of the season our flock had almost reached the Jordan Valley.

Then came the harvest. As he did every year at that time, our father directed us in the storing of grain, the lugging of water to the animal troughs, and the sheltering of our flock inside the barns and pens. Each member of the family labored in preparation for the coming winter. The three of us boys picked up Andrew's portion of the work with no trouble. He'd been little use to us when he was there.

Our mother and Sophina gathered the wheat, corn, and vegetables from our gardens. They ground the wheat and corn into grain and pickled or dried a portion of the harvest, reserving a decent amount for our table.

In Andrew's absence, the rest of us continued to assume his duties. We were faithful to honor our father's edict not to utter my brother's name. Our entire household remained in a state of silent grief. Our two sheep dogs moped about next to the enclosure and buried their noses in the soil, like two old women mourning the loss of a loved one. Even the bleating of our sheep sounded long and low, like a funeral dirge.

I needed to cry, but the sorrow had lodged in my throat, like a big, stubborn lump, though I didn't shed a single tear. If I could only release my grief, perhaps I'd feel normal again.

Winter approached. The women stored preserved fruits and vegetables on shelves already overflowing with pickled cucumbers, bags of nuts, and dried figs and raisins. In the corner stood huge sacks of grain and corn. We had enough food to get us through the harshest of winters.

Bartimaeus and Eli set about butchering two sheep and a

goat. They preserved the meat with salt and a thick coating of olive oil. They hung the carcasses from a rafter inside the barn and out of reach of the two hungry dogs. Of course, I assisted wherever I could, but being the youngest of the brothers I simply followed orders. While I was as adept as anyone in tending our flock and selling the animals in the Holy City, I still had a lot to learn about the rest of our work.

Many of our young ewes were not ready for breeding. We penned them for the winter and fed them dried grass, ephahs of grain, and vegetable peelings. Eventually, we paired them with our best rams, selecting different females at their appropriate time of the month. At least half of them were heavy with child in the spring. After birth, the mother and offspring remained together for several months, until the time of weaning and the selection of the unblemished lambs for sacrifice.

I had accepted this as my life's labor, though there were times when I may have followed Andrew's choice. It had been more than a year since he left. I could only imagine how he was living and what fascinating places he had visited. I didn't have the courage to do as he had done and leave the comfort of home, never to see my family again. Though I obeyed my father's command and never spoke my brother's name aloud, Andrew was always in my thoughts. The old man's edict had me outwardly in obedience, but he could not control what I was thinking. And so, I could remain in a state of mourning for as long as I needed.

Though I was curious about Andrew's different life, something more powerful than my father's order kept me from leaving Beit Sahour. Her name was Ariel. I would miss her greatly if I ever left. I looked for her whenever I went to the village. I couldn't go one day without seeing those sparkling blue-green eyes or catching a glimpse of her long red hair slipping from her veil and caught by a breeze.

One day in the final weeks of winter, I went to the Beit Sahour market to purchase a new set of knives in preparation for the next shearing. Sharply honed blades made our work much easier and protected our animals from the nicks and cuts they sometimes suffered from the dull, rusted blades we used.

I had completed my purchase, which the seller wrapped in parchment, and I was about to return home, when Ariel drew up beside me with a vial of liquid in her hand. Her red-streaked mane swayed with each step. There was a sparkle in her eyes that set my heart fluttering. As she drew closer, a beautiful smile spread her dimpled cheeks. I couldn't help but smile in return.

"May I walk with you?" she said, her eyes drifting to my purchase.

"Knives," I explained, lifting the bundle.

She raised the vial of medicine. "My father prepared this for Sophina. He was concerned about your sister's fever."

I nodded. Sophina had been ailing for the last few days. Hilkiah had come to the house the day before and had promised to send more medicine. He apparently had asked Ariel to deliver it.

I turned a corner, and Ariel got in step beside me.

"I can take the medicine home," I offered, sparing her the long walk.

She shook her head, and her flaming curls swung with the movement. "Thank you, Jesse, but I want to visit Sophina." She stammered then, "To—to make certain the medicine is working."

I smiled at her shyness and kept walking. Unable to get my tongue moving, I kept quiet, though a million thoughts circled inside my head.

"Have you heard from your brother Andrew?" she asked, breaking the silence.

I stopped walking and stared at her. "I am not allowed to speak of him."

She responded with a curious frown. "But, he's your brother."

"That is true, and I will always think of him as my brother, but my father has disowned him and will not allow us to speak his name in our home. Please, Ariel, whenever you visit, honor my father's wishes."

She nodded but remained curiously silent. A dark shadow swept away her beautiful smile.

Then she brightened. "We're not in your house now," she persisted, her smile returning and an impish sparkle in her blue-green eyes. "So I can say his name. Andrew, Andrew, Andrew."

I laughed at her boldness. But I still held back, unsure of my commitment to my father.

"I have not spoken of my brother since the day he left." I said, a wave of guilt sweeping through me. "But I have thought of him often."

"That's a good thing, to keep him alive in your thoughts."

"I suppose it is. I do miss him."

We walked on quietly. Ariel's mention of my brother had revived the pain I'd been trying to suppress. I wanted to speak his name, wanted to acknowledge him no matter where I was. At the same time, I needed to obey my father's command. Ariel must have understood my struggle, for she didn't say another word about it. Placing her hand on my arm, she changed our conversation to the crisp winter weather we were having, the upcoming Passover Celebration only three months away, and the widening of the western road, a project of the Romans who had invaded our land. I allowed her to talk on and enjoyed the sound of her voice.

We arrived at my house before I was ready to say good-bye. I wanted to spend more time with Ariel, but it wasn't to be. My mother was already at the door. She welcomed the vial of medicine with a grateful smile and dropped a few coins in Ariel's hand, payment for her father.

"I'd like to see Sophina," Ariel pleaded.

My mother shook her head, but she offered the girl a compassionate smile. "Dear Ariel, I am sorry, but Sophina is asleep. Perhaps another day."

Then she looked past the girl at the darkening sky. She turned to me. "Jesse, It will soon be dark. Walk with Ariel and assure her a safe arrival home."

I eyed my mother with suspicion. As though aware of my heart, she had given me more time to spend with the girl. Without hesitation, I turned away from the door and guided Ariel onto the path. We walked side-by-side along the winding road that led to the upper part of the village. As we walked together, she talked about a new friend she had made, a girl whose father had opened a metal shop in the village. I hardly paid attention to a word she said, I was so overwhelmed by her beauty. All I could think about was the kind of life we might have together. I had great plans for my sheep business, had already planned to increase my flock by interbreeding with higher quality animals. But I also needed a wife, a helpmate to support me in my chosen work.

"Alabaster jars are so much better than common pottery, don't you agree?" she said, drawing me back to the present.

I stammered an agreement, then looked around, suddenly aware that we had entered the part of the city reserved for the wealthy. The setting reminded me of the great division between our two families. Ariel was rich. I was poor but comfortable. Ariel was an only child. I had three brothers and a sister. She lived in a mansion. I resided in a small cottage, hardly big enough for a family of six. She wore fine clothes purchased from the better merchants in the Holy City. I wore a shepherd's humble tunic and sandals that were nearly coming apart.

But Ariel didn't dwell on our differences. In her many visits to our home, she never boasted about her station in life. Nor did she comment about the sorry state in which she found me. In fact, she appeared to be fascinated by my work as a shepherd. Whenever I spoke about my sheep, her full lips lifted at the corners, and she cocked her head and listened to my every word. On a couple occasions, she begged to walk among the flock with me, and even now, as I walked her home, she asked about my sheep.

"How is your flock enduring these bitter days of winter?" she said gesturing toward the myrtle trees, their branches weighted with frost.

It surprised me that the daughter of a wealthy physician should take an interest in something as ordinary as animals grazing in a field.

"They are well," I responded, though perplexed. Then, encouraged by the curious expression on her face, I plunged into a long speech about my sheep—the battle for dominance, the birthing of newborn lambs, the weaning, the feeding, the selection of the finest for the temple sacrifices. She grew silent, her eyes wide with interest.

"Each one has its own special need," I said, unable to suppress the pride that stirred within me. "Besides feeding and grooming them, I have to be their doctor, in a sense." I kept on, aware that I had mentioned a profession close to Ariel's heart.

She giggled. "What kind of ailments do sheep have?"

I numbered the list on my fingers. "Nose flies. Infections of the feet. Stomach ailments. Attacks by wolves."

"Wolves?!" Her face looked stricken.

I nodded. "At those times I tend to their scars, stop the flow of blood, and apply the proper ointments and herbs."

"Sort of like a physician does?" she said, brightening.

"I suppose. Of course, there is a big difference between caring for sheep and caring for people."

"I know something else about you and your sheep," she said, her tone teasing.

I stared at her with questioning eyes.

"One day while I was in the field picking wildflowers with Sophina, you called out names, as though your sheep were children and you were their father." She giggled then and my face flushed with heat.

I released a sigh. "You're right, Ariel," I confessed. "I've named many of my sheep according to their behavior. Each one is different from the others. Like people."

She released a little chuckle, then eyed me with interest. "Like people? Tell me more."

"Every herd has its own order of command. We call it

butting order. The strongest and most aggressive end up being leaders of the group, while the meekest and weakest tend to follow slavishly. Not only the rams. Even the ewes fight for dominance. Kind of like people, I guess."

I glanced at her to make sure she was still listening, then I continued. "My most aggressive ewe I named Sarah after Abraham's wife. The story says she attacked the handmaid that bore his first son. Sarah's lamb became Isaac. Then there's Hagar, the weakest of the herd. Her offspring is Ishmael."

Ariel laughed, and her eyes sparkled with mirth. I couldn't help but laugh with her. Renewed confidence spurred me on.

"Abigail is the fattest and proudest of all my ewes. She's my favorite. I love her lamb, which I named Reuben, and I never want to lose either of them. Then there's Esther. She's the prettiest of all, but terribly proud. She acts like a queen. When I comb her wool, it lies as it should, no tangles or briars. She tends to stay away from the brambles and the bushes, almost as if she knows they will damage her coat. Her face is flawless, like a queen's, and she lifts her nose in the air, as if she knows she is beautiful. The good thing is, she avoids butting the other ewes, simply allows them to achieve their status, and so she has no battle wounds."

I was aware I had begun to ramble, but Ariel's beaming face urged me on.

"One of my smaller ewes I named Eve. She cries a lot, I suppose because she lost her lamb before it had a chance to take a breath. She's vulnerable, like the first Eve who succumbed to the snake's temptation."

Ariel shook her head in girlish pleasure. "I never met anyone who named his sheep after people from the holy scriptures." Her eyes sparkled with delight. "Or after anyone, I suppose. You must truly care about your animals, Jesse."

She gazed up at me with unmistaken adoration. The sound of my name on her lips sent my heart in a whirl. I couldn't stop myself. I immediately launched into a long, boring speech about the feeding and bathing of my sheep, the brushing of burrs from their wooly coats, and the proper bedding of dried grass and hay for their enclosure. Then there was the shearing process and the gathering of wool for the market. I spoke about guarding my animals when we were out in the field, even exaggerated accounts about driving off wolves, bears, lions, and robbers that came down from the hills. Ariel responded with wide eyes and breathless gasps.

We had entered the upper part of the village, and I suddenly became aware once again of our differences. I had been trying to impress this girl with my life as a shepherd. I had gone beyond the truth and had even made myself into a hero. In all of that chatter, I had forgotten that sheep herding was looked down upon as a lowly profession, one that generally received ridicule from the offspring of doctors and lawyers, not praise as I assumed I was getting now.

The closer we got to Ariel's home the more worthless I felt. Once again my tongue was bound. I had stepped outside the life I was accustomed to and had entered an unfamiliar world. We approached her gate, and all I could do was stop and let her pass.

I stood back as Ariel entered a broad courtyard which in the summer teemed with flowers and vines, but for the moment had lost its color with its life hidden beneath a blanket of frost. Like the buried garden, I had portrayed myself as a wise shepherd when in reality I was a simpleton inside. I stared at Ariel, painfully aware of my low estate. How could I have presumed this girl might accept a marriage contract from someone like me? Such a suggestion would only bring more ripples of laughter, the worst kind.

Still smiling sweetly, Ariel turned to wave farewell. I could not read past that smile, could not determine if she thought me foolish or entertaining. She thanked me for walking her home, and then she disappeared inside. I walked away, humbled, dejected, feeling utterly hopeless. I headed down the hill toward the miserable dwelling I shared with my family. What promise was there for a lowly shepherd boy and the daughter of a prosperous physician? The reality was, no other girl had captured my attention as Ariel had. Was I to remain unwed for the rest of my life?

If I had Andrew's confidence, nothing could stop me from pursuing my dream, no matter how unattainable it appeared. If I were bold and forceful like Bartimaeus, I might loudly take charge and no one would oppose me. If I had the soft-spoken self-assurance of Eli, I could claim my prize with quiet certainty.

My brothers possessed the kind of qualities I desired. The truth was, my adversary Abijah had a better chance of winning Ariel's attention than I had. Though also a shepherd, his father mingled with the higher class citizens in the village. He'd grown rich at the expense of other men he had tricked into a contract with him. He hadn't let his shepherding business stop him from making friends with the elite, but had used it to his advantage.

I had caught sight of Jedediah one day in the Jerusalem marketplace. He boldly approached a group of Pharisees, broke into their circle, and had them laughing in seconds. Abijah also could talk to anyone without hesitation. It was no wonder he had better success than I did in the marketplace and with the temple priests. They had found success as shepherds, not because their sheep were so much better than what the rest of us raised, but because they had the courage and self-assurance we lacked. For certain, Abijah had only to ask for a contract with Ariel and I had no doubt the two fathers would heartily agree.

I arrived home, passed by the animal pen, and went into the house as though walking on a cloud. Ariel was still on my mind. Nothing drew me back to reality, not the bleating of the sheep, not the bustling of my mother in the kitchen, not the aroma of a hot dinner on the table.

I retreated to the upper room, dropped onto my mat and buried my face in my pillow. I lay there for a while, wallowing in self pity, until a nervous whispering wafted up from the kitchen. I strained to hear what my parents were saying in hushed tones on the floor below. I caught the name, "Andrew." It was my mother's voice, breaking my father's long held rule. Though curious, I pulled the sheepskin blanket over my head and tried to fall asleep.

Chapter Seven

Thou art with me

~Psalm 23:4b

I awoke in the middle of the night to a harsh groaning from across our upper room. I lifted my head and rubbed my eyes to clear them. A beam of moonlight illuminated Bartimaeus' strained face. He was writhing on his mat, his nightshirt soaked with perspiration, his mop of hair tangled. I'd witnessed a similar decline to his health many times before. There was no doubt his distress had come from his overeating and drinking to excess.

I raised myself off my mat and dragged myself to my brother's bed. I leaned close, listened for his breathing. A sour odor rose from his lips. He gasped for air. There was one other time, perhaps a week ago, when Bartimaeus struggled to breathe, but his distress lasted for only a short while. I held my breath and waited, but there was no change.

"He's failed again." Eli drew himself up to a sitting position, his mat a short distance away. "Go down and tell mother to bring the potion."

A spirit of annoyance came upon me. Why didn't Eli go down for the potion himself? I was about to question him, when Bartimaeus cried out in agony. Concerned for the big oaf, I flew down the outer stair toward the main house, nearly colliding with my mother on the bottom step. She was already ascending with the vial in her hand.

"Only a few drops remain," she said, tipping the bottle so I could see. "This won't be enough. Quick, Jesse, run to Hilkiah's home, and ask him for another vial."

"It's the middle of the night," I reminded her. "Why don't you use the medicine Ariel brought for Sophina?"

She shook her head. "No, it's a different mixture. Hers is for fever, not for this. Please, go."

Still, I hesitated. "Hilkiah will be in bed."

She gave me a gentle shove toward the exit. "The physician will understand. Go, Jesse, please go."

Mother pulled two coins from her pocket and slipped them in my palm. Sighing, I grabbed my cloak from the hook by the door and started along the upward path to the home of Hilkiah. I had been there only a few hours ago when I walked Ariel home, and now I was returning. The sun had set leaving an icy cold blanket over the town. For the second time that night, I made that same trek up the hill, and for the second time, imposing structures rose up on both sides of the street, once again reminding me of my low estate.

Along the way, I prayed Hilkiah would not chastise me for pounding on his door at that hour. And what about Ariel? She'd likely be huddled beneath a blanket in her own quarters at the back of their dwelling. Perhaps my knock on the door would also awaken her. I imagined getting one more look at the girl, perhaps in her nightclothes. I quickly dismissed the image. I was on a mission to help my brother.

My feet flew over the cobbled path. My heart also had wings, for I was still thinking about Ariel. I worried that this nighttime interruption might damage my chances with the girl. I passed into Hilkiah's courtyard and tapped on the doorpost, gently at first, then louder. I expected one of their servants to answer. But Hilkiah, himself, came to the door in his nightshirt. He did not bear the look of annoyance. Instead, concern overtook the physician's face, and he nodded his head knowingly.

"It's Bartimaeus again, isn't it?" he whispered.

"Yes. My brother is in distress. And it's worse, this time."

Hilkiah's concerned wrinkles relaxed, and he gave me a nod. "I've told your brother many times before, he must leave the spicy foods alone. And he must give up the wine. A little is good for the stomach, but not the amount Bartimaeus consumes. If he doesn't heed my warnings, he will experience more nights like this." Hilkiah's frown returned. "Or worse."

I knew what "worse" meant. The word brought to mind Josebad, the old woman who used to sell handmade napkins in the local market. She drank heavily and died last year of a stomach disorder. Now I feared the same judgment might fall on my brother.

"Please, help him," I pleaded.

Hilkiah released a heavy sigh and raised his hand as though asking me to wait. He slipped back inside the house. Moments later, he returned with a small vial that brimmed with the all-too-familiar, foul-smelling potion that had successfully soothed Bartimaeus' stomach in the past. I winced at the sharp odor that wafted from the bottle. Then, pressing the two coins in Hilkiah's palm, I left the dwelling and ran down the hill toward home.

When I arrived at the house, my mother was waiting in the doorway, craning her neck to get a better view of the road. As I drew near, she snatched the vial from my hand and hurried up the stairs to Bartimaeus. I followed close behind. My brother now lay on his side and had drawn his knees up to his chest.

Our father and Eli hovered nearby looking more hopeless than I'd ever seen them. Sophina peered from the top of the stair, a sheepskin blanket around her shivering frame, her tear-filled eyes wide. The innocent child wept without restraint, for she dearly loved Bartimaeus. An overgrown child, himself, he'd given much of his free time to entertaining our little sister. I always marveled at how someone as big and clumsy as my brother could lower himself to the floor and roll around like a big dog at play.

Now he lay helpless on his mat, and it was up to the rest

of us to bring him back to life. Following our usual custom, our father lifted Bartimaeus' head, while our mother drizzled the bitter liquid into my brother's mouth, spilling a little onto his beard.

Bartimaeus lurched about and gasped for air.

"Help us!" my mother cried out to Eli and me. I rushed to her side and grabbed Bartimaeus' arm. Eli knelt on his other side and did the same.

"Please! Hold your brother still," our mother shouted.

"We're trying to," Eli whined. "He's a big man and too strong for us to control."

Even in his weakened state, Bartimaeus was stronger than both of us. He pulled his arm free of my grasp and struck our mother on the side of her head. She cried out, more in surprise than in pain. Our father put all his weight across Bartimaeus' chest. But the big man kicked free and almost rolled off his mat, taking Eli and me with him. It took all of us working together to hold our big brother still while Mother continued to pour the bitter liquid into his mouth.

When the bottle was empty, she gave us a nod, and we released him. He let out another wail and curled his body into a tight ball. This was far worse than anything he'd suffered in the past. Perhaps instead of getting the potion, I should have summoned Hilkiah himself to the house.

Then, without warning, Bartimaeus unfolded his frame, dropped back on his pillow and fell asleep. A steady groan escaped his lips assuring me he was down for the night.

Our father wanted someone to stand guard for the rest of the night. "Take separate watches," he said to me and Eli. "Don't stop until the first rays of daylight. Then, summon me."

Eli let out a grunt and looked at me. "You go first," he said.

Though I was tired from all the running around and the battle over Bartimaeus, I agreed to take the first watch, certain Eli would take a turn in a few hours.

After everyone else went off to bed, I walked to the edge of our rooftop, leaned against the waist-high wall, and turned my face toward the east where the temple stood unseen beyond the rise of hills. I imagined myself traveling up the layered hillside, past Beit Sahour, past Bethlehem, beyond the city wall and through the temple gate. Being invisible, I could go beyond the curtain to that sacred place where only the high priest was allowed and then only once a year on the Day of Atonement. I imagined myself entering the Holy of Holies and kneeling before the Ark of the Almighty, pleading for my brother's life. I even thought about offering my own life as a sacrifice in his place. It was one of those, "Take me instead," prayers that rarely made it past the tip of my tongue.

As Moses begged God for the life of his sister when she sinned against him in the wilderness, so also did I beg for the life of my brother. Moses had uttered a simple prayer. *"Heal her now, O God, I beseech you."* I repeated those same words and inserted my brother's name. "Heal Bartimaeus now, O God, I beseech you." A simple prayer but one I trusted to reach the ears of an all-seeing, all-knowing God.

Surely Yahweh had been pleased with Bartimaeus for his faithfulness in spreading the good news of the arrival of the Messiah. On that night long ago, my brother began his mission immediately upon our return to Beit Sahour. He still spoke about that night, spreading the word to people who came to our house to buy sheep and cornering people at the marketplace to tell them the good news.

My mind scrambled through the psalms my father had recited to us over the years. One in particular surfaced in my memory.

"There shall no evil befall you; neither shall any plague come nigh your dwelling."

That promise gave me some hope. Then, with fervent courage, I devised a petition of my own.

"Don't abandon us, Almighty God," I whispered. "Show us your power, your mercy, and your everlasting love. Please, heal my brother." I hesitated, then boldly added, "And please, Yahweh, make it possible for me to marry Ariel."

I don't know how long I stood there, praying, but sometime during the night, I lay prostrate across my brother's body. After checking to make sure he was breathing, I retreated to my own mat and continued whispering prayers into the night. Sometime before morning, Eli stirred, grunted, and rose to take his watch.

At the first light of dawn, my mother roused us all. To my amazement, Bartimaeus was sitting up in bed. He'd recovered and was pleading for something to eat.

"Not until I have the physician take a look at you and declare you healed," Mother insisted. Then she caught my attention and I knew the look. Without saying a word, my mother was ordering me to run again for the doctor. Though I'd gotten very little sleep, I breathed a sigh of resignation, donned a fresh tunic, and headed out the door and down the outer stair.

With the gray light of morning to illuminate my path, I ran to Hilkiah's home, taking each hill with renewed energy. My brother was alive! Bartimaeus was healed. God had answered my prayers.

Once again I rapped on the doorpost. This time, a servant opened the door, and Ariel came up behind him.

I gazed at her, awestruck like I was seeing a vision, and I was immediately taken back to the field and the angels. I blinked hard against the aura that surrounded her, illuminated by the oil lamps stationed around the room. I knew it wasn't one of those angels. It was the physician's daughter, and she was standing there, her red-streaked curls aglow and her cheeks bearing a crimson flush. Still wearing her night clothes, she quickly reached for a veil and wrapped it around her shoulders.

"Your father," I said, breathless from the run up the hill. "We need Hilkiah to come to our house. My brother Bartimaeus has recovered, but my mother needs your father to give his assurance."

Hilkiah came out of the shadows and stepped up beside his daughter. He was still in his nighttime attire. He quickly slipped into his physician's clothing, a simple linen tunic, belted at the waist. He put on an outer cloak, then he slid his feet into a pair of leather sandals. Ariel handed him his physician's scrip, a wooden box filled with the necessities of his trade.

"It's not like before," I told him. "Bartimaeus suffered much through the night, but he has awakened, and he is begging a meal."

Hilkiah let out a chuckle. Then he nodded. "And your mother refuses to feed him until I have a look."

I gave an awkward shrug.

With his scrip in his hand, he slipped past Ariel and joined me in the street. We hurried together to my home, with me praying quietly and the thick-chested dwarf of a man, gasping for breath in an effort to keep pace with me.

The moment Hilkiah set his eyes upon Bartimaeus, his brow furrowed with concern. He placed a hand on my brother's forehead, then gently pressed him back against his pillow. Our mother stood nearby wringing her hands. Father and Eli joined me at our brother's side. No one spoke.

"I feel fine," Bartimaeus insisted. "I simply want something to eat."

We remained silent and turned our attention to Hilkiah.

The physician shook his head and dropped to his knees beside the mat. With practiced hands, he examined Bartimaeus from head to toe, his hands moving gently over the big man's entire form. Finally, Hilkiah spoke.

"I'm afraid he is far too big for the tomb you selected, Osiah," Hilkiah concluded with a wink to our father. He shook his head with feigned sadness. "It's best not to feed him. I'm afraid it's already too late."

"I need to eat something," Bartimaeus persisted. "I haven't eaten since yesterday morning."

Hilkiah ignored his complaint and signaled our mother to come near. "What about the potion I sent? Did he take it?"

She nodded. "All of it, except for a small amount that spilled onto his beard." She wrung her hands again and appeared to be about to weep.

Hilkiah sighed. "No sense in wasting any more potion," he said. "This man is beyond help."

Bartimaeus tore open his night shirt and bared his hairy chest. "Look at me!" he cried out. "I'm as fit as you are, physician. But I'm hungry. Do you hear me? I'm hungry!"

Hilkiah ignored him and shook his head again. He sent another wink to my father, then he glanced at Eli and me. He rose to his feet and straightened his back with a sigh. "What arrangements have you made, Osiah?"

"Listen to me!" Bartimaeus lurched upright. He was raving mad now. It was all I could do to keep from laughing. I struggled to keep a worried look. Eli appeared to be doing the same, then about to burst out in laughter, he turned away.

"Now, we wait," Hilkiah continued the deception. "There is nothing more we can do. We will simply have to wait for his passing to be complete and then we can prepare him for his burial." He looked at my mother. "Have you assembled the proper spices?"

Mother caught on quickly. "Yes," she said. "And more than enough linen strips to wrap his entire body."

Eli began to pace the rooftop from one side to the other, his body shaking. I crumbled to my mat and moaned. Mother drew close to Bartimaeus and bent beside him, weeping and mumbling incoherently.

Father tore at his robe and plucked hairs from his beard. "Oh, my son, my son. How will I go on without my firstborn?" he wailed.

Poor Sophina, huddled inside a sheepskin blanket, her dark eyes wide as she gaped at the four of us. The innocent child hadn't yet understood what was happening. Were we truly in mourning or simply giving a terrific performance before a sick brother?

Bartimaeus wanted no more of this. The big man flew off his mat and leaped to his feet. He stomped toward the open door, then turned and faced the physician.

"You will not touch me with burial clothes or with oils and spices," he ranted. "I am as healthy as you are, physician. I intend to go down to our mother's kitchen and find something to *eat*."

He was about to leave the upper room, when the rest of us burst out laughing. Then Father grabbed Bartimaeus' arm and guided him back to his bed.

"Marita, you may get our idiot son something to fill his stomach," Father said. "But be sure to follow the physician's advice. No spicy foods. And definitely no wine."

Hilkiah stepped up to my brother and waved his finger in his face. "This is what will happen if you don't listen to me. I have told you before to refrain from eating food that has been seasoned with too many spices. And stop drinking so much wine. You must control your urges, Bartimaeus. A little wine is good for the stomach, but you go beyond what is good. And food? Your father has told me how you stuff yourself until you can't breathe." Hilkiah shook his head, then gestured toward Eli and me. "Look at your brothers, how healthy they are. They know when to stop eating. They know when to put the wine away. Be wise, Bartimaeus, or we surely *will* be planning your funeral."

For several weeks, Bartimaeus submitted to the physician's demands and ate only the food our mother set before him, keeping to small portions most of the time. He didn't drink wine anymore, at least not that any of us saw. The physician's performance in the upper room had frightened him into obedience. He'd been ill multiple times before, but now he'd nearly died.

He began to lose weight, gradually at first, and then the pounds started coming off. His face grew gaunt, his eyes looked sunken, and he lost his tendency to make jokes about everything. Our cheerful, fun-loving, big cow of a brother had turned into a sad wisp of a man who cared little for the work that needed to be done.

Chapter Eight

Thy rod and thy staff they comfort me.

~Psalm 23:4c

One evening, a neighbor brought a basket of spiced peppers to our door, and while Eli and I eagerly sampled them, Bartimaeus shrank back from the basket and retreated to the upper room.

My concern grew for my brother. He'd lost so much weight his clothes began to hang on him, like the rags on the homeless beggar who sat by the city gate. He discarded his own shirts and cloaks and began to wear Eli's. He became so weak, he often left his duties unfinished, no longer helped with the lifting and the raking and the digging. He did the minimal amount of work, just led his sheep out to pasture and then found a place to sit and sulk.

With our aging father less able to help us, and with Andrew gone, we needed Bartimaeus more than ever. Eli and I had to take on his duties in the care of our animals. We made all the repairs to our barns and enclosures. And if there was something heavy to lift, we couldn't call on Bartimaeus as we did in the past. It took both of us to do the job our big brother could have done by himself.

"There are only three of us to do the work," Eli said to Bartimaeus one day as we made our way home from the barn. "Think about it, Bartimaeus. The hired men come only in the spring when we drive our sheep onto the plain and prepare them for shearing. During the fall and winter, we bear the full load of our labors." He drew close to Bartimaeus and snarled into his face. "You lazy oaf. We need your help. We need you to fix the enclosures that are falling apart." He nodded toward the house. "If nothing else, you could help our mother with household chores. Bartimaeus, we need you to do *something!* If you don't help, our entire family will suffer for it."

Bartimaeus didn't strike back. That emaciated skeleton of a man simply bowed his head and slumped off to a fallen log or found a rock to sit upon, then he spent the rest of the day in misery.

Eli went about his work moping and groveling. All his efforts had failed. He'd been unable to goad our brother into the high-spirited, hardworking jester we once knew and loved. Then something Eli had said troubled me. *Our entire family will suffer.*

I drew up beside him. "Are you certain, Eli? Will our family suffer without Bartimaeus' help?" I shook my head in dismay. "What has become of our family, Eli? Father remains in the house, pulling leaves off the corn. Andrew has left. And Bartimaeus is useless. Now, I wonder, what will become of *you?* How long do you plan to stay and labor beside me? When will *you* leave? Will you follow after Andrew, perhaps marry one of the village girls and have your own farm? Will I be forced to take on this responsibility alone?"

Placing his hand on my arm, Eli looked me in the eye. "You will be fine," he said. "Take one day at a time, my brother, and simply do what needs to be done. I'm not going anywhere. I have not yet decided which of the young girls appeals to me, but when I do choose a wife, why wouldn't she want to come and live here?" He waved a hand toward all of our property and grunted, as though he might be offering some lucky girl a life of luxury.

"Anyway," he added. "Father will never consent to a match until we get Bartimaeus married off, and that is impossible. So stop worrying."

I frowned at the realization. If the firstborn never married,

Eli and I might remain single for the rest of our lives. Surely, there was a law that protected us from such a fate.

It was obvious Eli had a high opinion of himself, like he was the prize catch of the village, which, I had to admit, was probably true. But I had seen Eli's flaws. His pride could be his downfall. Didn't one of Father's scripture readings say that? Eli's need to be the strongest, handsomest, most desired man in Judea showed how weak he really was. He never went to the village without first grooming himself from head to toe. Scented oils for his hair, his best shirt, and not a hint of sheep dung on his sandals.

"Without Bartimaeus to help us, what are we supposed to do?" I persisted.

Eli raised his chin to my challenge. "We will simply go about the business of tending the sheep," he said, then he began numbering our duties on his fingers. "We start by choosing a pair for the mating pen. We keep the bins filled with grain. We carry water from the well and pour it in the troughs. We prepare the garden with fresh seed." Then, he raised his hands toward heaven. "Finally, we give it over to God." He faced me then. "So you see, Jesse, there is so much to do. In the end, the passing of time will help to ease the pain of losing Andrew, we'll learn to do it all without Bartimaeus, and we'll accept the decline of our father. It's you and me, Jesse." Then he roughed up my hair and laughed.

I released a sigh. "Father forbade us to speak Andrew's name," I reminded him, tears flooding into my eyes. "Now we've both broken Father's rule. But, I miss my brother, and I fear I will never see or hear from him again."

Eli gave an indifferent shrug. "We may never be able to let go of him completely," he said. "But we must keep moving ahead. Bartimaeus is still with us. In time, he will be his old self again. I expect he will entertain us with funny stories about people he met in the village. He will once again fill our home with laughter. He might even start eating again."

A shuffling of feet drew our attention to a nearby path.

Bartimaeus had returned and had heard Eli's last words. Without speaking, he headed for the house. Curious, we both followed him and found him in the kitchen, poking his face into cupboards and moving bottles and bags, creating as much noise as humanly possible. Bottles scraping against the stone shelf, bags crinkling beneath his search, the heavy stone lifted from the cold pit in the floor where Mother stored the goat's milk and cheese.

"I have not eaten a decent meal in weeks," Bartimaeus whined.

He'd complained before. And I knew the signs. My brother was about to fall into his old ways. According to his pattern, he refrained from eating and drinking until he could no longer control himself. This last time was the longest he'd gone without, prompted, I supposed, by the threat of certain death. My big, bold brother didn't know how to control his passions. Moderation. That's what he was missing. Now he was about to resume his former weakness, and there wasn't a man or woman alive who could stop him. Not Mother. Not Father. Not the physician. And certainly not his brothers. The good thing was, whenever Bartimaeus put on a few pounds and regained his strength, he also sprang back to life and became the best worker on the farm. Nevertheless, I feared the change might also bring on another bout of illness, or worse.

I had to admit, I liked Bartimaeus better as the big, lumbering man of the field, the brother who couldn't control his impulses, said whatever came into his head, and made a joke about everything. I welcomed the day he again ate and drank whatever he wanted, and, as I had predicted, with his newfound strength he plunged into the work once again.

One spring day, at the onset of Pesach, we led our sheep onto the plain and prepared to settle there for the night. As darkness began to fall, and we penned our flock inside the stone enclosure, I was reminded of the night the angels came. Two years had passed, and the memory had left me with a lot of questions. I used to share my concerns with Andrew. In his absence, I had only Eli or Bartimaeus to confide in. What a choice. Bartimaeus jested about my questions, and Eli usually brushed me aside like an annoying insect. But something had been troubling me, and I had to talk to someone. I settled on Eli. At least, he was sober.

I found him on the very knoll where our father sat the night the angels came. The old man had stayed behind at the cottage, tonight, so in his absence, it was Eli who started the campfire, Eli who oversaw our work, Eli who gave his approval when we presented a newborn lamb. I approached him with a load of twigs and offered to help. Once he got a blaze going, we settled on the grassy knoll and warmed our hands. I drew a handful of raisins and nuts from my pack and, shared them with Eli.

He raised his eyebrows and looked directly at me. "You have something to say?"

I nodded and drew in a breath. "Do you remember that day on the plain when the angels appeared to us? We were in this very spot."

He frowned in puzzlement, then he lifted his chin. "Oh, yes. I remember it well."

"I don't," I confessed. "My memory of that night has faded somewhat, like it was merely a dream."

He let out a derisive grunt. "You were young." He waved a hand as though dismissing me.

I persisted. "Tell me, Eli—the angel's message and the child in the manger—was it all real or was it only a dream? What do you think happened that night? Did someone play tricks on us?"

Eli breathed a long sigh. "It couldn't have been a dream, Jesse. You weren't the only person there. We *all* saw it. Father, Andrew, Bartimaeus, even our hired workers, plus all the other shepherds who gathered around us that night. Then, after we visited the babe in the manger, the shepherds ran off singing and praising God and wanting to declare the news to others. Some of them went around Bethlehem that night. Others said they wanted to tell the whole world." He leaned toward me and placed a hand on my shoulder. "Now you can answer *my* question.

How could so many shepherds have the same dream? How could so many want to carry the report to the ends of the earth?" He didn't wait for me to answer, but kept on. "Do you honestly think it was a trick of the eye? Impossible!" He shrugged and then used a stick to stir the embers. "I admit there are demons and devils and false prophets who want us to believe in visions, but could they deceive so many at one time? Jesse, this was a message of hope and peace, a godly message that the deliverer we had long awaited had finally arrived. And *we* were chosen to convey that message."

He shrugged. "So, the Messiah came as a baby. It *is* possible."

"I wish I had proof."

He picked up a pebble and tossed it. Then he picked up another and I wondered if he might be stalling, that maybe he didn't know how to respond.

I thought I caught a flicker of sympathy in his dark eyes. "I can't give you proof, Jesse. You merely have to believe, that's all."

Eli released the other stone. Then he leaned back on his elbows and gazed at the sky. "The angel said a Savior had been born in Bethlehem. Think about the babe in the manger, Jesse. You were close enough to touch him. Hold onto that memory. If you choose to believe now, then someday you will have no doubts. As for me, I'd rather believe we were chosen, that we were special."

The fire had grown too hot for me. I scrambled to my feet and stepped away. Breathing deeply of the cool night air, I left my brother, his last words swirling around in my head. *If you choose to believe now, then someday you will have no doubts.* I entered the sheep enclosure and wove through the clusters of ewes, stirring them to life. They moaned softly, because a friend was near. Eli believed in the miracle. But my brother was certain it happened because of how special *he* was, and that troubled me.

✝✝✝

It was raining the day Ariel appeared on our doorstep with a basket of raisin cakes and a smile that started my heart thumping. My mother welcomed her into the kitchen where our family had gathered for the midday meal. Ariel removed her veil. I sat transfixed by the glow of red streaks in her hair.

"Please stay and eat with us," Mother said, and she gestured toward a cushion. In our culture, it was a rare event for females to dine with the men, though I'd known other families who did so regularly. Now Mother was extending an invitation to Ariel, and I couldn't have been happier. She accepted Ariel's basket of sweets and placed them on the long, low table beside a platter of seared goat and a wooden bowl filled with roasted vegetables.

Ariel modestly gathered her dress around her legs and lowered herself to the cushion. I couldn't believe how she went from standing to sitting in one graceful motion. Bartimaeus leaned close to me and nudged my arm. Startled, I looked into my brother's smiling face. He winked a twinkling eye at me. There was no doubt my fun-loving brother was back.

I looked across the table at Eli. He too was smiling. His eyebrows went up, like he had a happy secret. My face flushed with heat. For a moment, I allowed my mind to escape from the gathering, and I sat like a dumb sheep that had lost its way.

"Be sure and thank your mother for the basket of sweets," Mother said. Then she swept her hand over the table and offered Ariel a taste of the foods displayed there.

My mother had a knowing smile on her lips. Suddenly, for no apparent reason, she brought up the same concern that had been on my mind.

"Has anyone set a claim on you, Ariel?"

Ariel blushed and lowered her eyes. "Not yet," she mumbled.

"Isn't that something that should be discussed between parents?" Eli spoke up. "Don't they make such arrangements soon after a child is born? And isn't it done in private?"

Mother opened her mouth to speak, but it was Father who answered him. "You are correct, Eli. In our house, your mother and I chose to wait until you children were grown, so we could more rightly judge what sort of match is best." His eyes drifted from Eli to Bartimaeus and then to me. Then his eyes fell on Ariel. Again, she blushed a deep pink, which got my heart to fluttering.

I winced. Father had not matched any of us boys with the young girls of the village. Not at birth, not when we were young, not ever.

My mother sent Eli a harsh look. "I am simply asking our friend if any promises have been completed for her future."

The hairs bristled on the back of my neck. Poor Ariel. The flush on her face and the shock in her eyes nearly brought me to my feet, but I remained frozen, my mouth sealed shut.

Eli did not let the moment pass. "And who, dear mother, might have made a proposal of marriage to this girl? Look at her. She's not yet full grown."

More embarrassment. I gritted my teeth, unsure how I might rescue my beloved.

Our mother raised her chin. "There is word in the village that Abijah has set his heart on Ariel. I'm merely trying to find out if that is true."

I froze. As I had feared, my worst adversary may have put his claim on the girl of my dreams.

Eli nearly came out of his seat. "Abijah?" he shouted with disdain. "That boy is a scoundrel. His father, Jedediah, treats his wife badly. He shouts commands at her, sometimes shoves her out of his path. I even saw him slap her once. You can be sure, Abijah will treat his wife the same way."

Sophina let out a gasp. Ariel appeared to have shrunk in fear. She fumbled with a cup of water, brought it to her lips, and then held the cup to her chest. I seethed with sympathy for the poor girl. My mother had embarrassed her, and my brother had frightened her nearly to death.

"But," Mother went on, her voice softening. "Until a contract is signed, no one can make a claim." Her eyes landed on me, and I nearly collapsed from humiliation.

Ariel raised her face and straightened her back. "I have no intention of marrying Abijah—or anyone else," she said with newfound strength. "When the time comes for a decision, my father—a sympathetic and kindly man—will allow *me* to make the choice."

But my mother didn't let it rest. "Surely, he will want you to choose the son of another physician, someone from Jerusalem perhaps?" Her eyebrows shot up. "Or perhaps a boy of more humble means has caught your attention." She flashed a glance in my direction. I nearly crumbled to the floor.

At that moment, my father struggled to his feet and straightened in a gesture of strength. "I am the head of this home. I will say what will be and what will not be, in marriage contracts for our children, and in dinner table talk with our family and guests. Now, let's eat." He returned to his cushion, reached for a piece of meat and dipped it in the broth.

My father's display of authority struck me that one day I, too, would be the head of my own home. I did not want to be the kind of husband and father who made unreasonable demands on his family. I wanted to guide them with gentleness, and show my authority when necessary, the way my father moments ago had done. But one thing troubled me. My father expected to control my future. There was no doubt he liked Ariel. He had always welcomed her into our home. Who could deny such a match? If another shepherd like Jedediah could propose a marriage contract for his son, then my father could also do so for me. But time was running short. If I truly wanted to be wed to Ariel, I had to make my request known—and soon.

I began to look for opportunities. Like when Father finished reading another scripture. Or while he was overseeing my work. One thing was certain. I needed to wait until I could get him alone. Then, he'd have to give me an answer.

Chapter Nine

You prepare a table before me in the presence of my enemies.

~*Psalm 23:5a*

One morning, Jedediah's dark-skinned, young servant came to our house with a beautifully woven, blue-and-yellow sheepskin blanket. Another gift for Sophina, he said. He'd already brought two lacy shawls and a silver bracelet on previous days. I was shocked when my sister accepted the gifts. As she turned away, I caught a glimpse of her face. She was smiling. The servant boy also was smiling as he spun toward the open door and strolled off, his back straight, his feet nearly dancing on the path. I narrowed my eyes and scowled after him.

"What is this?" I said, tugging at the blanket in Sophina's arms. "Who is sending you gifts? Is it Abijah?"

She flushed a bright red and shook her head, her curls bouncing like shiny black coils. "I hope not Abijah." She sneered and wrinkled her nose.

"Then, who?"

She turned her face toward the open road and the image of the servant boy, now growing smaller in the distance.

"Jedediah's servant?!" I recoiled in shock. "Isn't he Egyptian?"

She lowered her eyes and pulled the blanket to her chest. Then she disappeared behind the veil to her tiny sleeping quarter. I peered through the slit in the veil. Sophina was cuddling with the blanket, her scrawny legs drawn up to her chest, that mysterious smile still glued to her face. She looked like an angel, lying there with her eyes closed against the real world. And I knew, my little sister had found love. But with it was sure to come extreme pain.

The gifts continued to come from the house of Jedediah. A beaded purse, like the ones the Roman women carried. A handkerchief made from the sheerest linen and trimmed with lace. A gold bracelet. Always carried to our door by the same young servant. His name, I learned, was Jahzeel, and he'd been hired by Jedediah to pay off a debt the boy's father owed. Whether Jahzeel could ever pay off that debt, I didn't know, but whenever I passed by the neighbor's property I could see the dark-skinned little Egyptian laboring in the field with the sheep, and taking far better care of them than Jedediah and his son did. I wondered how a servant boy could afford such costly gifts. I supposed he could steal them. Or perhaps, he'd been able to glean a portion of funds from his father's account for his own use. Whatever the case, I sensed disaster for my sister and her young lover.

As I should have expected, Father and Mother presumed the gifts had come from Abijah. My temper flared that my greatest rival had set his mind on marrying my sister. But I knew the truth. A different bonding had taken place. A bonding between Sophina and Jahzeel. A bonding that had little hope of fulfillment.

Abijah's interest in Sophina became a reality when his mother came to visit my mother. Though they spoke in low whispers, I suspected they were talking about a match. When the woman left, my mother stood in the open door, her arms crossed and a smirk on her lips. I breathed a sigh of relief. Whatever had transpired between the two apparently did not have a satisfying end.

Then came the day I met Abijah in the Jerusalem marketplace. Unlike our former encounters when he cursed at me, this time he called out a friendly greeting. Then he backed off of a sale so I could sell my lamb to the buyer. He simply smiled, asked about my sister, and then walked away in search of another buyer.

You fool, I thought, staring at his departing form. *You pursue my sister, and she loves someone else.*

Then more trouble arose when I went to the physician's home for another bottle of potion for my brother Bartimaeus. As I arrived, Abijah trotted up to Hilkiah's door carrying an armload of sheepskins. His gift was eagerly received by the man's servant, who quickly showed them to Ariel's mother. The woman let me stand there without so much as a friendly greeting, but she smiled sweetly at Abijah and even invited him inside the house. That's when it struck me. Abijah had set his eyes in many directions, and I couldn't help but wonder who else had he approached with gifts? Perhaps he had an entire harem holding their breath to see which one he might choose. I didn't want my sister to be one of them. What's more, I was concerned that he now had included Ariel.

Abijah was taller than I was, and more muscular. He had a broad forehead and a flat chin, and his nose had a slight bend to it. Some might say he looked masculine. I thought him ugly. But what might a young girl think if he won her attention with gifts?

I began to imagine how such a tangle of hearts might benefit Abijah's father. Perhaps Jedediah intended to use his son's courtships to improve his own business. If Abijah were to wed Ariel, Jedediah would be instantly related to the town physician, giving him higher status than the rest of us lowly shepherds had achieved. If he were to wed Sophina, his father could get access to our flock. The man already owned the finest rams in all of Judea. But his ewes were lacking, mostly because of poor care. On the other hand, my father's ewes were among the finest in all Judea. A blending of the two flocks could benefit both families. Or so it appeared.

Then I thought about the workload. Since my father's abilities had declined, and we'd already lost Andrew, Jedediah could easily take over full ownership of our combined herds. If our father agreed to such a deal, what might become of me and my brothers? Instead of inheriting our father's business, we could lose everything.

For the moment, I held my peace and chose not to share my concerns with my brothers. But my suspicions came to light one day when Jedediah and his wife, Ischa, came to our door seeking an audience with my parents. I was in the sheep pen, gathering the straw. I looked up in time to see my father welcome them into our cottage.

I dropped the rake, ran to the house and paused inside the doorway. My mother stood rigid, her arms crossed against her bosom. She lowered her eyes and quickly turned away from the visitors. My father stood facing Jedediah, and to my dismay, he was smiling. I wondered if an agreement had brought those two to our doorstep. Irritated, I spun away and went to find my brothers.

As usual, Bartimaeus was nowhere to be found. I assumed he had escaped to the village and was reveling with his friends. Weeks ago he had ignored Hilkiah's warning and had gone back to his former life. He'd already gained enough weight to fit into his own clothes, and he spent many a night drunk on his mat in the upper room.

I found Eli deep in the sheep pen pulling burs from one of the ewes that had gotten tangled in the brush that morning.

"Did you see who came to visit?" I said, breathless.

He nodded, pulled more briars free and tossed them aside.

"I'm going home to find out why they are here. Do you want to come with me?"

He shrugged and went back to his chore.

"It could be about Sophina," I said. "We've got to protect our little sister. Can you imagine what her life will be like if she marries that beast, Abijah?"

When he didn't respond, I turned away and hurried back to the house.

I stepped over the threshold and was shocked to find the

four parents standing face-to-face in the center of the room. To my dismay, it looked like they'd already reached an agreement. Jedediah offered my father the right hand of fellowship. I crept along the wall to a dark corner of the kitchen and squatted on the floor.

Suddenly, Eli entered the house and settled on the floor beside me. His eyes were on our parents. "Father must be out of his mind," he whispered.

I nodded. "I have great concerns. Those two must have come here to request a contract with Sophina. I can't imagine any other reason."

I turned my attention to our little sister who sat huddled in her usual corner of Mother's kitchen. Tears of distress filled her eyes and she appeared to be shuddering. I had a strong urge to protect her. If she had set her heart on Jahzeel, I needed to help them be together. I already knew what it was like to have your dream depend on someone else's decision.

My heart broke for my little sister. I rose from my place beside Eli and slid over to her corner. Lowering myself to the floor beside her, I wrapped an arm around her and drew her close. Her small, olive-shaped eyes looked up at me, pleading. Drops spilled to her cheeks. I brushed them away with my thumb.

"Don't worry, Sophina. I'm here," I said, my throat tightening. "I'm not going to let anything happen to you." I said the words, and I meant them, though I didn't know how to fulfill that promise.

The four parents settled around the low table where we ate our meals. Mother's servant girl set out a small feast of figs and dates, grapes and cinnamon bread. The two fathers were lifting cups of wine to their lips, and I suspected it was already too late.

"Do you know what's happening, Sophina?" I whispered.

Her cheeks were flushed and soaked with tears. She nodded. "I overheard Mother and Father talking this morning." A sob broke from her throat. "They are deciding my fate, Jesse. Please help."

"Not only *your* fate," I told her. "Did they also discuss the blending of our flocks? Such a union will affect our whole family."

Her shoulders slumped with resolve. "Then there is no hope."

"You must not give up." My mind scrambled for a solution. "I'm going to do whatever I can, Sophina. You favor Jahzeel, don't you?"

She nodded shyly, more tears spilling from her shimmering dark eyes.

"How did you come to know him?"

"One day, in the marketplace, I dropped my basket of vegetables. They spilled everywhere. Then, from the side of the road, Jahzeel rushed to my aid and helped me pick up every one. We spoke briefly, and before I left, he asked me to meet him there again on the following morning."

"Oh, Sophina," I said, shaking my head slowly. "Surely, you knew this friendship had no hope of enduring."

She shrugged shyly. "I had an immediate connection with Jahzeel. It was as though our spirits had bonded." She bowed her head for a moment, then raised it with determination shining in her dark eyes. "We have never had a harsh word or an indecent plan between us. Our love is pure, clean, unhampered by the rules of the world."

Her innocence overwhelmed me. In a way, I understood about such a bonding, for it was the same way I felt about Ariel.

"Have you promised yourself to Jahzeel?" I finally asked.

She leaned back from me. "Please, don't tell Father. He could have Jahzeel sent away—or he could have him stoned."

I scowled with concern. "Oh, Sophina, don't you know our father? He is not so unkind." I offered a sympathetic smile. "You're so young, my sister. Too young to make a decision about the rest of your life. But I know what a broken heart feels like, for I, too, have set my heart on someone, and I don't know if my future will go the way I want it to."

She smiled. "You love Ariel, don't you?"

My face grew hot, and I couldn't speak.

"I thought there was an attraction," she said with wisdom beyond her years. "I witnessed it in Ariel too."

"You did?"

"Oh, yes, Jesse. She likes you. Whenever she comes here, she looks around to see where you are. She's my good friend, but I think she comes here to see you."

My breath caught in my throat. If Sophina was aware of the attraction, perhaps our mother and father had seen it too.

The clearing of a man's throat drew our attention to Jedediah. He had risen to his feet and was lifting his cup. Our father did the same. Ischa also was on her feet, but she retreated behind her husband and had melted into his shadow. My mother was still sitting on her cushion, her body rigid, frowns of worry on her forehead, her lips tightly pressed together. It was the same look of doom she'd displayed the day Andrew left.

"Don't worry," I whispered in Sophina's ear. "They are not all in agreement. Look at Mother. She also must give her approval."

Sophina shook her head. "But Father—"

I raised my hand. "Shhh. Listen."

"Yes, this may be a positive union," Our father said, his voice bearing a tone of command. "But I have not yet discussed this with my wife and my sons. They also own this farm."

A thrill of hope surged into my heart. Not only had Father halted the transaction, but he also had included the entire family in the decision. I shifted my gaze to my mother. She was still sitting there with her arms crossed over her chest and her chin raised in what appeared to be stubborn opposition. Though he often boasted about being the master of his house, my father had said he will not make such a life-altering decision without her approval. Once again, my opinion of my father soared. I paid closer attention to the conversation.

"There are some concerns," Father said to Jedediah. "My flock is larger than yours. If we combine our herds the result would not be as favorable for me as it would be for you. I have three sons and several hirelings to help with the work. You have only Abijah and how many hirelings?"

"I have enough," Jedediah growled. "Enough to take on half the work, if necessary. Plus a worthless servant boy to help."

Sophina flinched in my arms. I could only imagine what was going through her head. The man had insulted Jahzeel.

"You do own a better breed of rams," Father conceded. "I am confident they will mix well with my ewes. But, my herd is larger and in better condition than yours is."

Jedediah stepped back. "Are you saying I don't take good care of my animals?"

"I only know what I have seen with my own eyes."

"Then you must be aware this is a profitable agreement," pressed Jedediah. "I, too, have seen *your* flock. Seventy-three ewes and twelve lambs of excellent condition. And your nine rams are far less virile than my own. Your twenty-two goats are a possible asset. But I have at my disposal the better grazing land. My field stretches nearly to the Jordan where the grass grows thick and moist."

I frowned with suspicion. How did Jedediah know how many animals we owned? Had he gotten close enough to spy on our flock? When did he do the numbering? I had never caught him anywhere near our property, nor on the portion of the plain where we usually grazed our sheep.

My father raised his eyebrows, aware, I presumed, that Jedediah had been keeping a record of our business.

Ignoring my father's questioning gaze, Jedediah cleared his throat and continued.

"A marriage between my son and your daughter and a joining of our flocks will prove profitable to both of us," Jedediah persisted. "I have three donkeys and two large drays, while you have only one. I am able to send many more animals to market at one time. Why delay? You cannot deny you will benefit from such a union."

Our father's continuous nodding troubled me. I knew he

was merely taking in everything that was being said and needed to make his decision later. But Jedediah had the ability to draw people into his plans, always for *his* benefit. I was aware of his transgressions, and I knew people who'd been hurt by him.

There was the shepherd who agreed to increase his flock, when Jedediah suggested they blend their herds together, but with Jedediah in control. Three years later, he was the sole owner of the flock and the other man was homeless and subject to debtors' prison. That evil man had worked their deal to his advantage, and he did so lawfully with the help of several officials in Jerusalem.

I could foresee Abijah carrying on his business the same way his father did, doing what was best for him and robbing the other party of a fair share. I did not want Sophina to be traded off in such a pitiful deal. Nor did I want to see my family's business wrenched from our hands.

I had learned from past experience that timing was all-important when approaching my father. If I tried to reason with him when he was tired, I'd fail. If I approached him during his more active moments, the old man might be too busy to stop and discuss my concerns. I needed to look for the right opportunity.

At the moment my father was in the midst of making an agreement. There was no way for me to offer an opinion. I could only hope the old man had not been taken in by Jedediah's promises. I had one saving thought. *Perhaps my mother will speak words of caution to him.* Then another thought struck me. Everyone in the family knew my father refrained from making a decision of significance without first going to God about it. I knew what I should do. I needed to immerse myself in prayer and ask the Almighty to bend my father's will and end this insanity. And I had to arm myself with scriptures he could not refute.

Without discussing it further, Father led Jedediah and Ischa to the door.

"I will reserve my judgment for another day," he said, his tone firm.

No paper had been signed, no hands had made the traditional clasp to finalize the agreement. All they'd done was drink a glass of wine together. I looked at my brother, still sitting against the far wall, a worried wrinkle on his forehead. Eli looked back at me and shook his head. He came over to where Sophina and I were crouching together on the floor.

"We need to approach him soon," Eli whispered. "But we have to take care how we speak our mind. Father needs to retain his position of authority. I know how he thinks, Jesse. If we say anything to stop this agreement, he will be forced to approve it." Eli shrugged. "How else can he prove he is the head of our home?"

Sophina shuddered. I tightened my grip on her arm. She gazed up at me, like a helpless baby lamb. I smiled to reassure her. I couldn't help but straighten my shoulders, the big brother protecting his frail little sister. I had to do all I could to keep Abijah from getting his hands on her, even if it meant a physical confrontation. Abijah was a year older than I was. He already had chin hair, and he was taller and more muscular. But I could move with surprising speed. The score was even.

Jedediah and Ischa stood waiting by the door. Not a word had passed between the two women. If and when the marriage contract was signed, the two of them would take charge of the festivities, whether they agreed with their husbands' decision or not.

But there was nothing festive about what had transpired in our house that day. For one thing, I did not sense a harmony between the two fathers. They were simply two men discussing a possible agreement but had not yet agreed to anything.

Jedediah paused outside the door and looked our father in the eye. His voice was gruff. "Do not waste too many days, my friend," he snorted. "There is another herder in Bethlehem who has a large flock of fine animals, and a daughter as well. And," he said, raising his chin, "there's always the physician's daughter. Though he has no sheep, a marriage contract may allow me to summon a doctor whenever I need one."

"Then why did you not go to one of them first?" my father challenged him, and I couldn't help but smile.

Jedediah shrugged. "Abijah is about to turn 18. He wants a contract with Sophina. Consider yourself fortunate that I came to you first."

Those last words brought a scowl to my father's face. Now he spoke, not from his head, not even from his heart, but from his stubborn flesh. Osiah ben Shallum needed to keep charge of his family and his farm, at any cost.

"It's time to end this meeting," he said, his voice filled with defiance. "I will give you my answer after the Sabbath and not a day sooner."

Jedediah grabbed his wife's arm and stomped away from our house. I peered from the doorway as he hurried down the path, his wife tottering along behind him.

A sense of relief poured over me. I returned to Sophina and reached for her tiny hand. "You're safe for now, little sister," I said, my heart overflowing with love for her.

I thought about Abijah, and a flash of anger erupted within me. He was about to turn 18, his father had said. Sophina was almost 15. Their betrothal period needed to take at least a year before the marriage. My father had said he'd make a decision after the Sabbath. I knew he intended to pray to Yahweh. Perhaps our great God might lead him to refuse the contract. Another thought struck me. If Abijah didn't succeed in winning Sophina, he might choose Ariel. In the end, I might save my sister but lose the girl I loved.

Chapter Ten

Thou anointest my head with oil.

~Psalm 23:5b

The next morning, I was still thinking about approaching my father in my sister's behalf. I couldn't do it alone. My brothers and I had to convince him to reject Jedediah's offer. I didn't want to lose Sophina to that family. And joining our sheep with that man's flock could destroy the rest of us. Hadn't Father said he needed to discuss the plan with his wife and sons? Why hadn't he done that yet? As a man who spent much time reading the holy scriptures he was about to make the poorest business decision of his life.

It was obvious Jedediah wanted to take over most of the sheep businesses in Judea. He'd already acquired the flocks of several other shepherds. Stories of his misdeeds had circulated. Not only did he cheat the shepherds, he often charged more for his animals than what was acceptable, especially when encountering foreign visitors who came to the area. He grazed his animals on the lush pastures lying closer to the Jordan, often trampling across the farmers' fields before their harvest was done.

The rest of us shepherds waited until the farmers had pulled in their wheat and corn before allowing our sheep to graze on their land. It had been a profitable arrangement. But Jedediah pushed ahead of us and allowed his animals to forage freely, often trampling the precious crops in their path. That selfish man had transgressed an unwritten law and ruined the relationship we had with the men of the field. If he and his son continued to provoke the farmers in this way, we would all be banned from some of the best pastures in Judea. I hoped my father wanted nothing to do with a man who behaved in such a manner.

Such was the bitterness that swirled inside my head as I made my way to the barn in search of Eli and Bartimaeus. As expected, Bartimaeus had already run off to the village.

I found Eli raking animal droppings from one of the stalls. "We have to speak to father," I said to his back.

Eli turned, acknowledged me with a grunt, and went back to raking.

"Jedediah will expect an answer after the Sabbath," I reminded him.

Eli nodded and kept raking. I puffed out my frustration and was about to turn away when my brother stopped working.

"I suppose we *should* speak to our father," he said, at last. He propped his rake against the wall and turned to face me. "We must choose our words carefully, Jesse. Father can be a reasonable man, but he will not bow to demands. We must not question his position as head of the household. We need to let him think it is *his* decision."

"What can we say then? How can we convince him?"

"We need an advocate," Eli said, scratching his head. "Someone Father trusts."

I snickered. "Father doesn't trust anyone except those ridiculous scrolls of his."

"Then the scrolls must be our advocate."

I frowned in puzzlement. "The scrolls? How?"

Eli smiled down on me. "We can look through them and find verses that speak about this very problem."

I shook my head. "I already thought of that, but I don't know where to begin."

"Look," he said, brightening. "Tomorrow Father will go to the marketplace in Jerusalem to buy vegetables for the evening meal. He searches for items we don't grow in our garden. You know how our mother loves to add a little variety to the evening meal." He raised his eyebrows and gave a little shrug. "While he is gone, you and I will search through his precious scrolls."

"Yes," I agreed, thoughtfully. "Tomorrow."

As Eli had predicted, our father left for the village early the next morning. After the donkey carried him out of sight up the hill, we hurried down from our rooftop abode and went directly to the corner of the kitchen where Father stored his scrolls.

Eli carefully pulled one of the tattered parchments from the cracked jar. He handed it to me and reached in to grab another for himself. We sat on the stone hearth and carefully unfurled the scrolls.

The shame of secrecy swept over me. I glanced around the kitchen. No one else was there. Mother and Sophina had gone to the well for water. Bartimaeus was still snoring upstairs. He had returned, tired and weary, before dawn.

We remained there, perusing the scrolls, but finding nothing to address our problem. Oh, there were plenty of praises, instructions for young men, and advice about warfare, but we found nothing about the plight of a young woman doomed for an unhappy marriage and even less about losing one's property to an evil neighbor.

Then a thought came to me. "What about the babe in the manger?" I stared at my brother. "If he truly *was* the Messiah, we should send up a prayer, and he will hear us and give an answer. I had prayed before about different problems. There was the time I misplaced a new shearing knife, and, immediately after I prayed, I found the old rusted blade wedged between two stacks of hay on the floor of the barn." I rolled up my scroll. "Do you think we should simply pray?"

"I do," Eli replied, nodding. "The Almighty does not want us to be yoked in business to a man like Jedediah."

"There's one problem," I said with weakening faith. "If the babe in the manger was the Messiah, then where is he? Why has nothing more been said about him? Is he still in Bethlehem? Did he return to heaven, or go somewhere else?"

"Do you still have doubts?" Eli said, incredulous. "Don't you recall the changes that came over us after seeing him? Think about it, Jesse. I walked away from that manger with a confidence I never had before. A joy overcame our father. And Bartimaeus. Do you recall how our brother became wild about spreading the news? Andrew also glowed with passion. His leaving wasn't only about finding a new life for himself. He believed the journey would allow him to spread the news that the Messiah had come."

Eli had broken our father's rule by saying our brother's name. I chose to ignore the slight, and instead, I paid heed to our problem. "Then where is the Messiah now? Why hasn't anyone said anything more about him? I'd like to believe we can pray and he will answer, but—"

Eli raised his hand. "Listen, Jesse. What happened that night was real. We were given a special calling. Now we need to believe the Almighty himself will help us protect our sister and preserve our family business."

I stared at Eli and found strength in the set of his jaw and the straightening of his back. He had a confidence I still lacked. "As my older brother, you should take charge," I conceded. "Protect our little sister and our flock, and I will stand with you."

"I will," he said, a hint of arrogance slipping into his voice. Eli returned the scrolls to the jar, and I left the house, convinced my older brother was in control.

Mother returned with a water jug on her shoulder. Sophina was not with her. Concerned for my sister, I went looking for her and found her behind our cottage, pulling weeds from the garden. As had been her habit over the last few days, she was hunched over, wiping at a never-ending flow of tears. I knelt beside her and lifted her chin, saddened by the pools of sorrow in her eyes.

"Don't be afraid, little sister." I said, leaning close. "We won't let anything bad happen to you. I promise. Eli and I are going to talk to Father. If we succeed, you will not have to marry Abijah."

Her sad, olive eyes stared up at me. Within their depths lay a broken dream, for even if we were able to stop her betrothal with Abijah, Father could never permit her to wed the Egyptian. I knew it, and so did she. Still, she forced a smile, and my heart melted even more for her. Planting a kiss on her forehead, I left her there in the garden, pulling weeds. I went back to the barn to complete my work for the day.

As always, Bartimaeus' work had fallen to Eli and me. Whether he lay sick in bed or was off drinking with his friends, the result was the same. Without saying a word about it, Eli and I set about opening the gates. We led a portion of our ewes into the pasture. I lowered the wooden gate and secured the latch. The danger to our animals went beyond wolves and bears. Now it included men like Jedediah. He treated his own animals with little care. Why wouldn't he do the same to ours?

Without having a word pass between us, Eli and I spent the day repairing the fences and stalls. At dusk we filled the mangers with corn, carried water to the troughs, and as the sun was setting, we led our animals back inside the enclosures. We bathed at the laver and hurried inside the house, our stomachs screaming for supper.

Our mother had already set out a meal of lentil stew and an array of colorful vegetables from the load our father had brought home from the marketplace. We gathered around the table, our hungry eyes on the food, and obediently waited for the usual blessing. Mother offered a quick invocation of the Almighty's blessing, aware that she had a gathering of hungry men seated before her.

With a resounding grunt, our father delivered a helping of stew to Sophina's bowl, once again inviting her into the circle of men at the table. Eli lifted his cup of wine and nodded his approval. Bartimaeus had not yet returned from the village, and I could only guess that he might be reveling with his questionable friends. I expected Bartimaeus to stumble in after dark as he often did, and fall, amply fed and full of wine, onto his mat. The stupid man continued to ignore the physician's advice.

Father glared at Bartimaeus' empty place at the table. Releasing a huff, he turned his attention to his own plate. Andrew's place also remained vacant, but there was no acknowledgement of our lost brother. Though our father had commanded that his name not be mentioned again, I believed that not only I, but perhaps all of the family, including Father, eyed his empty place with regret.

For a long time our mother had wept tears over the departure of her third son. I was concerned for her health, for she suffered greatly. I suppose a little of my mother died the day Andrew left. Gone was the amused sparkle that once dominated those sharp black eyes. She didn't hum anymore as she labored amidst her household chores. And I hadn't heard her laugh in a very long time.

As for me, I missed my brother's stories about the outside world he so longed to visit. Though I had no desire to leave Beit Sahour, Andrew's battle for free will had instilled in me the courage to pursue my own goals. But I had something at work inside me that Andrew didn't have. Fear of the unknown. I was still the shy, withdrawn little brother who couldn't envision anything beyond the place where I had been living.

The outside world offered challenging obstacles. There were mountains to climb, long roads to travel, town after town of strangers who might not accept a poor shepherd from Judea. Questions swirled in my mind. How could I find work? I couldn't imagine doing anything besides sheep herding. I could starve to death, or die of the cold, or suffer with an unfamiliar illness. I might encounter robbers who were said to come down from the hills and attack weary travelers, take all their money, and leave them for dead.

No. I couldn't leave home. Andrew already had driven a knife in my mother's heart. Why would I thrust it deeper? And how much more could Father endure if two of his sons were gone? I thought of Eli and Bartimaeus, stuck with all the work without Andrew and me to help them. And what about Sophina? Being close in age, she'd miss me most of all.

When I went to bed that night, I tried to imagine my brother somewhere beyond the borders of Judea, free as the wind, making money at whatever trade he'd chosen, and spending his evenings with one of those consenting Gentile women he sometimes raved about. Did I want that kind of marriage? I knew who I wanted to be with, and I was already convinced there could be no other.

In the midst of all those fleeting images, the face of the child in the manger came before me, and with it came still another hesitation—a conviction, perhaps, that such desires were selfish and even sinful. Whether a babe in a manger or an all-seeing eye in heaven, the Messiah frowned on such behavior. I was certain of it. The only answer was to stay in the life I'd been born into.

I fell asleep, content that I had accepted the right decision for myself. The problem Jedediah and Abijah had brought on us was my only concern at the moment.

He placed one finger against his lips, urging me to silence.

"Jesse, we need to talk. Come with me away from the house. I have a plan."

I rubbed my eyes and squinted into the darkness. "A plan?"

"You want to stop Sophina's betrothal to Abijah, don't you?"

"Yes."

"You want to save our flock, don't you?"

I nodded.

"Well, I believe I have found a way, but I'm going to need your help."

I tossed aside my sheepskin blanket, and the two of us crept past Bartimaeus' slumbering form, crossed the rooftop, and descended the outer stair. Once we had traveled beyond the sheep pen, I stopped walking and placed my hand on Eli's arm. We had gotten far enough away from the house to a place where no one could hear us.

My brother took a deep breath. "What was Father's proposal?"

I frowned. "Proposal?"

"You know, what reason did he have for matching Sophina with Abijah?"

I shrugged in ignorance.

"We both know what Jedediah's reason was," Eli reminded me. "He wanted to join our flocks in business. He claimed it was profitable for himself. But what about Father? What about *us*?"

I gazed in the direction of Jedediah's field, adjacent to our land. It struck me then how different our two pieces of property were. After hours of hard labor, our fields and barns were immaculate. Jedediah's fields needed to be reseeded, his barns were in dire need of repair. It was no wonder he led his sheep onto other pastures closer to the Jordan.

"That lazy man was trying to convince Father to join our sheep into one flock and combine our hired men," Eli said. "In doing so, his son also could marry Sophina."

"I already know that."

Eli went on, more excited. "The only thing Jedediah could offer to the deal is his much larger flock of ewes, though ill-kept, and several perfect rams," Eli said. "Jedediah convinced Father that such a partnership served both families equally."

"The man lied," I snarled. "Such a deal would not serve both families equally. Only Jedediah stands to benefit."

"That's right," Eli said, patting my shoulder. "His past dealings with other shepherds have proved him a liar and a cheat. Think about it, Jesse. In every situation, Jedediah came away the surviving owner of the combined herds, and the other shepherds ended up serving *him*. Eventually their share fell into ruin, while Jedediah walked off with the better animals."

I stared into his face, now illuminated under the light of a strange new star in the sky. "You're telling me things I already know."

"I am certain the man will do the same to our father.

But I ask you, Jesse, what could disturb the balance of such a partnership?"

I shrugged. "I suppose if father let go of his hired workers or if Jedediah lost his seven perfect rams. Then there could be no deal."

Eli stepped back and smiled as though waiting for the truth to hit me. I pondered over what he might be suggesting and my jaw dropped.

"So, you want to set Jedediah's seven rams free? Maybe lead them to a cliff and send them falling off the edge?" I shook my head. "Eli, we can't."

Eli was almost bursting with excitement. He snorted. "Toss them over a cliff? That is a child's way. Jedediah could run after them and round up any that survived the fall. No, Jesse. We won't simply run them off. We will *destroy* them."

My heart leaped in astonishment. I eyed my brother with concern. He pinched his lips together in a tight, determined smile. His eyes took on a wicked glow that frightened me.

"Think about what you're saying, Eli. If we are caught, we would be brought before the council. Wayward sons who'd committed a crime. We could be stoned to death. Except for Bartimaeus, who is worthless much of the time, Father would be left to tend our flock alone. He'd have to agree to Jedediah's deal, and Sophina would lose anyway."

Eli's evil laugh troubled me. "You worry too much, my brother. If we do this right, no one will ever know. We have no choice but to slay those rams. And we will do it in secret."

"I suppose, the Law of Moses might simply call for us to replace animal for animal," I suggested. "But if Jedediah demands our lives, no one would fault him for it. The law is clear, Eli. Stoning. Isn't that the punishment?"

"Stop your ranting, Jesse. I've looked at all the possibilities. This is the only way. It's quick. It's easy. And if you keep your mouth shut, *no one will ever know*."

I caught my breath and took a step back.

"What about Father's rule that the eldest must be wed first? Doesn't that protect our sister for a while?"

Eli sneered. "I think he meant it only for us boys. Sophina is simply a possession to be bargained away." He gazed at me with resolve. "Think about how distraught she was. We need to protect our little sister, and we need to do it soon. Once the betrothal is agreed upon, it will be impossible to break it. Jedediah said he wants an answer after the Sabbath. Abijah also will want a quick answer. Those two will not stop until Father's will is broken and he agrees to their demands. They've already offered a contract. All they need is for Father to approve it."

"Perhaps if we wait, we can try another way," I offered. "No one has set a dowry or a bride price as yet. There is still much to be done."

Eli's face turned like stone. "Didn't you see Jedediah drop a bag of coins on the table before he left?"

I nodded but remained quiet.

"Afterward, Father sorted through Mother's jewelry. Despite her pleadings, he separated the best pieces into a wooden box, then he slid it under a pile of sheepskins, separating them, I suppose for the big day. I suspect he's been adding to that store of treasures for weeks." With surprising force, Eli grabbed my arms and held me fast. "We have no other choice, Jesse. We must do this thing, and we must do it tomorrow night."

I shook my head. "Instead of killing Jedediah's prized rams I'd like to stab Abijah and watch *him* die," I said, laughing. I imagined the deed, Abijah bloodied and flailing helplessly on the ground. Then I let out a gasp. Had I really considered *murder?*

"There must be another way," I said. "Why don't we simply take Sophina away for a while? We could return in a few weeks and restore our sister to our home. Hopefully, our parents will have mourned over the loss, and by then, perhaps Abijah will have found himself another wife."

I believed this to be a far better plan. Even if Abijah shifted his attention to Ariel, though my heart would be broken, I was willing to make the sacrifice for my sister.

Eli was already shaking his head. "That won't work, Jesse. As soon as we return, Father and Jedediah will resume their original deal."

"Why don't we go to Jedediah and tell him our sister has been promised to someone else?" I offered, still grabbing at other ways to solve the problem.

Eli huffed his displeasure. "Jedediah might demand proof, a written contract revealing the young man's identity. Besides, during their visit, Father never mentioned that anyone else had a claim. There's no other way, Jesse. Stop trying to find an alternative. We must slay Jedediah's rams. Don't leave me to do it alone."

I left Eli, determined to find another way to stop the agreement between our father and Jedediah. I didn't sleep well that night. The problem continued to weigh heavy on my mind the next day while I did my work, when I sat down to eat, and as I tended to my sheep. I found little comfort as I ran my hand over their wooly coats and bent my ear to their friendly bleating. I clicked my tongue at Reuben, inviting him to follow me as I went to sit on a log. He turned his face up at me, his dark eyes sparkling with what appeared to be adoration. My will began to crumble.

Shedding my doubts, I sought Eli out in the field. "All right. Let's do it," I mumbled. "Tonight."

Chapter Eleven

My cup runneth over

~Psalm 23:5b

Ⓜy brother smiled, winked at me and went back to work. I turned my eyes toward the heavens. The bright star from the night before was hovering overhead, brighter than the sun, larger than any star I had ever seen. Shading my eyes, I went to the house for a piece of Mother's date bread and a horn of goat's milk. I went outside and found a place to sit in the shade of an acacia tree. While I ate, I gazed with appreciation at the barns and enclosures, the vast stretch of pasture, our tiny cottage, our sheep grazing in the field. It will all belong to me and my brothers one day. We had to do the right thing to preserve it.

The huge ball of light shed its light on me. I was instantly aware that as I was looking up, someone else was looking down. Someone far bigger and wiser than the rest of us. On more than one occasion, Father had told us boys the Almighty could see everything we did, that He heard every word, and even knew every thought in our heads. A shudder ran through me. Did the Creator of all the earth also know the sin my brother and I were about to commit? Part of me—the part that listened to my father's scripture recitations and set them to memory—wanted to stop our plan and trust Yahweh with my sister's future. But another part of me reasoned that if the Almighty had wanted to stop the arrangement, He could have done so already. Now the outcome depended on Eli and me.

I spent the rest of the day arguing with myself. Even as I brushed burrs and tangles from our ewes' matted coats, wiped their ears and noses with olive oil and herbs, and cleaned their cloven hooves, I thought about the terrible plan Eli had conceived. I had nearly finished grooming the last of the ewes when Eli arrived, looking, to my surprise, amazingly well-rested, though he'd been toiling in the field all day.

Unlike me, he had not lost sleep over what we were planning to do. I eyed him with contempt. Though he helped me finish bathing the sheep we had selected for market, I resented my brother. He was whistling and humming the entire time we worked. Then, with a bounce in his step, he placed the chosen ones in a separate pen and turned away. My brother had become a stranger to me. Did I love him? Of course I did. But I didn't like the man he'd become.

With the help of our hired men, Eli and I sealed all the enclosures for the night and set up the first watch. With each passing moment, I became more and more uneasy. The time was drawing near for the two of us to go to the neighboring farm and begin the slaughter. Doubts filled my head. What if Jedediah had set a watch? What if someone saw us sneaking onto his farm? I toyed with my supper, couldn't get the food to slide down my throat, and finally gave up and ascended the outer stair to the roof. Eli soon followed.

Within the quiet of the upper room, my brother repeated his plan. Though riddled with doubts I nodded in agreement. We were alone. Bartimaeus' mat lay empty. He had not come home for two nights. I shrugged with indifference. The big man could take care of himself. I had enough troubles of my own. I did not share Eli's confidence. He moved about our quarters collecting knives and towels and stuffing them inside two packs. He handed one of the packs to me. I refused to take it. He thrust the pack at me again. Heaving a sigh, I accepted it and set it on the floor beside my mat.

Eli's sharp eyes sent a warning to me, then he settled on his mat, and we waited until our parents and Sophina retired for the night. When the house grew quiet, Eli sprang to his feet, grabbed his pack, and signaled for me to follow. Slowly, I descended the outer stair a few steps behind my brother. With the packs slung over our shoulders we stalked along the path that led to Jedediah's neighboring property. The trail ahead was brightly illuminated by the strange star that was still shedding its light on the world around us.

I turned my attention back to the trail, and off in the distance, the shadow of Jedediah's house and barns loomed before me. As was the custom of most shepherds, he most likely placed his sheep inside the enclosures for the night. His ewes and their lambs had separate pens, apart from the rams.

As I walked beside my brother, my step faltered, and I stumbled over the stony path. My breath came in short gasps, and my hands trembled. In fact, my entire body was seized with shaking.

"What's wrong, Jesse? Are you nervous?" Eli snickered.

I shook my head and moved on, though I wanted to turn around and run home. Sophina's troubled face came before me. She had wept so pitifully. The image convinced me to keep going.

As we drew closer to Jedediah's property, Eli withdrew the long, sharp knife from his pack. My hand shaking, I did the same. Our blades glinted in the light of the big star. Eli had spent an hour that afternoon honing them. He had tested one on a large coleus leaf, slicing it in half with ease. What we were about to do was the most humane way to kill a sheep or a goat. It was the same method the priests used when they readied an animal for sacrifice. One slash across the throat not only severed the vocal chords so they couldn't cry out and be rejected, it also ended the animal's life quickly and painlessly. Knowing this should have brought me some peace.

It didn't.

As we approached the gate, my eyes darted from one

section to the other. The hired men had apparently left for the night. Jedediah and Abijah must have gone to the house. There was no guard at the gate, not even a dog, and no sign of human life at all.

"Don't fret," Eli said to me. "I've been prowling around Jedediah's property for several nights. It's always the same on his farm. The animals are secured, and no one is standing guard."

I followed Eli into the enclosure. We passed through the entrance, then skirted the shearing pen. Stepping cautiously, I didn't speak, didn't cough, barely even took a breath. We slipped past the enclosure that housed the ewes. They moaned softly and shifted their weary bodies. We approached the enclosure where the mating took place. The pen for the rams lay just beyond.

Eli signaled with a raised hand. He entered the rams' enclosure. I followed him inside and quickly numbered them. All seven were present.

Eli immediately began the slaughter. Without hesitation, I raised my knife. We moved like lightning, slashing throats and allowing the animals to fall in a heap at our feet. Blood flew everywhere. We hurried through the pack so fast there was no time for the animals to resist or cry out. Then, suddenly, as one of the rams fell, his leg came up sharply. Its hoof bit into my shin. Blood splattered my clothing, my hands, my face. A small amount had come from my wounded leg, but most of the bloody stains erupted from the carcasses as they went down. When all seven rams lay still, we paused and viewed the carnage. Bile caught in my throat. My eyes burned with tears. A blanket of bloodied wool lay across the pen. Jedediah's loss was disastrous. He wouldn't be able to unite his farm with anyone, not for a long, long time.

I spit out a swill of bile, then stepped around the carcasses and slipped out of the pen. We wasted no time but returned home the same way we had come. I was confident that no one had seen us, but sick of myself for what I had done. The task was too easy. As Eli had predicted, Jedediah had neglected to post someone at the gate. I was relieved he hadn't, for what would Eli have done? Killed him too?

As I walked the path back to our own field, overwhelming guilt swept through me. I stopped along the way and wretched out the contents of my stomach. I was disgusted with myself that I had taken part in such a slaughter.

Eli paused beside me and waited until I finished vomiting. I wiped the spittle from my mouth and looked him in the eye.

"Do you think anyone will suspect us?" I needed to know.

He laughed. "Not possible."

"Why do you suppose there was no guard?"

"I told you, I spied on Jedediah's farm for several nights. That ignorant man and his foolish son regularly neglect one of their main duties, the guarding of their sheep at night. It's their fault this has befallen them. If it hadn't been us, it might have been wolves or wild dogs that destroyed their prize rams.

I shrank back in disgust. My brother smiled in triumph. His cheeks were flushed and his eyes shone with satisfaction. It was as if he had enjoyed the slaughter. From that moment he no longer was my idol to follow. Instead, I was filled with great disappointment, not only for him, but also for myself. I'd been weak, merciless, and brutal. I was shocked at myself for having committed the worst of sins.

"By morning, the birds of prey will have finished our work," Eli said with a heartless grin. "The carnage will be so complete, no one will be able to tell if it had been done by a human with a knife or by a pack of wolves."

A disgusting lump settled in my throat. Those rams were a man's livelihood. More than that, they were creatures of God, created for the pleasure of man. The Law of Moses spoke clearly about such things.

"If a man steals an ox or a sheep, and slaughters it or sells it, he shall pay five oxen for the ox and four sheep for the sheep."

Four sheep for one? Where could we get two dozen excellent rams to replace Jedediah's seven? This was a time when we were trying to build up our flock. We could not give them away. The truth was, none of our rams could compare with the special breed in Jedediah's barn.

My hands began to tremble, and I shuddered.

"Are you cold—or scared?" Eli said, his tone mocking.

"I-I'm troubled."

"Ha! Don't worry, my little brother. No one saw us. No one heard us. Now, let's go to the burn pit, shed these bloody rags, and set them afire. Father will be snoring away. Mother will not yet have risen. We can return to the upper room without being seen."

After destroying our blood soaked clothes, we mounted the outer stair, wearing nothing but loin cloths. We hadn't gone far when a footstep scraped on the stair below us. From out of the shadows stepped Sophina. The star's brilliant light illuminated her face and revealed her wide-eyed amazement.

"What are you doing?" she said. "And why are you both naked?"

"We're not doing anything," Eli whispered. "Know this, little sister. You can sleep better now. There will be no marriage to Abijah."

A curious frown swept away her shock. "But, how?" she said. "And why?"

"Don't concern yourself," Eli snapped. "And don't say anything about seeing us out here tonight, dressed like this."

Sophina giggled, then she turned her face away, embarrassed.

"Go to your bed," Eli ordered her, and she quietly disappeared inside the house.

I looked into Eli's face, now bathed in the light of the big star. The man exuded confidence, like he had completed a difficult challenge and was ready to receive his crown. He lifted one finger to his lips and smiled at me. Then he hurried up the stairs to sleep away the rest of the night.

I froze on the stair and watched after my departing brother with interest. Another wave of disappointment surged through me. The brilliant star still hovered overhead. There'd been talk that a procession of elaborately attired royalty on camels and horses had come from the east in search of the King of the Jews. I wondered, did their journey have anything to do with that star? Another thought struck me. Did the star have anything to do with the babe we had seen in the manger nearly two years ago? A thought entered my mind that perhaps I could leave with the caravan when it departed. I could find my brother Andrew and perhaps make a new life for myself. Maybe then I could forget about the terrible deed I had committed that night.

But as always, my sin followed me wherever I went. I couldn't run away from such a horrible transgression. Bent beneath the weight of my sin, I mounted the stairs to the roof, certain I would miss another night of sleep. As I dropped onto my mat, I whispered a prayer, but I had no assurance the Almighty was listening. Didn't the scriptures say the Lord did not hear the prayers of the guilty?

Mt father had recited a warning by the prophet Zechariah. *Woe to the idle shepherd who leaves the flock! The sword shall be upon his arm, and upon his right eye: his arm shall be clean dried up, and his right eye shall be utterly darkened.*

Though my father had spoken that warning against idleness—for he wanted to encourage us boys to work hard for our family business—those words now held a different meaning for me. I was suffering from overwhelming guilt over what I had done that night. I wished I could revisit the manger and beg the child to forgive me. I trembled as I recalled his steady, knowing gaze. It was as if he knew I'd one day disappoint him.

The next morning, I was overcome by another surge of guilt. First, I cursed Eli for suggesting such an evil act, and then I cursed myself for taking part in it. I skipped the morning meal, ignored my mother who stood by the door, with her mouth open and a raisin cake in her hands.

Shoulders bent under the weight of my sin, I shuffled off to the sheep pen and began to prepare the flock for a day on the field. Though the onset of winter promised less grazing land, I followed the usual routine my father had established, as had his father and grandfather before him. I suppose that's what made my work easy. My routine had already been set. I didn't have to think up new ways of doing things. What my ancestors had established had worked well for many years.

I paused for a short while and stared at the field my father had inherited. A host of stories had come down regarding that piece of property. Once inhabited by Canaanite tribes, the field eventually went to Jacob who buried his wife Rachel in one of the nearby caves after she died giving birth to their son Benjamin. David's great-grandfather Boaz met Ruth in that area while she was gleaning grains of wheat from his harvest. With such a powerful history I wondered that we shepherds had lost favor among the people. Now I could no longer question our low estate. I deserved to be shunned. Or worse.

Downcast, I went about my day and led the sheep from one grazing area to the next. Around midday, the gnawing ache of hunger gripped my stomach. I left the sheep under the care of our hired workers and wandered back toward home. I stopped short of the house, for I'd caught sight of the town gossip, Hannah the Hawker, shuffling along our path.

The woman frightened me. When I was a young boy, I ran in the opposite direction whenever she appeared on the road before me. She was so thin her clothes hung like tattered rags. She had small black eyes, a long, pointed nose, fingers that looked like chicken bones, and her hair resembled the matted straw in the bottom of our sheep pen. She winced with each step, likely because of the painful bunions that stuck out of her sandals. Holding her hand out for alms, the woman made her way about the village, and on some days she even took her gossip to the sheep farms outside of town. This was one of those days.

My brother Eli came up beside me. We stood very still as Hannah rapped on the door of our house.

"She's a witch," Eli sneered. "She invokes curses, makes

things happen to people she doesn't like, and then she talks about what happened to them. It's better if Mother doesn't welcome her inside."

"Mother believes her to be a harmless, old woman," I said. "A prophetess even."

A servant girl opened the door, and Mother stepped out and reached for Hannah's arm. As we had feared, she welcomed the old woman inside the house. There was no doubt, Hannah had come with a story to tell.

"Do you suppose she found out about Jedediah's rams?" I said, quivering.

Eli nodded and sucked in a noisy breath. "Most likely. Such a report travels fast."

I gritted my teeth and took another step toward our house. Then I cast a sideways glance at my brother. "What should we do?"

Eli shrugged. "We need to find out what the old woman has to say."

At that moment, our mother burst through the door and nearly knocked me over. She ran toward the barn, screaming for our father, "Osiah! Osiah! Come quickly! Such a tragedy."

Chapter Twelve

Surely goodness and mercy shall follow me all the days of my life.

~Psalm 23:6a

Our father rose from inside one of the sheep pens and shuffled toward the house, shaking his head and mumbling. He did not like to be disturbed in the middle of his labor, little as it was. He passed Eli and me on the path, waved a hand at our mother, then seeing the distress on her face, he quickened his step.

Hannah emerged from the house and tottered along the path close to where I stood, frozen like the ice that weighed heavy on the trees in winter. As she passed me, I shrank back from the odor of sour garlic. She cast a dark glance in my direction and kept going. My throat tightening, I followed my parents and Eli into the house.

Mother stood in the middle of the room wringing her hands, her brow lined with anxiety. Sophina rose from her cushion in the corner. She laid aside the dress she'd been mending and drew close to Mother's side.

"A terrible thing," Mother whimpered. "A terrible thing."

"What terrible thing?" Father prodded, his impatience evident. "Speak, woman."

"Jedediah's prize rams—all dead—mercilessly butchered during the night. Osiah, do you know what that means? There will be no business partnership. No marriage for our daughter. Jedediah will be forced to withdraw his offer."

Father frowned at her. "You said you were against the arrangement. You cautioned me to wait and to think about what that meant for our daughter and for our business. Now what are you saying, woman, that you approve of the contract?"

Mother gave a weak shrug. "I changed my mind. The union of our two families is a good thing. People in the village will respect us. You will have less work on your shoulders. Our boys and Jedediah's hirelings could take care of all the duties, and you can relax at home." She shook her head. "But now, there will be no contract, no joining of flocks, no increase in our income, and no marriage for Sophina."

My little sister was beaming. I appeared to be the only one who saw her relief.

"Only his prize sheep?" Father said, frowning thoughtfully. "The rest of Jedediah's flock remained untouched?"

Mother nodded, but the lines of distress remained.

"Was it wolves?" Father wondered.

"Hannah didn't say. I don't think she knew for certain.

"I will go and speak with Jedediah," Father decided. "We can perhaps make a more fitting agreement."

Sophina let out a little gasp. To think our father wanted to continue to pursue the agreement made no sense.

Mother simply shook her head. "No, husband. There can be no contract, for yet another tragedy has struck."

Father's frown deepened. He tilted his head in question. I also held my breath. What more could have happened? Did Jedediah suspect us? Was judgment about to fall on Eli and me?

"Even without the business arrangement, there can be no marriage," Mother said. "Jedediah blamed his son for the attack. He had ordered Abijah to guard the sheep gate, but as soon as he and his wife went to bed, the boy ran off to the village with his friends. The hirelings had already been dismissed for the day. The rams were left unattended. There was no guard at the gate. No Abijah. No hired servants. No one to keep them safe."

Father ran a hand through his hair. He walked to the window and looked toward the property owned by Jedediah. Then he turned and faced Mother.

"The boy—is he—?"

Mother brushed a tear from her cheek. "Hannah said Jedediah flew into a rage, took his rod, and beat his son severely about the legs. He left Abijah badly crippled. There will be no marriage for that boy. Not now or ever."

A hard knot clenched my throat. *Abijah crippled?* I dropped to my knees, gasping. Sophina came running to my side. "Why are you upset, Jesse? Isn't this what you wanted? Didn't you say I won't have to marry Abijah, that you could protect me?"

Father caught every word. He narrowed his eyes at me. "What do you know of this, Jesse?"

I shook my head. "I know nothing, Father," I lied, and I hoped the sudden flush in my cheeks and the trembling of my hands did not reveal the truth.

The old man took a step toward me. "Are you respons—"

Eli lunged between us. "Jesse knows nothing. He was at home last night, asleep on his bed."

My brother's strong hand pressed against my shoulder, holding me back, and silencing me. If I confessed, I'd be exposing him as well.

The truth was, I was no longer an innocent shepherd boy who had been led astray by his brother. I had willingly sinned. I was as guilty as Eli, and I deserved to be punished.

Our father eyed the two of us with suspicion. He was a wise old man, but he didn't know the truth, not without a confession.

He folded his arms and faced the two of us. "What do you boys know about what happened to Jedediah's sheep?"

Eli shrugged but said nothing. I lowered my gaze and swallowed hard. I'd never been able to fool my father before.

"Tell me the truth!" he shouted, his face inflamed with rage.

He shook his head at us. "Did the two of you go into Jedediah's sheep pen and slaughter his prize animals?"

I was about to admit my sin, but Eli raised his chin, not in defiance, but with a strength I didn't have.

Disappointment crept into our father's eyes. Frowning, he softened his voice.

"I am your father, and I'm responsible for everything you do, the good and the bad. I want you to tell me if you were involved in killing Jedediah's rams."

Mother stepped up. "It could have been wild animals. A pack of wolves may have broken into the enclosure and killed them."

Father waved her aside. "Wolves? Wild animals? Unlikely. He drew close to us and stopped when his face was mere inches from mine. His eyes pierced my own and then shifted to Eli. "I believe the slaughter was done by a man, perhaps someone with a sharp new knife."

We remained silent, with Eli setting a firm jaw, and me holding my breath.

"Your sin will find you out," Father said, and he reached inside his shirt and withdrew a shred of cloth that bore stains of blood. "I found this in our burn pit this morning. Somehow, this evidence escaped the flames."

My heart pounded in my throat. It was the tail of the shirt I had been wearing last night. I lowered my eyes, unable to look into my father's condemning gaze.

"If we bury our sins alive, they will rise from the grave one day," he said.

I was about to confess, when Eli slipped in front of me and forced our father to take a step back.

"That's the tail of *my* shirt," he said, reaching for the bloodied cloth. "I did it, Father, and I acted alone."

Our father frowned with disappointment. The displeasure in his eyes was ten times worse than what he had displayed when Andrew told him he was leaving.

Eli dropped to one knee. "Father, please understand, it was the only way I could stop the contract. I had to protect my little sister, and I needed to discourage the combining of our flocks. Such a bargain would bring disaster on our family. There was no other w—"

Father threw the soiled cloth on the floor in front of my brother. His lips drew back in a snarl. "Not only have you broken the Law of Moses, you have brought shame on our house. You committed a terrible crime, Eli." He paced to the window that overlooked Jedediah's property, came back to us, then went back to the window. When he turned he seemed deep in thought. "Your punishment must be severe," he said. "You must feel the weight of your sin."

I shuddered. Eli had not included me in his confession. I needed to admit my part in it, but again my brother pressed his hand against my shoulder, silencing me.

"Who helped you, Eli? Was it one of the hirelings?" Father continued to question him. Then he turned his eyes on me. "Or was it you, Jesse?"

Again, Eli came to my defense. "No, Father. I told you, Jesse was asleep. No one helped me. I acted alone."

Our father stepped back from us and did not speak another word. We waited. Eli in his shame, and I in my cowardice.

At last, Father released a deep breath, raised his chin and glared at my brother. "Here is my decree. First, you will not mention this to anyone. Such a report will only bring more tragedy. Jedediah could rightfully demand a stoning. I know the man. He would not be kind."

I trembled at the thought of a stoning. My brother could be killed. Still I said nothing.

Then Father did something surprising. He offered mercy. "Knowledge of this crime will die with us," he said, his voice softening. "You will never speak of it again."

Hadn't he said when a person buries a wrong it will come out of the grave, one day? Now he was burying the truth. I waited for the rest of his decree. It came immediately.

"Tomorrow, you will take seven of our finest rams to Jedediah and offer them in an act of kindness," he said, his eyes still on Eli. "You will then go to the temple, take two of your unblemished lambs, and offer them for sacrifice. You will beg the Almighty's forgiveness. In this way we will make restitution without bringing shame upon our home."

I opened my mouth to speak, to admit my part in the crime. I looked at Eli. He shook his head and mouthed the word, *No*, at me. Filled with shame, I bowed my head and choked back my confession.

Sophina stood still through the entire discourse, her hands pressed against her face, her eyes revealing her terror.

Father looked down at her. "There will be no match with Abijah," he said.

Sophina's face lit up with hope. "Then, Father, will you approve another?" she boldly asked.

Father smiled. "I have already considered another. The village rabbi has offered his son. It will be an even better match."

I gasped in shock. The rabbi's son?! He was an ugly boy with a large nose and a mole on his cheek.

Sophina fell to pieces. Sobbing, she dropped to the floor at our father's feet. "No, Abba. Please. Not him." Then, she rose up and bravely faced him. "There is someone else, Father. I want to be promised to Jahzeel."

Father lurched back in surprise. "Jahzeel? Who is Jahzeel?"

"He is a servant in the home of Jedediah," she said softly.

He grunted. "That dark-skinned servant boy? This will never happen. I will not match you with a heathen."

She shook her head. "He's not a heathen, Father. He embraces the God of Abraham."

Father stomped his foot. "You will *not* be wed to this Jahzeel. I and I alone will select a match. Someone from the village, perhaps. The rabbi's son or possibly another. But never Jahzeel."

"You are condemning me to a life of misery!" Sophina spun away, her eyes filling with tears. She fled past Mother, stumbled beyond the veil to her sleeping quarter and fell on her mat, wailing. Mother hurried in after her.

Father turned away, passed his eyes over the rest of us, silently declaring his authority, and walked out of the house.

I faced my brother. "Why, Eli—?" I said. "Why did you protect me. I was willing to share the blame."

He shrugged. "It's a gift, my brother. Accept it."

I stood dumb as he walked away and took the outer stair to the upper room. Sophina's weeping poured from beyond the veil. I went to her tiny quarters and pulled back the curtain, found her lying there, sobbing and trembling, with Mother helpless to appease her.

I was brought back to the crime Eli and I had committed. We had not accomplished anything. My sister's future was still set. She had to marry the person our father selected. And the combined flock? Now lost, but what did it matter?

I only knew the Almighty had to be angry with us. Eli was going to make a sacrifice, two unblemished lambs to appease our mighty God. I needed to do the same. I needed to take one of my lambs to the temple, and offer the animal to be slaughtered on the altar. An animal sacrifice had to serve as my atonement.

I went directly to the field and surveyed the few lambs my ewes had given me over the past year. None were as perfect as Reuben. My heart ached, but still I located Abigail and her lamb, Though fully weaned, Reuben had remained with his mother. I looked him over. As Eli had predicted, he was flawless. I hesitated, but I knew the truth. For my sacrifice to be adequate, I also had to feel the pain, and nothing hurt me more than to offer my favorite.

I stepped into the fold and pulled Reuben from his mother's side, ignoring the bleating and the wailing. I flung a rope around his neck, and led him from the pasture. Tears poured from my eyes. I forced myself to keep going. Every step up the hill toward Jerusalem sent waves of agony through me. I arrived at the temple near sundown, as the priest was getting ready to make the final sacrifice of the day.

I knew the fate my little one faced. The priest would place his hands on Reuben's head and make an atonement for my sins. He would then slit Reuben's throat with a sharp blade, collect the flow of blood in a basin, and sprinkle it on the altar. Then another priest would come with a knife and cut him into pieces, offering his perfect head and all of his fat on the altar. He would wash the legs and entrails at the laver and present them too. The remains would be cast into the ashes. The ritual would be over in minutes, but the aroma of charred meat would remain within the spiral of smoke drifting upward to the heavens.

With tears in my eyes and my entire body trembling, I reluctantly delivered my precious Reuben into the hands of the priest, who smiled his approval. It was like handing over my own son to suffer for the sin I had committed. I quickly turned away, unable to stand by as my favorite little sheep was about to be slaughtered. Tears blocking my vision, I passed through the Sheep Gate and stumbled down the hill to Beit Sahour. I turned only once to see the smoke rising from the pinnacle of the temple, and I knew my Reuben had paid dearly for my sin.

But by the time I reached home, a feeling of uncertainty came over me. Did slaughtering a young lamb atone for every evil I had done? What about all the other sins I had committed throughout my life? Did one lamb pay for it all? Or did I have to repeat the ritual over and over again, like so many of my people did, bringing sacrificial lambs, month after month and year after year, to the temple?

Surely, I needed to do something more, something far more worthy to appease the Almighty Judge of all the earth. I thought about the animals Eli was preparing to take to Jedediah. There could be no apology, only an act of kindness, my father had said.

Then I thought of Abijah, now crippled. Because of me. How could I make restitution for the pain I had inflicted on my adversary? Though we had vied with each other for years, I had never wanted to destroy him.

An idea came to me. Abijah was unable to do his work. I

could offer to help him. I could make time every day, after my own work was done, and go to Jedediah's farm and complete Abijah's chores. I could put aside our enmity and be his friend. Perhaps then the Almighty will smile down upon me. Perhaps then I will have paid the full price of my sins.

Chapter Thirteen

And I will dwell in the house of the Lord forever
~Psalm 23:6b

Following the Sabbath, I altered the notches on the ears of three of my rams, easily changing them to Jedediah's mark, and I offered them to Eli.

My brother raised his eyebrows in shocked surprise. "Thank you, Jesse," he managed. "I didn't expect you to do this."

"And I didn't expect you to take the blame," I said with heartfelt appreciation.

Eli prepared four of his own best rams, also altered with Jedediah's mark. Then we went together to our neighbor's property, leading the seven rams behind us. Hopefully, Jedediah might see our gift simply as an expression of good will and nothing more. I couldn't imagine the terrible judgment he could bring upon us if he suspected the truth.

As it turned out, our neighbor tearfully received our gifts. "Osiah has raised a family of fine sons," Jedediah murmured, unaware that he was speaking to the very rascals who had destroyed his rams. "I would have been honored to blend our two families through marriage and our two herds in a business agreement. But now—" he gave a hopeless shrug. "Now, such an arrangement is impossible."

For the first time, I pitied the poor man. Our cruelty had brought him immeasurable grief, and our kindness now served to humble him. I returned home with an unexpected weight on my shoulders. Though I thought I'd find atonement by giving my rams to the man, after seeing how broken he appeared, I was more sorry than before. The sinful act Eli and I committed had destroyed a neighbor and made little difference in our sister's future. Father did not approve of Jahzeel. He intended to look elsewhere for a spouse for Sophina. He and he alone had to select the boy who was to wed his only daughter.

Meanwhile, Sophina did not hide her pain. She moped about the house, weeping, her head down, her hands carrying out her household duties as though someone else were moving them. It was as if someone had died—and maybe someone had, at least within the broken heart of this sweet young girl.

The news of my sister's suffering reached Ariel. She wasted no time coming to our home to encourage my sister in her grief. The two of them squatted on pillows in the corner of the kitchen. They wove blankets from the sheep's yarn and assisted Mother with the baking and the cooking. They chattered like two squirrels, laughing, and erasing the pain that had drawn my sister down. Ariel's lighthearted encouragement summoned Sophina from her misery and brought an atmosphere of peace back to our home. I looked upon her with appreciation, more aware than ever that she was the one girl I wanted in my life.

Then one day, our visitor turned her conversation in my direction. With a flutter of eyelashes and a raising of an eyebrow, she awaited my reaction.

"What are your thoughts, Jesse?" she urged. "I asked if you agreed that Hannah the Hawker has been living in such great poverty we should all be helping her."

The intensity of her blue-green eyes paralyzed me. I didn't know what to say. I had never thought much about the old woman, only that she made a pest of herself, begging at people's doors, pretending to know things we didn't. But how could I express those thoughts to Ariel, who obviously cared about the Hawker.

"I suppose we should," I said, though I had no intention of helping the old woman.

"There are so many things we can do for her," Ariel persisted. "We can take a basket of bread and fruit to her house. We can weave a new cloak to keep her warm in the winter months. We can bring kindling for her fire, stones to repair her hearth, clay to patch the holes in her walls. The poor thing has no husband or family to care for her."

I had nothing to add, could only nod in feigned agreement. Though my head reasoned that doing those things for Hannah was a waste of time, my heart kept me tied to whatever Ariel wanted to do for the old hag.

Mother eyed us from the hearth, then turned away, smiling, and lowered the kettle to the flame. Feeling discomfort, I decided it was time I left the house and got back to work. I quickly departed for the sheep pen, but I barely made it to the barn when Mother hollered after me.

"Wait, my son. You forgot your midday meal."

Ariel came running after me carrying a basket of raisin cakes and a horn of goat's milk. She drew up to me, out of breath and her face aglow.

"Where's Sophina?" I mumbled as I accepted the food.

"Your mother said she should stay and cut the vegetables for the midday meal."

I took a bite of raisin cake and lifted the goat's horn to my lips. "Thank you," I managed, my tongue a little tangled. Her smile disarmed me, and I started to turn away.

"When do you begin sheering your sheep?" she said, stopping me.

I turned to face her. "Soon." In my discomfort it was all I could say.

When I didn't offer more information, she backed away and slowly returned to the house.

I wanted to kick myself. Ariel had shown an interest in my work, and I had brushed her aside. I nearly choked on my next bite of the raisin cake. After washing it down with another sip of goat's milk, I set aside the provisions, grabbed the rake that was leaning against the wall of the barn, and began clearing the floor of debris. My sharp movements did little except to strew the hay in every direction.

Moments later, Mother stepped out the door of our house and called my name. I set aside the rake and ran back to the house. I entered the house to find Mother with her arms crossed and a scowl on her face.

She pointed at a corner of the kitchen where several tiles had lifted from the floor.

"You need to fix this, Jesse, before someone trips on these broken tiles. Go now and make a paste of mud. Then fill the cracks and press the tiles back in place." She raised her chin with an air of authority.

I peered out the window at the barn. "My work—"

"Your father and brothers can handle the work," she said, her tone firm. "I need you here."

Though she tried to sound gruff, her eyes shifted from me to Ariel who was sitting cross-legged on the floor with Sophina. The two girls were staring at me as though waiting to see my reaction.

"Yes, Mother," I said. I hurried outside to prepare a paste of mud and straw. I returned to the kitchen, and avoiding Ariel's steady gaze, I bent close to the broken tiles.

My mother stood over me, smiling. I didn't know if her satisfaction came from my repair of her precious tiles or if she had another reason for the sparkle in her eyes. I recalled how she had pressed Ariel to find out if she'd been matched with anyone yet. Whether or not she knew how I felt about Ariel, she never said, but in her own way, my mother was already giving us her approval.

Mother's desire for a match became even more evident, when two days later, she devised a way for me to have time alone with Ariel, who'd come again to visit my sister.

"Sophina," she called out. "We need to wash our family's clothes. Come with me to the stream. With both of us pounding the rocks, the work will go quickly."

"Should Ariel help?" Sophina innocently suggested.

My mother was quick to answer. "No. She's our guest. You and I will do this. Now come along."

Sophina didn't resist, but trudged off obediently, a bundle of clothing balanced on her head. Mother lifted another bundle. Then the two of them hurried off to the stream, and I found myself alone with Ariel. I stood speechless in the doorway, a warm flush surging to my face. I should have been out in the field, tending to my sheep, but I hesitated, unable to move.

Ariel cocked her head and gazed at me with what appeared to be sympathy.

"Let's go with them," she said, and she led the way out the door. I cast a glance at the meadow, then quickly followed her.

We walked side-by-side along the path, and though I tried to keep a suitable distance from her, she narrowed the gap between us.

"Did you hear the report?" she said, her eyes brightening.

"What report?"

"A great party of kings came to Judea last week. Hannah the Hawker has been spreading the word. She said they came here in search of a miracle child many believe is the Messiah."

I was immediately taken back to the babe in the manger. If the report was true, then the child was still alive and had remained in Bethlehem the entire time. He had to be about two years old now.

"Hannah said they came from afar, from somewhere in the east," Ariel went on. "They were ornately attired and carried costly gifts with them."

I eyed Ariel with compassion. The poor girl had fallen into one of Hannah's traps. I snickered. "Hannah claims to be a prophetess, the only one in Judea. But there is no proof."

Ariel stopped walking and her tone turned solemn. "It's

sad," she said. "Have you seen how thin that woman is? People don't help her like they once did when she brought news to their door. Some even accuse her of being a witch."

"A witch?" I didn't doubt it.

"I don't think she's a witch," Ariel said, her lips forming a sad pout. "She's a lonely old woman. She has no work. No income. No relatives to care for her. And she has a gift. She knows things before they happen."

I looked into her eyes. The sparkle had gone and the blue-green of them looked like a pond of still water.

"Why do you care for her so much?"

She blushed. "I wish I could help her, but I don't know how."

I stared with awe at a young, kind-hearted girl who could have looked down on people like Hannah. But not Ariel. Her care of my sister, her kindness to my mother, and now her concern for a useless old woman revealed what lay within her heart. She was not the spoiled daughter of the town physician, as some might think. Though clothed with fine silk and an array of jewels, the real Ariel beneath all the glitter was humble, unselfish, and sensitive to the needs of others. The world she came from was not the world she had chosen. Our difference in status did not matter to this girl. I conceded that I did not deserve her. Not because of her wealth, but because of her heart.

We settled on a grassy slope a short distance from where my mother and Sophina sat on the rocky bank with their wash. They pulled shirts and towels from their bundles and bent close to the stream. Mother plunged each piece of fabric in the water, rubbed on a little soap, and pounded the cloth against the rocks. Then, she passed them to Sophina who waved them in the air and slapped the dampness away. Their pounding and slapping and waving sent sprays of river water in all directions. The *snap, snap, snap* of the wet pieces of cloth competed with the flutter of birds in the air and the screeching of crickets in the brush.

Ariel nudged my arm. "What are you thinking about?" she asked, a sparkle of interest in her eyes. I gazed into them with fascination. They had been dark green when we were in the shadows inside the cottage. Now they had become tiny mirrors of the cloudless blue sky above.

"What?" I blurted. "I'm not thinking about anything."

"What I mean is, what do you think about Hannah's report of royal visitors?"

I shrugged. "I don't know what to think."

She let out a rippling laugh that matched the movement of the nearby stream.

"All right," I conceded. "Do you know what I think? I think Hannah sometimes makes up stories and expects people to believe them. People tell her a little gossip, and then they wait to see what she does with it. If she knows anything beyond what people tell her, she claims she got the message from God. No one knows if she's speaking the truth or telling a story. When she's not aware, they point a finger at her and laugh."

The sparkle in Ariel's eyes faded. "The poor soul," she said.

I was appalled to see tears spilling down her cheeks.

"Sometimes, we don't know what to believe, what is true, and what is false," I admitted. "Poor Hannah may be no different from the rest of us. She may simply be looking for a friend. And I think she found one in you." I poked Ariel's arm and grinned.

She brushed the tears from her face. "Some say she has magical powers, that she once healed a leper of his disease," she said in Hannah's defense.

I cocked my head and eyed her with disbelief. "It could have been a simple rash, or a reaction to something the man ate. Ariel, your father is a physician. He could have offered a cure."

"That's what was so amazing. My father tried to cure the man and couldn't relieve him of his sores. He sent him to the priest for examination. But on the way, the man stopped to see Hannah, and by the time he got to the temple, the infection was gone." She was shaking her head. "That woman amazes me. She may have more powers than we suspect."

"There has to be another answer," I said, frowning. "Hannah

may be a witch, as some say. Or a magician. She can make people believe something happened when it didn't, except in their minds." I drew upon a story my father had read from the scriptures. "You know the tale about Moses contending with Pharaoh's magicians, don't you?" I said, and then I related the story the same way my father had told it to me.

Ariel listened with childlike interest.

"What Moses did was real," I concluded. "But what the magicians did may have been a trick of the eye, or the work of the devil himself."

Ariel shuddered. She grew quiet then and appeared to be lost in thought.

"So Hannah could be hearing from the Almighty, or she could be a servant of Satan?" she asked, scowling. "I want to believe she's a servant of Yahweh. She rarely delivers a report without first saying a little prayer. That's proof enough for me."

Then she blinked it all away and tilted her head like another revelation had come to her mind.

"Have you seen how the children run off when they see Hannah coming?" she said.

"I did the same when I was younger," I chuckled. "The truth is, children sense what is good and what is evil. My friends and I once passed by Hannah's house chanting curses against the evil we were certain resided there." I snickered. "The poor woman hasn't a friend in all of Judea."

"I want to be her friend," Ariel insisted. "She must live a lonely life." Then she brightened, and her azure eyes caught a glint of sunlight. "I recently learned that her husband and son were killed in a raid on the road to Galilee. Evil men came down from the hills, took their donkey and all their money, and left them to die by the side of the road. Someone later came along, buried them, and brought the sad news to Hannah."

I listened in horrified silence. Ariel went on, and I could tell from the sadness in her voice that she sincerely cared about the old woman.

"She lives alone," Ariel went on. "She survives on a tiny garden she grows behind her house and from whatever kindness people show her. Once I was so overwhelmed with pity, I saved portions of meat and potatoes from my supper and brought them to her."

I snorted. "I think that woman may have put a curse on you."

"You're wrong, Jesse. She is harmless. Just a lonely old woman without a friend in the world."

"Except for you," I said with a smile.

A deep pink flooded to Ariel's cheeks. "Except for me," she acknowledged with a smile.

No longer was Ariel a giggling young girl who had befriended my little sister. No longer was she the unapproachable physician's daughter. She was a sensitive young woman who loved the unlovable and had a desire to help the poor. I didn't deserve her, and it had little to do with our position in life. I had done evil, and she sought only to do good.

It amazed me that this sweet girl had come out of the house of Hilkiah. The physician was a powerful man who had little tolerance for gossips and beggars. Ariel's mother was an elegant but outspoken woman of leisure. She used her husband's wealth to flaunt her position among the other women in the village. And she also had a temper. When angered, her shrew-like voice carried over the rooftops. Somehow, the steadfast physician and his nag of a wife had given birth to a soft-hearted, sensitive girl named Ariel. There she was, an arm's length away from me, pining over the welfare of a lonely old woman, and I was only beginning to get to know her.

I couldn't help but wonder if a match between a wonderful girl like Ariel and a lowly shepherd like myself might be possible. Though I hardly deserved her, I sensed she wouldn't refuse me. Perhaps Hilkiah might approve of the union, but how could I ever impress her mother? Did I first have to change my life's work, like my brother Andrew had done?

As we sat on the grassy knoll pondering the fate of Hannah,

I moved beyond my fears and asked the question I'd been mulling over for weeks.

"Has your father made a contract with anyone for your—your betrothal?" I said, recalling that my mother had embarrassed her with the same question.

I glanced at my mother, who had her back to us, consumed with pounding the soil out of our wet clothing.

Ariel allowed an uncomfortable few moments to pass. Then she gazed at me, her eyes dancing with mirth. "Why do you want to know, Jesse?"

Lowering my eyes, I rose from the grassy knoll and stumbled onto the stony path that led toward home. "It's time we returned to the house," I said. "I have work." Then I straightened my shoulders and glanced back at the riverbank to see my mother and Sophina still kneeling beside the water.

"Wait," Ariel called out. She leaped to her feet, brushed the wrinkles from her dress, and was at my side in seconds. "You didn't answer my question."

I'd had enough of her game. I looked her in the eye. "I was merely wondering, Ariel. It was a question, that is all."

"I don't believe you," Ariel said raising her chin. Her eyes flashed a challenge. "I think you had good reason to ask. I believe we have bonded."

I gave her a little shrug, but said nothing.

"Jesse," she said, her sweet face turned up at me. "I am not opposed if you want to approach my father on my behalf."

I laughed softly with discomfort. According to the laws of our people, *I* was supposed to be the one to suggest a union, not Ariel. And *I* wasn't supposed to approach her father. My father was supposed to do that. Still, a wave of confidence flowed through me. Ariel had revealed her interest in me. She'd opened the door, and it was up to me to step through it.

Though renewed hope surged through me, as we walked back toward the house, I couldn't help but compare Ariel's jeweled sandals with my own shoes, barely held together with hemlock twine. My eyes traveled to her veils, soft and of the purest linen, fluttering in the breeze, while my frayed linen tunic hung unevenly to my knees. Ariel's hands were like glass, smooth and clean, while mine were rough from years of labor in the sheep pen, and dirt clung to my worn nails. I admitted the truth.

"I want nothing more than to have my father approach your father, Ariel, but I fear they will never agree to such a union. Your father probably prefers the son of one of the wealthy merchants in the village or the heir of another physician, perhaps someone from Jerusalem. And my father will likely settle for one of the village girls."

She listened intently, then she shook her head, her long red waves billowing with each movement.

"We have to try," she insisted.

"My father will never agree to my wishes," I argued. "He's about to choose a match for Sophina. Why should he do any different for me?"

I tried to smile, aware defeat must have showed on my face. "You have forgotten, I am but a poor shepherd. And you?" I stopped walking and stared at her with eyes that must have conveyed my desperation. "You are a princess," I whispered.

My remark caused her to laugh. But it wasn't in jest. It was a ripple of joy mixed with what appeared to be admiration. Then she stopped laughing and exhaled slowly. "You don't know my father," she said. "He is the most generous, forgiving man I have ever known. I doubt he will hold your status against you."

"What about your mother? She flaunts her wealth in the village. I've seen her strutting about the marketplace, selecting this piece of jewelry and that swath of silk, with her eyebrows raised and never a concern for the cost of anything. She walks past me without acknowledging my presence."

"Don't worry about her. She will bow to my father's wishes," Ariel said with confidence.

"No one else has approached him on your behalf?" I said, fearful of her answer.

"Oh, yes. Several young men in the village and also a few from Jerusalem."

I frowned. "Then, what chance do *I* have?"

"My father wants me to be happy," she said. "He has always asked me if I am interested in the young men who come to our door, their pathetic faces pleading for acceptance. And always, I have told him no. Until now. If you ask him, Jesse, I will not say no."

Reality struck. "You live in a wealthy home. I can't offer you the same."

She smiled sweetly. "I'm a simple girl, Jesse. I don't need all the fine furnishings my mother treasures. I prefer a simple life. I love the fields and the flowers. I breathe the outside air with pleasure. And I adore your sheep. I would be content—and proud—to be the wife of a shepherd."

Know ye not that the Lord He is God: it is he that made us, and not we ourselves. We are his people, and the sheep of his pasture.

~Psalm 100:3

I wasted no time to present my desire to my father. After the next day's morning meal, I invited him to join me outside to the fallen log where we'd had many talks in my growing up years. Usually, the talks surrounded lessons my father wanted to teach me, always using the scriptures in support of his thoughts. This time, I was the one who had requested an audience. My hands shook like reeds in a windstorm. I tucked them inside the folds of my cloak. My lips were dry as a potsherd. I kept licking them, to no avail.

Though I'd pondered this talk throughout the night and slept little, I now searched for the right words. How do you tell your father you want to commit the rest of your life to one girl? How do you win his approval when the match is a difficult one?

At my hesitation, he raised his eyebrows in question. Still, he held his tongue and waited with his hands folded on his lap.

I took a deep breath and hesitated.

The old man turned toward me. "You have a confession?" he said. "Or a request?"

"Perhaps both, Father. A confession, and yes, a request too."

He nodded his assent. "Then speak it or leave me and go to work."

His patience was declining. I drew in another breath and forced my shoulders to relax. "My confession first," I said, drawing on hidden courage. "I have developed a friendship with Ariel, and we have talked about the possibility of a contract."

Father nodded, frowned, but said nothing.

"Now my request," I said with increased boldness. "I ask you to approach Hilkiah and seek an agreement."

Like an animal that has exposed its throat to an attacker, I awaited my father's response. Did he understand the desire of a young man's heart? There was a time when he also had made a contract to wed my mother. Did my father make the request or was it thrust upon him?

He didn't answer immediately. He was staring off in the distance, beyond our farm, as though remembering. Then he blinked it away and faced me. I shrank beneath his stern gaze.

"You are young, my son."

"Yes, Abba, but many contracts are made long before this—some before a child is even born."

He nodded. "That is true. My own contract with your mother was decided when I was a year old."

I frowned at the thought of the two of them being promised with no knowledge of the other. Yet, they appeared to be deeply in love, and they had worked out a suitable blending of authority. My mother had charge of the kitchen and garden. My father had control of everything else.

"Were you content with your parents' choice?" I dared to ask.

He nodded, then made a confession of his own. "There was another."

Shocked, I backed away from him. "Another woman?" I said, appalled.

"You already know her, Jesse. It was Jedediah's wife."

"Ischa?!" I scowled in disgust. The woman couldn't hold a candle to my mother. She was dark, not in skin color, but in nature. "She's—she's ugly!"

I regretted my response. But it was true. The woman rarely

put a comb to her hair. Deep bags had settled beneath dark, lifeless eyes. She stood tall and menacing, yet she behaved like a mouse around her husband, always bowing to his demands. She stepped back in Jedediah's shadow when the two fathers met to discuss a match for Sophina. The woman had no life in her. She was like a living corpse, dark and withered and showing no spirit.

"You couldn't have chosen that woman over Mother," I said aloud.

Father chuckled and lines of mirth crinkled the skin around his eyes. "Never. *She* had chosen *me*. She pleaded with her parents to have my contract with your mother annulled. They refused and matched her with Jedediah. As for me, I was content with my parents' choice."

I breathed easier then. "So you married the woman you loved."

"And still do," he acknowledged. "We came from the same mold. As you know, her father was also a shepherd. She understood my work." He released a long breath, like he was preparing to recite a psalm or teach me some truth about life. The mirthful lines disappeared. I froze in expectation.

"Such is not the way with you and Ariel," my father said, frowning. "Her father is a physician of great standing in the village. He has much wealth. But we are humble shepherds. We live a comfortable life. Yahweh has been good to us. But we are not wealthy. We are not respected for our work. A great divide rests between our two families."

I nodded. "I've already thought about our differences. I mentioned my concerns to Ariel. She told me our status doesn't matter to her. She feels as I do, Father. She also wants a match and is going to speak to her father about it."

His eyebrows descended in a deep frown. He gazed at me, his eyes piercing my soul. "I have seen her comings and goings to our home, sometimes bringing a gift to your mother, sometimes with a vial of medicine, sometimes to visit with Sophina. I also was aware when she set her affections on you."

My father was about to pass judgment. It was the most helpless moment of my life. What then? Should I do as Andrew had done? Run off and make a different life for myself? Perhaps take Ariel with me?

His frown faded. "You will have to be patient, my son. I will discuss your proposal with your mother. I know she likes the girl. But in the end, you will accept *my* decision."

Without another word, he rose off the log and strode toward the sheep enclosure. He grabbed his staff from the fence post where it had been resting, then passed through the gate as though planning to work. He entered the enclosure where we kept our ewes. He stroked their backs, enjoyed the feel of their soft wool, the warmth of their bodies, and he most likely was pondering the difficult decision he needed to make.

Then it came to me that perhaps I had asked the wrong authority for approval. Shouldn't I first have gone to the Almighty? Shouldn't I have asked for Yahweh's blessing? Surely, the God of heaven could move my father to give his approval. There could be no obstacles if the Lord God took charge.

I bowed my head in prayer, uncertain what I should say. Should I plead with the Almighty to give me my way, or should I bow my will to his? After listening to my father's preaching for years, I knew what was the right response, but the words caught in my throat. After a fruitless struggle, I lay my unspoken request before Yahweh. I needed to impress my father by working hard and allow him to see I was not a silly youth but a young man ready for a marriage contract.

I rose from the log and rushed into the sheep pen. Under the old man's watchful eye, I plunged into my work—cleaning, bathing, brushing, feeding, discarding the brambles and burrs, and finally, leading the sheep out to the field behind our house. I remained with the flock for most of the day. When one of them strayed, I hurried after the wayward animal and guided it back to the flock. Eli also was out there, numbering the ewes and the goats and keeping an eye out for predators.

When Bartimaeus and the hirelings took their turn with the flock, Eli and I returned to the enclosure and set about removing the sheep dung and sifting in fresh hay. Then we filled the troughs with fresh water. We took time to eat a meal delivered by Sophina, then, satisfied that I had done my share of the work, I left the remainder to the care of my two brothers, and I went off to the home of Jedediah with plans to help Abijah with his work. This had been part of my plan of restitution. Even after sacrificing my favorite lamb, I thought I needed to do more to win Yahweh's approval. Somehow, I had to prove to the Almighty—and to myself—that I was worthy of forgiveness and that I could fulfill the role of husband to the girl I loved.

I entered our neighbor's property with caution, uncertain how I might be received. I needed to let the man know I'd come as a friend and not as an intruder. But I'd no sooner stepped foot on his land when I heard the gate to the enclosure slam.

"What do you want here?" The voice was sharp and accusing.

I turned. Jedediah was marching toward me, his rod raised like he was about to attack.

I raised my hands in defense. "I-I came to offer my services, to help Abijah with his chores."

The big man lowered his rod, but he continued to eye me with suspicion. Realizing who I was, that I had come with Eli to replace his lost rams, the distrust faded from his face, replaced by an inquisitive stare.

"What I mean is, I came as a friend, to work alongside your son," I explained. I gave a nervous shrug. "My father has three sons to help, plus several hirelings. You only have Abijah. Your hired workers have their own duties. I merely came to help."

He narrowed his eyes. "Why are you proposing such a service? Your family already offered seven rams to help me renew my flock, though they are of lesser quality than those I lost. Don't you have work of your own?"

"I finished my work." I looked around but there was no sign of Abijah. "Where is your son?"

Jedediah nodded toward the house. "He's doing what cripples do. He's lying on his bed, alone, while his mother fawns over him."

I looked closely at Jedediah. For his age he was a man of great health, probably able to do his own work and Abijah's too.

"With your permission, I'd like to go inside and see him," I said.

Slowly, Jedediah nodded his approval, but the glimmer of doubt had returned. How could a man like that, who had taken advantage of so many people, how could he trust someone who offered free work? It made little sense.

I turned away from him and approached the door of the house. Once inside, I took a moment to adjust to the darkness. The room reeked of harsh cleansers. A lone oil lamp illuminated a corner of the room where Abijah lay on a mat of straw. I drew closer. The boy's face was twisted with pain. His mother stood nearby with a bowl in her hand. I looked her over, aware that I was facing the woman who had pursued my father. Again I breathed a sigh of relief. My mother had a sweet continence and a disposition to match. The one who stood before me now had an ugly face that must have been bred somewhere deep inside her heart.

Huffing, she lowered the spoon to the bowl and stepped back. Her bent shoulders denied the proud woman who had come to my door only a few weeks before seeking a contract with Sophina.

"What do you want, boy?" she snapped, and her face grew darker and her brow more knitted.

"To visit Abijah." My own voice came out weak and pitiful.

She grunted and turned away to the kitchen. Though she had disappeared into the shadows, the clatter of dishes rose from the dark corner of the room.

I drew closer to the bed of straw. Abijah blinked in recognition. The glow of the oil lamp illuminated his sad eyes. He turned his face away. "Leave," he snarled.

"Abijah, I'm here to help you, not to harm you."

He turned back and stared at me. "Help me? How can *anyone* help me? Look what my father has done." He pushed the linen blanket from his body and exposed legs that resembled two broken limbs of a tree, bent out of shape and with painful nubs protruding. "He has taken away my ability to walk. He has taken away my ability to work, to marry, to become a man. He has taken away my *life*."

Abijah's mother sighed from the kitchen and resumed the clanking of bowls and spoons. Then came the swish of a broom against the floor.

I stared in shock at the boy's mangled legs and shook my head. "You must be in a lot of pain, Abijah. I'm sorry."

He snorted. "Sorry? Why should *you* be sorry? You've won. I can no longer compete with you."

"I haven't won anything," I told him. "I was unkind to you in the past, always vying with you in the marketplace and in the village games, hoping to beat you at every turn. But I never wanted you to suffer. I want you to be well. To walk again. To tend your sheep, even if it means you will rob me of a sale or two. I merely want to be your friend, Abijah."

"My *friend*?" The boy's tone was filled with scorn. "How can *you* be my friend?"

"I can help you with your chores," I offered. "I can get you out of this—this bed of confinement, so you can do your work, with me at your side." I dared to step closer. "Will you allow me to do that, Abijah? Will you allow me to be your friend?"

Seeing the boy in such agony, I began to think less about making myself right with God and more about helping another human being who was suffering. I was amazed at my own transformation. No longer was I a self-centered youth who competed with Abijah in every aspect of life. My hatred had turned into compassion.

"What do you propose?" Abijah challenged me. He sat up a little, bracing himself on his elbows.

"First, let's get you out of this bed," I said, pulling the covers free. Again, I winced at the sight of his disfigured legs, and I doubted we could accomplish much.

"Have your parents summoned the physician?" I said. "Surely, he can help to straighten your legs."

Abijah grunted. "Hilkiah came immediately. He gave me medicine to relieve the pain, but straighten my legs? There is no hope."

I leaned close, gave a gentle tug to Abijah's arm and helped him to stand. We made it to the open door with me bearing most of his weight and Abijah dragging one foot behind the other.

He paused at the door and turned toward me. The look on his face was one of disbelief. "Do you really want to help me with my chores?"

I nodded and smiled with encouragement. "You will feel useful again."

He grabbed a small knife from a shelf by the door. "Come and see what my chores are now that I'm a helpless cripple."

"You're not helpless," I insisted. "And you won't be a cripple for long. You can do this, Abijah. You can take on your former work. But you have to try. And you need to have confidence. You need to believe."

I didn't know for certain that Abijah could work again. But I needed him to believe he could. There was a verse of scripture my father often recited whenever I'd been overwhelmed to the point of giving up. Now I chanced to repeat those words to Abijah. "*Though he slay me, yet will I trust in him.*"

Abijah nodded. "The words of Job. I had forgotten."

"My father won't let me forget," I said, chuckling.

Abijah laughed. "I know about a father's stubbornness," he sneered, though he was still laughing.

"Come on," I urged him. "Let's show your father what you can do."

Smiling past his pain, Abijah gripped my arm and together we passed through the door. The walk to the sheep enclosure was arduous. We stopped often so Abijah could rest. We passed through the same gate Eli and I had entered on that fateful night. Most of the animals were out in the pasture with Jedediah's hirelings, but six young male lambs remained inside. Abijah turned to me.

"These are not prize rams," he noted. "They are flawed, blemished, not fit for sacrifice."

He slipped out of my grasp, limped closer, and stumbled into the midst of the lambs. "My father wants the manhood cut from these animals. They are not good for breeding. They have little value except for the supper table"

I knew what Abijah was suggesting, and though my father did not approve of this mutilation I had already committed to helping him. I swallowed hard, then drew close to the lambs, lifted one, and flipped him on his back. Moving quickly, I grasped his back legs and spread them apart.

The knife in Abijah's hand glinted in the light of the sun. He kept his balance by holding onto a fence post. Then he raised the knife and swiftly made the cut, bent close and completed the deed with his teeth, emitting a loud sucking sound. Then he rose to his full height, pulled the pieces of flesh from his mouth and spit the blood in the dirt. Filled with disgust, I nearly choked on the bile that rushed to my throat. I released the lamb, expecting him to writhe in agony. Instead, he pranced away, blood dripping from his underside, yet surprisingly unaffected by the offense.

"We don't do this to *our* lambs," I told Abijah, my distaste obvious. "It's cruel. There is no need for it."

"These flawed ones are of no use to us," said Abijah. "We have to keep them from breeding with our ewes. Now they will grow fat and be more suitable for the table." He stared at me with a challenge in his eyes. "If you really want to help, let's take care of the rest of them."

Reluctantly, I lifted another lamb, spread his back legs, and waited for Abijah to lower the knife.

When we finished with all six, we left the pen and sat

together on a wooden bench with a basket of raisin cakes Ischa provided. She managed a smile, and I imagined she may have been quite lovely at one time, but never as lovely as my mother. Still smiling, she handed each of us a cup of goat's milk and a wedge of cheese, then she stood by with her arms crossed and waited for us to finish our meal. Abijah took a bite of his raisin cake and smiled at me. It turned my stomach to see him eating with the same mouth that had torn the masculinity from his lambs. He appeared unconcerned.

"Thank you, Jesse," he said with sincerity. "I could not have done that job by myself. Nor can I clean the enclosure or carry water from the well. One day, I'll have to tackle the shearing. That job requires having someone hold the animal still. Our hired workers are busy enough. I have no one to help with the shearing, no one to gather the wool, no one to wash it clean, no one to spread it out to dry, no one to carry it to the house for my mother to separate the strands and spin them into garments."

It was obvious what he was suggesting. I knew the job well. It was tedious. It truly did take two people. And now Abijah was hinting that I should help with that too.

"You have someone now," I relented. "I will come here again when my work is finished at home, and we will do another job together. And when the season is upon us, I will help you with the shearing."

Abijah's smile faded. Tears filled his eyes. "I'm grateful, Jesse. I don't know why you want to do this for me, but I am sorry for the many times I've offended you."

I patted his hand. "All is forgiven," I said, adding, "I'm sorry, too."

I walked away from Jedediah's property that day with a lump in my throat and a deep regret for the terrible harm I had caused. If I could have relived that fateful night, I would have refused to follow Eli's plan. Now regret consumed me, and I was determined to make things right.

I believe that was the moment when I made the transition

from a boy to a man. Something had changed within me, and it had nothing to do with the number of my age. Nor could the change be seen with the naked eye. Something good had happened inside me.

Quite possibly, the seeds of change had been planted in me more than two years before at the side of a manger in Bethlehem. Now those seeds had sprouted and grown. Now, I determined to pay for my sins any way I could and free myself from the guilt once and for all.

Chapter Fifteen

He shall feed his flock like a shepherd: He shall gather the lambs with His arm, and carry them in His bosom, and shall gently lead those that are with young.
~Isaiah 40:11

Despite all I'd done to relieve my guilt, my sins continued to torment me. I had given three of my best rams to Jedediah. I had offered to help Abijah with his work. I had sacrificed my favorite little lamb, an act that broke my heart until I thought I, too, might die. None of those sacrifices relieved the guilt that kept me in bondage. What more did the Almighty want from me?

Besides feeling guilty, I felt ashamed and unworthy of the angel's visit on that long ago night. I was unworthy of Ariel's affection. My father might never give his approval—and rightfully so. I didn't want to wait for his denial, had to put an end to my misery, one way or the other.

I decided to approach my father one more time. I chose what appeared to be the right moment. We were in the field, looking over our flock and discussing the breeding of some. We had completed our chores for the morning. There was no pressing job, no reason to hurry through our talk and run back to the barn.

"Abba," I said, with boldness. "I need to know. Are you going to seek a contract between me and Ariel?"

He shook his head and huffed with annoyance. "You cannot

expect me to approach a man like Hilkiah. I would look a fool, and so would you."

A lump caught in my throat. My eyes burned. "But Ariel said—"

He raised his hand. "It doesn't matter what Ariel said. She is a child and subject to her parents' authority." Ignoring my look of distress, he went on without sympathy. "My poor, ignorant son, you need to admit the differences between our two families. They live in a whitewashed home with a large courtyard and many servants to do their bidding. Their garden produces all they need, and their cupboards are full. Hilkiah sits at the city gate with village officials. I have no place with them. He dines with the rich and powerful, and can choose any one of their sons for his daughter. But you?" His sneer pierced my heart, yet he continued to hurl his insults. "Hilkiah will never agree to such a match. Nor can I rightfully ask for it. Look at yourself, Jesse. Though I am proud to have such a faithful, hardworking son, you are not fit for a girl like Ariel. Wake up. Choose one of the village girls, someone who labors in the field or serves in a home of the rich. I will not deny you."

I crumbled beneath my father's rebuke. Still, I pressed ahead, thoughts of Ariel and our last time together nudging me on. "Abba, you have recited scriptures to me for most of my life. Many of those promises from the Psalms have to do with trusting God and pursuing your dreams. Isn't that what I'm doing now? Isn't that what you've always taught me to do? Haven't you also said there is no shame in being a shepherd?"

He tilted his head and stared deeply into my eyes, as though I had caught his attention. Sympathy flooded over his countenance, and his next words were more tender. "There is a difference between a dream and what is real, Jesse. Our Creator placed us where we are. He did the same for Hilkiah and his family. Different places. Different ends."

"You don't understand, Father. My dream has already been fulfilled. Ariel wants an agreement as much as I do. She believes she can convince her father to give his approval. She has already refused the proposals of several suitors, and Hilkiah has allowed her to reject them. He's letting her choose, Father. And, she's chosen *me.*"

He snorted. "Jesse, haven't you listened to a word I've said? Take a look at yourself. Take a look at this place." His gesture took in our entire farm. "Look at our humble cottage, our poorly built sheep enclosures, the muddy ground, our limited grazing land." He grunted. "Have you not seen the worried lines on your mother's face when she peers into an empty cupboard? Do you want that spoiled girl to have those lines? Do you want Ariel to spend the rest of her days in near poverty? Wake up, my son. This union will not be good for either of you. Ariel will feel cheated. And you will labor beyond your strength to replace the treasures she left behind."

I stood frozen, allowing my father's words to enter my ears but blocking them from controlling my heart.

"Imagine this," he went on. "After two or three babies, you find your wife stooped and tired, her hands raw from scouring the floors, tears flowing from her eyes, her face flushed from laboring in the heat of the day. That's the moment when she will long for the comfortable life she walked away from."

I shook my head. "Now who's dreaming, Father? I can't live my life wondering if something like that will happen. I will work hard to make sure Ariel is well-cared for. I don't see my mother looking like you described her. She doesn't stoop. She doesn't weep and wail over her lot in life."

"Your mother came from the same background. Her father and all her ancestors were shepherds."

"That is true. I agree, we live a humble existence. But we have never failed to put food on the table. And you have generously provided a servant girl to help Mother with the household duties." I shook my head at him. "I am asking you to present our petition to Hilkiah. Let *his* word be final. I don't believe he will turn us away. He may have a fine house and an honorable profession, but he is a humble man who often gives to the poor. He will not deny his daughter's request. This match was meant to be, Abba. I have never wanted another, only Ariel, and you can't ask me to settle for less."

My father straightened. "You forget one thing," he said, a sternness returning to his voice. "I have said it before, and I say it again. Bartimaeus must be promised first, then Eli. You are third in line, Jesse. You will have to wait until your brothers' future has been settled."

"You can't be serious, Father. Bartimaeus will *never* marry. And Eli? He has too many young girls begging for his attention. He will not easily make a decision. I beg you, set aside this useless rule and grant me my request."

My father removed a handkerchief from the fold of his robe and mopped the perspiration from his forehead. Then he crossed his arms and gave a firm shake of his head, the same way he had done in the midst of every bargain he had made with the buyers of his sheep. And I knew I had lost.

I left him standing there and went about my chores without thinking about what I was doing. I completed my work with hands that moved without my direction and feet that carried me from the field to the barn and back. The work was done, but I was hardly aware of it.

More days passed. Still, my father did not repent.

"Has Father changed his mind?" Eli asked me one day as we were raking the ewes' enclosure.

Bartimaeus was also there, pretending to help, but making little progress.

I shook my head.

"No word yet?" Bartimaeus said. "You should give it up, Jesse. Pick one of the village girls. They are always available."

I tossed a burr in his direction, then continued to rake with more vigor.

After another hour passed, I left my two brothers to finish the work, and I went to Jedediah's home to help Abijah. I no longer thought of this labor as a chore. What had begun as an act of mercy had turned into time spent with a friend. From the first day I started helping Abijah, we had poured our hearts out to each other. I talked freely about my interest in Ariel, and he assured me he had never intended to make a claim on her. Our friendship had grown so that every day in the waning hours of the afternoons, I looked forward to working with him and sharing my life with him. I even regretted that he had not married my sister, making us brothers.

When I arrived at Jedediah's farm, I was surprised to see the man's sheep looking especially well-groomed. Then I caught sight of the reason. Ischa's houseboy, Jahzeel, had been laboring among the ewes. The youngster worked like a seasoned shepherd. He flashed a smile in my direction, then turned away and went back to his labor. I walked closer and stopped to speak with him.

"You make a good shepherd, Jahzeel. Jedediah's ewes have never looked better." His smile spread, exposing a row of sparkling white teeth, a stark contrast against his glistening dark skin. Not once did he ask after Sophina, though I suspected she was on his mind. I understood his pain, for I, too, yearned after a girl who was out of my reach. He gave me a nod and hurried out to the field to gather cuttings for the barn.

I went to the house and summoned Abijah outside. We went to the field and worked alongside Jahzeel, with Abijah wielding a sickle and me gathering the cuttings into a pile. I succumbed to a sense of pride over the wonderful change we three were able to achieve in Jedediah's pasture. Abijah's countenance also had changed. Instead of scowling and whining in agony, he was smiling and even laughed out loud when he swung the sickle too hard and fell to the ground in a heap. Jahzeel and I roared with laughter. Together we helped Abijah to his feet and got back to work again. What had begun with me trying to make amends for a wrong I had committed had turned into a daily enjoyment. The young man I once hated had become a friend. The work we did together had become a labor of love.

The truth was, between working with my father's flock, repairing barns, cleaning enclosures, and then helping Abijah, I had little time to pursue anyone, not even Ariel. At the end of each day, I fell, exhausted, onto my mat and was asleep within moments.

Though I should have grown tired of laboring on two farms, I counted it all joy. My friendship with Abijah grew, and though our talks centered around one day having our own farms, I couldn't help but mention Ariel now and then. Though I belabored my broken heart, he listened without complaint.

As it was, I managed to meet with Ariel on the Sabbath, when all other activities ceased. It was then we walked along the path near the spring or sat talking beneath the sycamore tree at the edge of her father's property.

One Sabbath morning, we dined on almond cakes and raisin breads she had snatched from her mother's kitchen. It wasn't long before the physician came out to the courtyard, set his eyes on Ariel and me, and, heaving a sigh, he shuffled back inside the house. Inevitably, Ariel's mother found an excuse to step outside—a rug needed batting, herbs needed plucking from their garden, a cook fire needed tending. She turned a troubled gaze on the two of us, arched a brow, then, without saying a word, she turned away and went inside. I could feel her eyes on us from the window, and I knew we were never completely alone.

Aside from wishing I could favorably impress Ariel's parents, I spent long hours thinking of ways I might win my own father's approval. When I was in the shearing house passing the knife over the backs of our sheep, I did the job with great vigor. When I walked among my sheep in the pasture, I also looked after those Father had given to my brothers. I even helped my mother and sister with their household chores, sometimes going inside to sweep the floor or carry a kettle out to the fire pit. All the while, I longed for my father's approval.

The truth was, my biggest battle was with myself. I didn't think I was good enough, strong enough, or skilled enough to pursue a life with Ariel. One main question continued to prick my mind. *Can a princess find happiness with a humble shepherd?*

Spurred on by my plan for a better life, I began to take a serious interest in our family business. I thought of new ways to enlarge our flock without having to seek a partnership with Jedediah or anyone else. I used some of my own money to purchase a few prime animals from a well-to-do shepherd who lived near the Jordan River, where the grass was thick and rich with minerals.

I hired another hireling from Edom, purchased a second donkey, built another dray, sturdier than the first, and I doubled our income during the festivals by hauling a greater number of sheep and goats to the Holy City. Apart from doing my own work and helping Abijah with his duties, I petitioned the temple priests for a job caring for the sheep they set apart for their meals. I went there every Friday afternoon, and I left before the Sabbath hour. The priests paid me well, and I discovered such employ-ment received great honor among the people. With Abijah unable to pursue such a position, I had no trouble securing it.

One afternoon, I sat outside the house on a rock-hewn ledge, a stylus in my hand, scratching financial figures on a sheepskin parchment. I was distracted when a hearty laugh rose from the path behind me. Turning, I caught sight of a tall, lanky youth pulling an overloaded donkey along the road from the west. I squinted my eyes against the harshness of the setting sun. The visitor—merely a shadow against the glow of the sunset—waved his arm and called my name. I leaped to my feet and let the stylus and parchment fall to the ground.

"Andrew!" I yelled and ran to my brother.

Chapter Sixteen

Behold, the Lord God will come with strong hand, and his arm shall rule for him: behold, his reward is with him, and his work before him.

~Isaiah 40:10

A rush of tears spilled from my eyes. Through the blur I gazed at my brother's face, surprised to see his chin clean-shaven and his curly hair cropped in the style of the Greeks, making him appear years younger than his actual age.

I rushed forward and wrapped my arms around him. "Are you home to stay?"

"For a little while," he said, stepping back from our embrace. "I have much to tell, much to share."

I looked him over, amazed at how well he looked. His skin glowed with a golden tan. His dark eyes sparkled with intensity. He'd shed the threadbare tunic and tattered sheepskin cloak he was wearing the day he departed. Now he wore fine clothes made of rich linen and embroidered with threads of colored silk. A leather belt encircled his waist, and on his feet were sandals made up of many straps held together with rings of gold. Silver and gold chains hung from his neck, and his first finger displayed a large emerald set in a gold band that reflected sparks of sunlight.

"You have acquired your wealth, after all," I marveled.

"Yes, my brother. And I've brought gifts." He gestured toward his donkey, piled high with three large packs. "Help me get these parcels inside the house, and I'll tell my story before the whole family." He paused and lost his smile. "That is, if Father will welcome me."

"We'll convince him together," I offered.

I assisted my brother in removing the sacks from his donkey. After tying the beast to a rail beside the trough of water, we carried Andrew's bundles into the house. The moment my brother stepped foot through the door, Sophina leaped from her place in the corner. Shrieking with joy, she flung her arms around his neck.

Our mother stood in shock, a soup ladle about to drop from her hand. She hovered there, beside the kettle of potato soup. Realizing her son had come home, she lowered the ladle into the pot, brushed her hands on her apron, and stepped into Andrew's open arms.

I left them amidst an animated discussion and hurried outside to summon Bartimaeus and Eli, certain they would be glad to see their wayward brother had returned. But Father? The old man had sent him away without any sign of remorse. I found him in the barn and told him the news. I waited as my announcement hung in the air.

"So the prodigal has returned," my father quietly mused. He stared at me for a moment, like he was having difficulty deciding what to do. He asked, "Did you witness any signs of repentance?"

I shrugged. "I don't know, Father. He looks wonderful, even prosperous. Won't you come inside and see for yourself? He said he has much to tell us. And he brought gifts."

Eli and Bartimaeus flew laughing and shouting toward the house, but the old man walked slowly along the path, still undecided, I supposed.

"You need to forgive him, Father," I urged the tired old man.

He shook his head, turned around and started back toward the barn.

"Abba, please," I implored him. "Andrew is with Mother this very moment, and he wants to see you. You should at least come inside and listen to what he has to say."

I searched my mind for one of father's favorite proverbs.

"Hatred stirs up strife, but love covers all offenses," I quoted.

My father hesitated, his eyes widening in remembrance. There was a softening of his brow, and he gave a nod and walked with me to our cottage. Upon crossing the threshold, he froze and stared at his number three son. Andrew rushed toward him and extended his arms. The old man resisted at first, then quietly gave in to the embrace.

My eyes darted back and forth between the two of them. Father and son in a moment of indecision. Which one of them had the courage to tear down the wall?

Andrew, of course, made the first gesture. He took our father's hand and led him to a wooden bench against the wall. Usually the one in charge of whatever was happening in our home, our father now had only to sit and listen. I laughed to myself over his discomfort, a rare sight to see.

With Sophina helping, our mother quickly put out a meal of potato soup, dried berries, strips of lamb, and flatbread basted with honey. The aromas wafted from our table, drawing me and my brothers to our cushions. After Mother recited the usual prayer, we directed our attention at Andrew, who remained standing, like an orator preparing his message.

"I want to make known to you the life I have experienced since leaving," he began, his face aglow. "My journey was uneventful, completely safe, even pleasant at times. I found Alexandria to be a wonderful place." He paced the room and waved his hands in wild gestures. "A magnificent lighthouse stands on the shore. The streets are wide and paved with pure marble. There's a huge marketplace with many shops lining the main road. There are no hovels in Alexandria. No miserable dwellings. Everyone lives in comfort with courtyard gardens that open onto the street."

"What are the people like?" Eli's face brightened with interest.

"The people?" Andrew grinned. "I found them receptive to an outsider. The day I arrived, a complete stranger offered me a hot meal and a warm bed. The furnishings in his home were not like ours. Their beds stand high off the floor and are hidden beneath piles of pillows and blankets of the softest materials." He gestured toward the rest of us reclining on pillows around our table. "They don't sit on the floor. They sit on platforms raised this high on four legs, and their tables stand equally high allowing them to dine in comfort."

Andrew paused to enjoy our reactions. Mother smiled and released a delighted sigh. Sophina sat clapping her hands and giggling. And all three of us brothers listened with eyes wide and mouths hanging open. Andrew's descriptions of that far-off land held our interest.

"Did you find work there?" Eli asked.

Andrew nodded with enthusiasm. "Immediately upon my arrival," he said, his chest appearing to grow wider. "A shop owner offered me a position selling his wares. He had an assortment of items—fine jewelry, porcelain vases, layers and layers of colorful fabric. After I had worked there for a couple of months, I had earned enough income to become a partner and to share, not only in securing supplies for the shop but also in dividing the profits. But, that isn't the best part," he said, his eyes glistening. "The best part is, I am attending school."

I held my breath, my admiration instantly hampered by a twinge of jealousy. I had never aspired to go to any school beyond the teachings at the village synagogue. Now my brother had stepped into another way of life that promised to raise his status even more.

He turned his gaze on our father, who'd sat listening with eyebrows raised in appraisal. "That's right, Abba," Andrew said, smiling. "I'm going to school. I used part of my inheritance to enroll in several different studies at the city's library. Scholars come from afar to teach many different subjects. I have chosen to sit at the feet of a teacher of the law."

"The law?" I was incredulous. He wasn't talking about the Law of Moses, which every young boy studied, even us poor shepherds. He was talking about a different law, one that governed people of all races and beliefs. One that took place in the courts of man.

"Yes, the law," Andrew responded with a confident nod. "I am studying to be a lawyer, so I can help people with their civil disagreements. When I finish my studies I will sit at the city gate and debate the state of affairs with the elders. I can return to Beit Sahour, or move to Jerusalem, if I choose. No matter where I go, I can recommend civic changes with authority. Lawyers and physicians are respected nearly everywhere. In Jerusalem they can be members of the Great Sanhedrin. In Beit Sahour, they work with the village leaders. What do you say, Father? Have I not chosen a worthy profession?"

Our father merely grunted, but I thought there was a hint of pride in his tired eyes.

Here I was, still struggling to learn all of my duties as a sheep herder, and my brother had entered a whole other world and was going to be a lawyer. Andrew had been gone from us for two years, and already he had stepped into a higher position than I could ever hope to achieve.

If I had gone with Andrew and attended school, perhaps then I might have been fit for marriage to Ariel. Perhaps I might even be a physician, like her father. I blinked hard against the realization that I had missed a great opportunity. I looked at Andrew, his face aglow, his short-cropped hair and ornate attire confirming his fondness for the ways of the Greeks. Should I be envious? Or frightened for him?

I turned my gaze toward our father and tried to make sense of the lines on the old man's face. Though Osiah ben Shallum had never admitted he was wrong to disown Andrew, it was obvious he now regretted doing so. I passed my gaze around the table, stopping at each family member and trying to determine how each one was receiving Andrew's news. Each of them appeared captivated. Except for our father. His face was as unreadable as stone.

After a tense period of silence, the old man finally spoke. "I need to know, are you here to stay, Andrew?"

Andrew straightened his back and slowly shook his head. "No, Abba. I'm sorry, but I need to get back to my studies. I merely came home to restore my standing with our family, and to let you all know I am content with my decision."

The room went silent as we all settled our attention on our father, awaiting his judgment.

He simply nodded but didn't speak. A moist sadness filled his eyes. He rose awkwardly from the bench, came to the table, and settled on the cushion in his usual place. He reached out with a trembling hand and gathered a handful of dried berries, then dropped them in his mouth, one at a time. The proud man was caught between admitting he'd been wrong and stubbornly holding onto his place of authority.

The chatter resumed around the table, with my brothers and me expressing interest in Andrew's new life. We showered him with questions, which he promptly answered.

Our mother simply sat with her lips parted in a big smile, obviously thrilled to have her family together again, though she had to know Andrew wasn't going to stay. Noticing the empty platters, she rose from her place and flew about the kitchen, directing her servant girl to provide more servings from the hearth. She asked Sophina to bring another cruse of wine. Then, satisfied, she settled on her cushion, and with a sweep of her arm, she beckoned Andrew to sit beside her.

He complied with her wishes, and she slipped her fingers through his arm, looking like she might never let him go. Her eyes sparkled with delight. The reunion, though temporary, had brought her great joy. I was grateful for my brother's visit, but I worried that Mother's moment of happiness would fade when he walked out the door again.

"Eat, my son, eat," she encouraged him, her face aglow with admiration. "It's certain you did not find the right kind of food in that big city across the sea. You are so thin, so frail. While you are home we will fill your belly and make you strong again."

Andrew smiled down at her. "You are correct, Mother. The food in Alexandria *is* different from what I was accustomed to. Although they also enjoy many of the same foods allowed by the Law of Moses—lamb, fish from the Great Sea, olives, nearly every kind of vegetable, and unleavened bread—they are not bound by our strict observances. But don't worry, Mother, I don't starve. And my thin appearance? It's my choice. I restrain myself from overeating, and I spend much of my time in my studies at the library."

Andrew had followed his dream and had become so involved in his studies he didn't worry about food. If anything, he appeared to be healthier than the rest of us.

More than that, my brother had increased his wealth. Conscious of the difference between us, I adjusted my fraying tunic and gazed with disgust at my dirty sandals, now discarded beside Andrew's fine-crafted shoes by the door. Perhaps Andrew had been right to leave.

Then as though seeing into my jealous heart, Andrew leaped to his feet. "I have presents," he announced. "Presents for everyone."

Sophina bounced on her cushion and started clapping. Eli and Bartimaeus straightened and gave their full attention to Andrew. He hurried to the corner of the room where we had tossed his bags. He opened one, and pulled out a huge object swathed in a silk cloth. Pulling away the wrapping, he revealed a beautiful blue vase with a rounded base and a narrow neck, covered with hand-painted images of birds and butterflies. He held it out to our mother. She didn't hesitate. Gasping, she reached out and accepted his gift.

"It's so fragile," she whispered, turning the vase over in her hands and eying every splash of color, every line of gilding. "Whatever will I do with this? It is far too lovely for our simple home." Still, she shut her eyes and clutched the vase to her bosom.

Andrew chuckled with pleasure. "Do with it whatever you

want, Mother. It's yours to put flowers in or to simply keep as a remembrance of your third son."

He turned away, opened another sack, and pulled out more gifts. There was a calf's skin vest for Eli, a leather scrip for me, a woven belt for Bartimaeus, and a sheer yellow veil and gold bracelets for Sophina. Finally, he withdrew a long-handled pipe and a leather pouch for our father. He opened the pouch and released a cascade of gold coins onto the table in front of the old man. The room erupted in shouts of surprise and laughter. Our father sat quietly examining his pipe, a sad smile on his lips. He looked up at Andrew, and nodded. This son that he had disowned and sent away had returned and had replaced his entire inheritance, and more. Father rose awkwardly from the table, stumbled over to where Andrew stood, and wrapped his arms around him.

"I have wronged you," he said. "You made your own way, and you proved me wrong. And now, you are sharing your success with your family. Will you forgive me?"

Andrew was already nodding, his eyes filled with happy tears. "I never doubted your love, Abba," he said. "But I had to prove to you that I had chosen the right path."

At that moment, a gentle knock drew our attention to the door. Mother's servant girl rushed to open it. Ariel stood in the open doorway, her hair aflame in the glow of sunlight beyond. She looked like an angel standing there in a simple white dress with a basket of breads in her arms.

Her eyes fell upon Andrew and a quizzical smile tugged at the corners of her lips.

"My brother has come ho—" I started, but my words were interrupted when Andrew stepped between us and gave a little bow.

"I remember you," he said, beaming. "You're Sophina's friend, the physician's daughter. You're Ariel."

He reached for her free hand and drew her into the room. Then he went back to his pile of bags and pulled a small package from the bottom. He yanked the string and pulled out a lacy shawl. It lay limp across his arm in a delicate spray of blues and greens. Ignoring the rest of us, he returned to Ariel and held it out to her.

"A gift for the prettiest girl in the village," he said. "Something to show off the color of your eyes."

A fire erupted inside me. Surely, Andrew hadn't expected Ariel to visit our home that day. Had he meant the veil as a gift for her? Or for someone else? She released the basket of breads to Mother and drew the shawl to her cheek. It was true. The mix of colors brought out the blue-green of her eyes. Andrew had chosen the perfect gift for her. My face was so hot, and my throat so tight, I couldn't speak. Eli was staring at me. He gave a little shrug and a half-smile.

Andrew needed to know Ariel had been *my* choice. Hadn't I confided this with him when he was living at home? Unaware of my reaction, he kept pulling more presents out of his bags. He handed Eli and Bartimaeus hand-carved tools and sharp metal knives with pearl handles. He tossed a linen shirt in my direction. And he poured a handful of glittering gems in Sophina's open palm. Ariel gasped in amazement.

I was sorry my brother had ever come home.

Like two simpletons, Eli and Bartimaeus pressed him to talk about the places he'd visited and the people he'd met. The two of them hammered Andrew with questions, until he nearly collapsed in exhaustion. I kept wishing my brothers hadn't praised him like a mighty conqueror who'd come home from the war. This was Andrew, our wayward brother, the one who had left us to do all the work. Why didn't they see that?

There was no doubt, my brother was a successful man, but, instead of being happy for him, I found myself resenting him. He had done something I could never do. He'd gone after his freedom. He'd taken control of his life. And now he was a huge success, and I was still a poor shepherd boy. What's worse, our differences were now exposed before the girl of my dreams. If only he'd also come home with a bride.

As though reading my mind, our mother asked Andrew if a young woman had caught his interest in one of those far-off places he'd visited.

My brother glanced at Ariel and sent another ripple of jealousy through me.

"None of the Greek girls compare with the beauties who live right here in our village," he said, still holding her gaze.

Ariel smiled shyly and lowered her eyes. A prickling sensation struck the back of my neck. I reached up to swipe it away. I had to keep control. I clenched my fists, straightened my back, and ground my teeth. Andrew glanced at me as though he knew he'd stirred up my anger. He gave a little grin, and continued his flirtation with Ariel.

"The Greek girls wear far too much paint on their faces," he expounded. "In contrast, the girls of Beit Sahour allow their natural beauty to shine through." He gave Ariel a wink, and I wanted to punch his face. This time she held his gaze far longer than I thought necessary.

My mouth went dry. An invisible sword carved a hole in my heart. I should have been thrilled my brother had come home, and earlier that day I was, but now I felt a bitterness I couldn't dispel.

The way the women in our house doted on Andrew, offering him sweet pastries and refilling his cup with wine, I believed I'd made a mistake not running off with him. What if I ignored the needs of my family and went off to make my own way in life? Then perhaps I could claim Ariel with no one to oppose me. Now she appeared to be captivated by my brother, swooning over him and clinging to every word he spoke. It was beginning to look as if I'd lost her forever.

Chapter Seventeen

He shall feed his flock like a shepherd.
~Isaiah 40:11a

I was relieved when the meal was over. I expected everyone might simply go about their business. But instead of helping Mother restore her kitchen, Sophina and Ariel left the work to the hired girl and the two of them knelt at Andrew's feet while he told story after story about life in the big cities ruled by the Greeks. He spoke about the shops, the merchants of Alexandria, the library with its thousands of scrolls, the market where he purchased those fine gifts he'd brought, the shop where he worked, and the ship that carried him back to Palestine.

I tried to ignore his boasting, but, in truth, I was filled with a strange mix of fascination and jealousy. After a while, I grew weary of the arrogance that spewed from my brother's mouth. He bragged about how he bargained with traders, always getting the better deal, how he'd made a great many friends, male and female alike, and how he had earned the respect of the town leaders, who offered him positions in their places of business.

At around dusk, Ariel bid us farewell and left, but not before she offered one more smile to Andrew and a whispered, "I loved your stories." The angry prickles returned to the back of my neck.

My mother summoned Sophina to help her ready our home for bedtime. Eli and Bartimaeus followed our father out to the pen to retire the sheep. I remained behind with Andrew.

"Will you walk with me?" I said, struggling to suppress my rage.

Somehow, I intended to address his behavior and remind him that Ariel was the girl I'd spoken of from our youth.

"Certainly, little brother," was Andrew's response, inciting further hostility within me. I grabbed his arm and steered him out the door.

"Don't call me *little* brother."

"Shouldn't you be helping Father with the sheep?" he said, his voice mocking.

I ignored him and dragged him to the log where Father and I recently had our own little *talk*. I needed time to choose the right words. Words that heal, not harm. Words that let Andrew know he was stepping on my dream.

We approached the fallen log, which allowed us a view of our two brothers leading the sheep in from the plain. As they moved through the gate, I gazed at the wooden structures, the fencing and the storage bins, and all that our family owned. This was what Andrew had given up to go out in the world and claim a fortune of his own. Eli and Bartimaeus were filling the troughs. The aroma of fresh cut hay and mashed corn wafted on a breeze, sweet reminders of the kind of work I had chosen.

I had intended to confront Andrew for flirting with Ariel. But the sympathetic look in his eyes stopped me. I had expected my brother to gloat. Instead, he looked the way he always had when we were young and told each other everything, even if it meant revealing secrets no one else should hear. I sensed I could trust him with the truth.

"A lot of things happened after you left," I said. With renewed trust in my brother, I told him about Jedediah's offer of a match between Sophina and Abijah and the business deal the man had proposed. The story was met with a shaking of Andrew's head and a puff of annoyance from his breath.

With sadness, I confessed the evil Eli and I had committed late at night, and I followed with the harsh punishment Jedediah had exerted upon his son. Despite Andrew's gaze of admiration, I bowed my head in shame. When I finished, he rested a hand on my shoulder. I looked at his face, expecting to find pity there. Instead he looked back at me with what appeared to be rage.

"I wish I had been there to help you and Eli in the slaughter of those rams." His back straightened, and he raised his chin, his former arrogance returning. "Was your crime discovered?" he asked.

I shook my head. "Eli confessed to Father. He insisted he acted alone. He protected me, Andrew. My brother took the full blame and let me go free. Then Father instructed us to keep quiet about the attack. As an act of good will he suggested we should take several of our best rams and offer them to Jedediah."

Andrew grunted. "The man with all the scriptures hid the sin. What a good example our father makes before his sons."

"And I'm a coward," I admitted. "I allowed Eli to take the blame, and I never told Father about my part in the crime. I've been punishing myself ever since. I even sacrificed my pet lamb."

"Reuben?!"

"Yes, it broke my heart, but I didn't know what else to do. And still, the guilt of my sin has not been resolved."

Andrew put an arm around me. My brother who had made a new life for himself had come home. It was like it always had been, before he went away. We were more than brothers. We were best friends. Now that he'd come home, I had someone to confide in again. I had been needing to confess my sin. Now that I had done so, I'd merely succeeded in reliving those bitter memories. It was like my father had said. *If we bury our sins alive, they will rise from the grave one day.* This was that day—or one of them.

"Don't punish yourself, Jesse. You did good. You prevented a marriage between our little sister and that horrible Abijah. Now our sister can make a better life for herself."

I shook my head with sadness. "Not so, Andrew. Poor Sophina. She had already set her heart on someone else, but Father has refused the match."

Andrew backed away frowning. "She's only fifteen. Who could she possibly have in mind?"

"She has made a bond with Jedediah's servant boy, Jahzeel."

"A servant boy?!" Andrew burst out laughing. "What is the matter with our sister? A servant boy. What other surprises has she planned?"

"Nothing is the matter with Sophina. She loves Jahzeel. I've met him, and I have to admit, he's a hard worker, and he appears to have a gentle spirit. But he is Egyptian, and Father will not allow any of his children to marry a Gentile."

"Ah," said Andrew. "I also have discovered some fine people among the Gentiles. For me, marriage to one of them won't be a problem. Father already knows I'm going to do what I want. But poor Sophina."

I nodded. "Yes, poor Sophina. She goes around the house moping daily for her lost love."

"You have to understand, Jesse, our father follows the old teachings of our people. He will deny Sophina her desire and match her with someone she could never love. Does he not understand how much he will hurt her?"

"Already he's mentioned the rabbi's ugly son—the one with the big nose and the mole on his cheek. My one hope is that the old man will die before the match is made final. Then the decision will fall on us, her brothers."

My own words shocked me. Once again I had wished for the death of someone. Another sin upon the mountain of sins I already claimed.

Andrew sighed and shook his head. Then the muscles in his jaw hardened. "Don't worry about Sophina," he said with determination. "I'll make things right for her. And I won't wait for Father to die to do it."

I wondered how Andrew expected to help our sister. My brother was the most mysterious person I had ever known. He did whatever he wanted, went wherever he wanted, and made decisions without seeking anyone's advice. We were only 18 months apart in age but many years apart in wisdom and courage.

I began to think I had overreacted to Andrew's flirtation with Ariel. Perhaps he was simply being kind to a family friend. Believing I could trust my brother, I asked if he might help me convince our father to arrange a marriage contract with Ariel. Besides making sure he knew I had a claim on her, I needed an ally, and who better than my dear brother, the one who had defied our father's authority and succeeded?

"Ariel?" he said. "She *is* a lovely girl." His eyes sparkled when he said her name.

"She's more than a lovely girl to me, Andrew. I want to marry her one day."

"Marry?!" Andrew was incredulous. "Jesse, you're only a boy!"

"I'm not. I'm almost 18, not much younger than you. And I know what I want. I want to be with Ariel."

"So, you want to get married."

"Someday." I didn't care for the condescending way he was looking at me. "Yes," I insisted. "Ariel has already agreed to a match. It's up to our fathers now."

He raised his eyebrows, like he had another idea. "Has our father proposed a betrothal contract?"

I suddenly felt very small. "No, Andrew. Father has delayed. He said a shepherd boy is not a fit match for Ariel. I haven't been able to convince him to approach Hilkiah. He believes her father will never accept me."

Andrew stroked his chin. Then he faced me, his eyes serious.

"Perhaps it's not meant to be, Jesse."

"Don't say that. It has to be. I love her."

"Perhaps someone else is a better match for Ariel," he said, pensively. "What if I, too, have an interest in the girl?" His arrogance struck me cold.

"What?! You can't possibly have feelings for someone you met only an hour ago."

"You're wrong, Jesse. I didn't meet Ariel today. I knew her when I lived here. I never pursued her before."

"You spent one afternoon with the girl, and now you're in love? Betrothals don't happen that fast."

"They do in Alexandria."

I clenched my fists. My entire body stiffened. I was like a wild animal, ready to pounce. He wasn't aware of the rage that was building inside me.

"In Alexandria," Andrew continued. "Men and women fall in love overnight, sometimes over a simple meal. They marry quickly, if they desire, and they don't wait for a parent's approval."

"This is *not* Alexandria, Andrew. And we are not heathens. We live under the Law of Moses. We follow the customs of our people. And our customs require that our fathers make the arrangements and the two families agree."

"Then I will go to Father and ask him to approach Ariel's parents on *my* behalf. After all, I'm prosperous now. I am a more suitable match."

I didn't know if my brother was merely poking fun at me or if he might truly be desiring a union with Ariel for himself. He'd teased me often enough when we were youngsters. But something in his demeanor had me thinking he might be serious.

Aflame with anger, I lunged at him. He held me back with one hand pressed against my forehead, and he was laughing as I swung my fists at him, missing every blow.

We tumbled to the ground, rolled over, and tugged at each other's hair. I fell on my back. Andrew hovered over me. He slapped my face. Blood trickled from my nose.

He was laughing. "Give up, little brother. You are fighting a losing battle."

I collapsed in tears, my chest heaving, my head throbbing.

"Don't call me—l-little—b-brother." I hadn't planned to attack Andrew, but there I was, swinging at him with every bit of strength I had, and still missing. He held me fast, with his knee upon my chest, slapping my face and snickering. It was like it had been years ago, two brothers fighting over a toy—a wooden carving of an animal or a musical pipe. This time it was over a girl.

Andrew released me and the air returned to my lungs. "I love you, Jesse," he said, rising. "But you are no match for me. I am older and I have learned much during my time away. Admit it now. I will be a far better match for Ariel. I can provide for her like no one else can, not even you. So why don't you wish me well and find another girl for yourself?"

I rolled over, pressed my palms against the stony ground, and struggled to my feet. Then I faced my brother, my eyes flaming, my fists clenched for another fight.

"You servant of Satan!" I said, spitting the words in Andrew's face. "I will never give her up. And Father won't agree to your wishes. He resented you when you left our home. Why should he do this for you if he won't do it for me?"

He laughed and raised his chin. "You forget, little brother. I have studied the laws of the Greeks. I have read the writings of the philosophers. I have learned their manner of persuasion. I know how to approach our Father. I only have to choose the right moment."

Andrew brushed the dust off his clothes and turned his back on me. I stood rigid, my face like stone as tears spilled from my eyes. Intense hatred rose up within me. For a moment, I wanted to go after him and pounce on his back, drag him down and beat him to death. But I stood helpless as Andrew strode toward the house, determined to take away my one dream.

Chapter Eighteen

He shall gather the lambs with his arm, and carry them
in his bosom, and shall gently lead those that are with young.
~Isaiah 40:11b

The evening passed with nothing more said between us. I watched Andrew carefully over the next two days, fearing he might already have conceived a plan to win my Ariel to himself. His behavior troubled me. How could my brother support me one minute and attack me the next? He'd developed an unreasonable arrogance during his time away. Or perhaps he may have been self-serving all his life.

To my shock, three days after our fight, Andrew approached our father in secret. But it wasn't in secret at all. I was leaning against the wall surrounding our rooftop abode with a perfect view of them standing in the open courtyard below. Though they waved their arms in active discourse, I couldn't discern what they were saying. Andrew appeared to be pleading, and Father appeared to be resisting. Then Father did something unexpected. He pointed at the roof where I stood in the shadows. Was he talking about me? Were they discussing Ariel?

Andrew paced a little, then spun around and faced our father, who stood with his feet planted firmly, his arms crossed over his chest.

I turned my eyes away from them and fixed my gaze on the town of Bethlehem to the west. That tiny village still held a sweet memory for me, and I wondered if the child I encountered there knew what was happening that night. Then I looked beyond Bethlehem, to the rise of tree-filled hills that hid the city of Jerusalem from my view. I had gone there often enough to be able to envision the massive temple with its broad stairway, dividing walls, and the Holy of Holies where the Almighty was said to reside. I sent a prayer on the wind.

"Please, God of heaven, turn my father's will in my direction. Stop Andrew's pursuit, and grant me the desire of my heart. You alone can—"

A footstep interrupted my petition. I turned, surprised to see Andrew coming up the outer stair. Standing tall and confident, he strode up beside me.

"It's a beautiful sunset, isn't it?" The distant horizon was aglow with streaks of gold and orange.

I nodded but couldn't speak. Was he there to tell me he had won, that my dreams had been dashed to stone?

"I'm leaving, Jesse."

I gaped at my brother. "Leaving?"

"Yes," Andrew said, nodding. "Father refused the match. You won, Jesse. He's going to speak to Hilkiah on your behalf."

Speechless, I swallowed the lump in my throat. "How—?"

"As I expected, Father has not gotten over my offence. When I left home I drove a wedge between us. It's still there. My gifts did not remove it." He shrugged. "I doubt we'll ever be father and son again. But," he said, his countenance brightening. "My plan worked. I gave Father a way to refuse your request by matching *me* with Ariel. Of course, he chose you."

My heart pounding, I frowned in disbelief. "What are you saying, Andrew? He chose me?"

"That's right, little brother," he said, his brief moment of humility fading and his arrogance returning. "I forced Father to make a decision. Don't you see? I did it to help you."

I was speechless. What he'd proposed hadn't sounded like help at all.

"Do you recall what I said, that I'd been studying with the philosophers?" He was grinning now. "They know how to get people to do what they want them to do without having them realize they'd been tricked into it." He laughed aloud. "My little scheme worked on you, Jesse. You thought I had feelings for Ariel. Then it worked also on Father." He grunted. "I had no real interest in Ariel. In fact, I've been spending my evenings with a lovely Greek woman who suits me well."

I cocked my head, still unsure I understood. "It's true, your trick worked on *me*," I said. "I thought you were vying with me, like we did as children. But this time it was over a girl. Now you're telling me you had no interest in Ariel?"

He laughed wryly. "You'll never know for certain, will you?"

That was Andrew. Always taunting. But we had been close enough while growing up for me to believe he also felt the pain of our father's rejection.

"Father did welcome you into the house," I said in an effort to appease him. "He appeared to forgive you."

"Yes, but the wall is still there. I feel it every time I look into his hard eyes. Father will never understand how I feel about the sheep business. Nor will he know why I needed to go off on my own, how I had to experience the life I was meant to live and not the one that had been forced upon me. Knowing this, I took the opportunity to help you win the girl you love. I forced Father to choose, and he chose you."

My compassion for my brother grew. "Father is old, Andrew. He's bound to the laws of Moses. He's living in the past."

I hoped I had eased his pain. But he stood tall, as though untouched, and he threw his shoulders back.

"Yes, he lives in the past, and I refuse to be stuck there with him. I am successful, Jesse. I have more money than I ever hoped and friends who accept me for who I am. Most of all, there is no father there to tell me what to do and to accuse me of being a reprobate. I am my own man. And being my own man, I'm going to fulfill my promise to our little sister. I will make things right for Sophina, so she'll be able to marry Jahzeel one day."

I was surprised and curious about this sudden announcement. "How will you hope to accomplish *this*?"

He raised his chin defiantly. "I'm going to take her with me."

I stepped back. Sophina? Leave our home? "No!" My fists tightened. Did I want to fight him again?

Andrew shook his head at me. "I will take charge of our sister, and I will make a new future for her. Sophina does not have to suffer because of Father's obsession with the Law."

"You can't be serious, Andrew. You're taking her with you?"

He nodded. "I've spent a lot of time with Sophina during the last two days. She shared her heart with me, how she loves that servant boy and has no desire to marry anyone else. I've won her trust, Jesse. She's gathering her belongings at this very moment."

My heart was pounding with anxiety. "You can't take her, Andrew. Father won't allow it. *I* won't allow it."

He stood firm. "I can, and I will. Father doesn't know my plan. He won't know she's gone until we are a great distance away." Then a softness took over his face, and he eyed me with sympathy. "I know you love her and want to keep her in this place always. But this is best for her, Jesse. There's nothing you can do."

I stepped closer to him and raised my fist. "Andrew. Don't do this."

He made no move to fight me. Gently, he pressed his hand against my arm and forced me to lower it. "I know you will miss her, Jesse. But this is the only chance she has to live a good life. She'll be safe with me. And happy."

"If you want to protect her, then stay here with us. You can protect her best if you stay."

"No, Jesse. My plan is set. Sophina will accompany me to Alexandria and live under my roof and under my care. I presented my plan to her this morning. She wants to go."

I was stunned. Now I was going to lose my precious sister. She was about to leave, and I had no power to stop her.

"Wh-When will you go?" I dared to ask.

"Tonight. As soon as Sophina is ready. Tell the family I will never forget them. Assure them that Sophina will be safe with me. Will you do that, Jesse?"

I nodded weakly. Unexpected tears rushed to my eyes. I wrapped my arms around my brother's waist and held him fast. He had said his final good-bye. Unlike the first time Andrew left, I feared I would never see him again. Or Sophina.

My brother stepped back and ruffled my hair, like he used to do when we were young. I reacted the same way I always had. I laughed and brushed his hand away.

"You're going to be fine, little brother," he said, and I was certain he choked on the last two words.

Then, he spun away and left the rooftop.

"Don't call me, little brother," I murmured after him.

I turned toward the railing and directed my gaze to the courtyard below. Father had already disappeared inside the house. No one else stood on the property. Not Eli. Not Bartimaeus. They were most likely at the laver, washing for supper. I was the only member of my family who knew about my sister's impending departure. I considered summoning my father, then I suppressed the thought. Andrew was right. This was the only chance for happiness Sophina had. I waited and held my breath.

Several minutes passed. Then Andrew emerged from the house. He brought his donkey from the barn and placed a large pack on its back. Sophina came out, carrying a small bundle, filled, I assumed, with all of her worldly belongings. Andrew added her bundle to the donkey's back, then he grabbed the lead and started out. Sophina fell in step beside him, skipping along the path. I couldn't move, couldn't pull my eyes away from the two of them. Sophina looked back only once. I stood there for a long time, my heart in my throat, as their shadowy forms grew smaller in the waning light.

To my surprise, they took an unexpected turn toward the

property belonging to Jedediah. I frowned in puzzlement. Then the truth struck me. That was where they would find Jahzeel.

Chapter Nineteen

There is a voice of the howling of the shepherds; For their glory is spoiled.

~Zechariah 11:3a

The departure of my sister weighed heavily on our family. I broke the news first to my mother, who shrieked in agony, poured ashes on her head and wailed as though mourning for the dead. My father's response also was quite loud. After rending his cloak, he shouted curses against Andrew, pounded his fist against the wall, and vowed to go to Alexandria and bring his daughter home.

Eli stomped about the upper floor, pacing back and forth. He accused me of compliance, said I had gone against the rest of the family.

No surprise, Bartimaeus fell to drinking and eating his sorrow away.

As for me, I pondered my last conversation with Andrew and agreed he was right to take Sophina away. She didn't deserve the life our father had proposed for her. Marriage to a man she didn't love? And being kept from the one she did? I was one person who could understand that kind of grief. There was no helping me, but Andrew had assured me he'd take care of our sister, and I believed him.

Sophina was destined to have a better life with Andrew as the head of their home. It was Andrew, not Osiah, who would decide Sophina's future. Andrew who now had the right to approve her choice in marriage and anything else she might want to do. My brother had accomplished so much for himself, I didn't doubt that he could help our little sister find happiness. I didn't tell the rest of my family that Jahzeel had gone with them. The only problem was, if his father's debt had not been fully paid, Jedediah would never let it rest until he brought the boy back. Then what would become of Sophina?

I needed to shut out the crying and the shouting, I left the house and strolled aimlessly along the road, but soon found myself on the path that led to Hilkiah's home on the hill. I approached the courtyard and peered through the gate. Ariel was there, squatting on the ground in the garden. Her slight frame was swathed in the blue-green veil Andrew had given her. She bent close to a flower bed and plucked weeds from the soil. My footstep startled her. She raised her head and looked at me, her watery eyes flashing with welcome. A sad smile spread across her lips.

As she rose to her feet, tears spilled onto her cheeks. Her eyelids looked puffy and her nose was red from what must have been hours of weeping.

"Has Sophina truthfully gone?" she said, her voice breaking.

"How did you know?"

"Yesterday morning, Sophina came here and shared Andrew's plan with me. I didn't want her to go, didn't want to lose my dear friend, but I knew it was best, so—I'm sorry, Jesse—I told her she should accept his offer."

"It wasn't your fault, Ariel. I agreed with them too. We have to accept that she won't be coming back. Eli wanted to pursue them, but Bartimaeus convinced him not to go. My father wants to travel to Alexandria and bring Sophina home. But he's old and unable to take such a long journey. Andrew will never let her go. Nor will she agree to come back."

My own eyes filled with tears. I choked back the surge of emotion. "A terrible sadness has fallen on my house. Once again my father cursed the day Andrew was born. And now he's cursed Sophina too."

Ariel stroked my arm. "That's so sad, Jesse. If only your father had agreed with Sophina's choice, perhaps she wouldn't have left. My own father cannot believe your father denied her the right to marry the person she chose."

I knew the reason for such trouble. It was my fault. And Eli's. The evil on our family had been set the day Eli and I broke God's law and ended the contract with Abijah. No Abijah? Then our father reserved the right to choose another. And it wasn't going to be Jahzeel.

If only we had restrained ourselves, Sophina would still be living in our home, our father and Jedediah may have completed the contract, and all would be well. Sophina might have married Abijah, but she wouldn't be wandering off to some unknown place with her wayward brother. We should have left everything in the hands of the Almighty.

I looked at Ariel, aware of her grief. How could I tell her the truth, that Eli and I had caused the whole mess? I had added sin upon sin, evil upon evil, and lie upon lie.

Ariel released a little chuckle. "My father has only me to look after. He will never know what it's like to raise four sons." She shrugged. "I suppose one daughter is headache enough."

"You said your father understands your desires. Have you spoken to him? Have you told him about me?"

A shyness came over her, and she gave a little nod. I held my breath.

"I approached him yesterday, after I learned Sophina was leaving. He has said nothing of assurance. I suppose having to promise his only daughter in marriage is one of the most important decisions a father might have to face. And there is the problem of our—our—" Her eyes said it all as they slid over my shabby tunic, down to my worn sandals. "our unequal status," she finished with an apologetic frown. "I have to be honest with you, Jesse. My mother wants me to marry someone from the upper city. She has several suitors in mind." Ariel stared at me like she was trying to see inside my heart. A surge of compassion flooded into her eyes. "Of course, I prefer to follow my heart," she added, and her sweet smile returned.

I straightened my shoulders, took a deep breath, and tried with all my might to appear unaffected by the obvious truth. Though we usually avoided talking about our unequal status, we both knew our paths had followed a different course. There was no denying it.

Despite the truth, I hoped that Hilkiah had already seen what a suitable choice I was for his daughter. He'd been to our home often enough to care for Bartimaeus, and then there was that time Sophina had a fever. He must have seen what hard-working people lived in that cottage, how well my mother kept her kitchen, how my father insisted we four sons adhered to the laws of Yahweh. There was no doubt, with the right effort, we could make my father's business more profitable. My hope was that one day shepherds will have earned the respect of the people of Israel. We filled important needs—food for the table, warm woolen clothing, oil for the lamps and for cooking, and unblemished lambs for the sacrificial altar. Yet, I had to admit, only one member of my family had elevated his position to a place of worth. And that was Andrew.

I had a fleeting thought of the way my beloved had shown interest in my brother. Still troubled, I needed to remove the threat.

"I suspected, a time or two, that you preferred Andrew," I ventured to say.

She burst out laughing. "Andrew?"

"But, the veil—" I gestured toward the blue-green swath of cloth still wrapped around her shoulders. "And you appeared to be captivated by his stories."

She shook her head. "I thought him funny. And interesting. Yes, the stories he told kept my attention, but only for a brief time."

I gazed into her eyes, looking for the truth. *Slay me now and I won't continue my grieving.*

A little pout spoiled her smile. "Andrew is too tall. Too skinny. Too unsettled to suit me." Her gaze softened. "I prefer a more responsible partner in life. And I won't care if my husband comes in from the field with dirt under his fingernails and shoes that ruin my freshly washed floors. It means he works hard, is dependable, and leads an honest life."

Works hard? No doubt I did. In addition to my own work, I was also spending my afternoons laboring alongside Abijah. *Dependable?* I liked to think I was. *Honest?* That's where I failed. I'd already proven myself a liar, over and over again.

Still, I basked beneath Ariel's admiring gaze, and I hoped she always looked at me that way, that the light in her eyes didn't dim after we'd been married for ten years.

"Don't concern yourself about my father," Ariel encouraged me. "My mother may try to wear him down, but he will bow to *my* wishes, not hers. I can think of no other place where I can be happy except in the care of my shepherd. If you take care of your household the way I've seen you handle your sheep—with gentleness and compassion—I can trust you with my life."

"You've watched me work?" I was appalled, had no idea she'd been near my field.

She bobbed her head, jostling her sun-streaked curls. Then, she leaned close like she was about to tell me a secret. "I sometimes walk down the hill to your property. I breathe in the fresh air, lift my face to the heavens, and with my eyes shut against the warmth of the sun, I listen to the birds and the baaing of your sheep. When I'm certain no one is looking, I step close to your fence and set my eyes on the frolicking young lambs and the ewes all bunched up together like the women at one of my mother's gatherings. Do you suppose your sheep are gossiping too?"

She raised her head, laughed, and her eyes sparkled with mirth. I stood in awe, comforted that this girl of means should find joy in the simple pleasures of life. My life.

"You speak to your sheep when you think no one is listening," she continued, her voice breathless. "You even call them by name. What shepherd calls his sheep by name, except you? I don't know of anyone. I can only say that if you treat your animals that well, then I can be sure my children and I will be safe in your care."

My head was reeling. I had never seen her anywhere near my family's property, never caught sight of her walking near our fields, never imagined she could find joy in such an encounter. I flushed with embarrassment.

"Are you prepared to marry someone who also eats with his favorites and sleeps with them? That is my life when I'm out in the field at night."

Her resounding giggle set me to laughing with her. But while I was laughing at my foolishness, she appeared to be laughing for joy.

"Jesse, that is funny," she said, suppressing a giggle. "Eating and sleeping with one's sheep? I don't know if I like that. I want my husband to eat his supper at *my* table and spend his nights in *my* bed."

I grew serious then. "That will never happen for us if your father doesn't give his approval."

"Don't worry, Jesse," she said, brushing my arm with her fingertips. "My 18th birthday is next month. My father will no longer be able to put off a decision."

At that moment, a voice came from the doorway. Ariel's mother stepped outside and beckoned her daughter to the house. The woman glared at me, and with a jerk of her hand she waved my beloved inside.

Chapter Twenty

Thus saith the Lord my God; feed the flock of the slaughter.
~Zechariah 11:4

As Ariel had predicted, the marriage contract was agreed upon the following month on her 18th birthday. To my relief, my father broke his rule that the elder sons should wed first. He willingly paid the bride-price, a large sheepskin blanket and the pouch of gold coins Andrew had given him. My mother reluctantly offered the beautiful vase, which Ariel's mother received with wide eyes and the first smile I had seen on the old shrew's face. Still, I was humbly aware that my family's contribution was less valuable than what other, more affluent, suitors might offer, but Hilkiah received everything with a grateful nod.

In return, the girl's dowry far exceeded our portion. Besides a pouch full of silver, Hilkiah promised to build us a house on land he purchased next to my father's field. He set the work to begin several months before our wedding day.

The hand of fellowship completed the agreement and the written contract was signed. The two mothers then took control of the wedding preparations. I was surprised when Ariel's mother eagerly participated in the plans and even took charge of the many details and expenses, though she did so with an ever-present scowl on her face. To Ariel's mother, everything had to be perfect, no mistakes, no opportunity for the Beit Sahour ladies to raise their eyebrows in disapproval.

During our engagement period, I spent Sabbath days visiting Ariel at her mansion on the hill, always under the supervision of her hawk-eyed mother. As he had promised, Hilkiah began the construction of our home on a stretch of fertile ground in the valley below my father's property. I couldn't believe our good fortune. We planned to start our marriage in a home of our own, and because of my own father's generosity, I already had the start of my own sheep herding business.

Eager to observe the progress on our house, Ariel and I often walked to the site and gazed at what was to become our future home. It wasn't a big house. Two rooms and a vast upper room that stretched from one end to the other across the flat roof. Like Hilkiah's home, plans for our house included a courtyard and a bathhouse. Though our home would be smaller than theirs, Ariel could take pleasure in many of the same luxuries she'd enjoyed while growing up.

Completely gone was my dream of following after Andrew, never to be revived again. Even my concern for Sophina eased a little. I needed to remain in Beit Sahour. I wanted to continue my work as a shepherd. I had chosen to live a modest life in reasonable comfort with the woman I loved.

We arrived at our property one afternoon after I finished bringing in the sheep. I stared in awe at the pile of glistening white marble by the side of the road. Hilkiah had spared no expense and had ordered the slabs from a quarry near Egypt. There also was a large pile of cedar logs, straight from Tyre on the edge of the Great Sea, and many buckets of mortar to seal the walls. Workmen moved about, assembling the walls, the roof, the room divisions, the large, flat roof and its enclosed upper room. Slowly the boards and stones were coming together to form what could be—in my eyes—the most beautiful house in Beit Sahour.

"It's going to be more magnificent than I could ever have imagined," marveled Ariel. She pointed toward the eastern end of the property. "That's where our garden will be," she said, "hidden from the rest of the world, but with enough vegetables to feed the entire village if we want. You have lots of room to build enclosures for your sheep and goats. And, with the house positioned right, I will be able to see you at work, even when you drive your sheep onto the pasture. And from our back door, we'll be able to see the distant hills and catch the rising of the sun each morning."

I chuckled at my bride's enthusiasm. A garden. Her husband at work. A view of the hills. It was obvious Ariel's love of the outdoors matched my own. From my early days I was drawn to the natural world the Almighty had created. I shook my head in amazement. Instead of raving about the huge indoor cooking area her father had designed for her or the precious materials for finishing our walls, Ariel dreamed about growing enough vegetables to feed the whole town.

Because of Hilkiah's generosity, I was able to provide my wife with a wonderful home. On my own, I could give her my love, and I could protect her from harm. And I could give her a houseful of children, if she desired. But being poor, I could not give her what her father had provided, so I was eternally grateful.

That evening, as we stood before the half-finished building, talking about our future together, we were interrupted by a harsh scraping on the path behind us. We both turned to see Abijah limping toward his home. He must have come from the marketplace for he was carrying a basket of vegetables in one hand and keeping his balance with a shepherd's staff in the other. He paused, cast a look at the half-finished building, and then continued on without saying a word. Surely, he had seen us. Why had he not spoken to me when I'd been spending hours at his side, helping him shear his sheep, helping him fill the mangers, helping him lug water from the well? We were supposed to be friends, weren't we?

I bit my lip, overcome by confusion. The half-built house suddenly had little meaning for me. But it had spoken great loss to Abijah. My prosperity must have reminded him of his own misfortune. Overwhelming guilt split apart my dream of a wedding and a comfortable home. By my sinful actions I had denied Abijah the chance to have a similar life. Through an evil impulse I had brought about the end I was seeking. Eli and I had stopped the agreement. My sister was free. And our farm belonged to us with no partnership. But at what cost? For Jedediah, it was his seven favorite rams. For Abijah, it was his ability to live a normal life. For myself, it was a loss of integrity, something I might never be able to recapture.

Ariel was to be my wife. My dream was coming true to make a future together, to raise our own children, to live in a fine house. But seeing Abijah again, like that, stumbling along the path, I knew the truth. A shepherd boy was crippled for life, and it was my fault. Did I deserve the blessings that had been bestowed on me? I doubted it.

Now a distant figure, Abijah struggled with his armload while trying to keep his footing on the uneven path. A tear surfaced in my eye, blurring the sight of him. I quickly brushed it away and forced a smile. But Ariel had seen my distress. She looked from me to Abijah, then frowned in puzzlement, but she didn't ask.

I left the building site that day, my shoulders stooped in shame. Someone was suffering because of my actions. I could never fix Abijah's legs. I could only help with his work and simply be his friend. Except for Andrew and, of course, Eli, no one else was aware of our transgression. But the Almighty knew I was offering Ariel a heart blackened with sin.

Unable to speak because of my remorse, I walked Ariel to her home. She didn't say a word, merely patted my shoulder before disappearing into her house. She knew something was amiss, and it was obvious my distress had to do with Abijah, but she didn't know what it was. Perhaps someday I might be able to share my guilt with her. That would be the true test of her love.

When I arrived home, more tragedy awaited. My mother was wringing her hands and weeping aloud.

"It's Bartimaeus," she managed to say. "I could not rouse him this morning. Now, here it is, late in the day, and he has not risen from his mat." She stepped toward me and grabbed my arm. "Please, help, Jesse. Your brother's face has gone pale and he writhes in pain."

I flew past my mother to the outer stair, then hurried up to the roof. "Bartimaeus!" I dropped to my knees beside his bed. "Open your eyes, Bartimaeus. Please, wake up!"

My mother shuffled up beside me. In her hands were wet towels. She carefully laid them, piece by piece, across my brother's forehead and behind his neck. I leaned close and grabbed his shoulders. I shook him, hoping the jostling might stir him awake. He groaned and rolled away from me.

"It's like before," our mother mumbled, lines of anxiety creasing her forehead. "Hilkiah warned him of this discomfort if he did not change his ways. Too much wine and far too much of the wrong foods." She bent over him. "It's my fault," she wailed. "I should have taken control." She collapsed against him. "Bartimaeus, my son."

This was her firstborn, the babe that had opened her womb. Her pain was beyond anything I could imagine. I knew a brother's love. I'd looked up to Bartimaeus as my big brother, a man who took charge and showed me the way.

"Where's Father?" I said. "And Eli?"

"Where do you think?" she moaned. "There is work to be done. And, where have you been?"

I shrank from the accusation in her voice. "I was at my land with Ariel. I walked her home and came straight here."

"You must go back to Ariel's house. You must summon her father." She stared at me, her eyes pleading. "Hurry, Jesse, or I fear your brother will die."

The desperation in her voice prompted me to go. Though darkness was settling on the land, I had one purpose, to bring the physician to my brother. I spun away from my mother and stumbled down the outer stair. I extended my legs, took long strides up the path that led to Hilkiah's home on the hill. My brother was dying and I had one goal—to summon the only one who could save him.

I raced into their courtyard, panting for breath, and pounded on the door.

One of the servants opened the door, stared at me through accusing eyes, and called for Ariel's mother.

"No," I shouted after him. "I need Hilkiah."

Ariel's mother came to the door and stared down her nose at me. "My husband is not at home," she said, almost with pleasure. "He has answered a call in Bethany. I do not know when he will return."

"Please, as soon as he comes home, send him to my house," I pleaded. "My brother Bartimaeus is ill again. This time, he may not survive."

She sniffed. "What else do you expect me to do?" Her voice was laced with hostility.

"Do you have access to the potion? Can you check Hilkiah's cupboard for a bottle? It's—it's a brown liquid. I might be able to identify it, if you could look. Please, try."

She shook her head, her lips pinched tightly together.

"Please—"

"I don't know my husband's business," she snapped, and she shut the door in my face.

This woman's daughter had been promised to me in marriage, but it was obvious she did not want to be joined to my family. On the day of the agreement, the contract had gone smoothly between our fathers. Ariel's mother had sat quietly, her arms locked together, lines of distress crossing her forehead. Ariel and her father had moved ahead, despite her objections, I supposed. She eyed me with distaste whenever I came around. Now she was refusing to help my brother. She could have sent a servant to find Hilkiah. She could have looked for the medicine. I raised my fist to pound on the door again, but I knew it was useless. I lowered my hand and left the house of Hilkiah, aware that my one attempt to get help had failed.

By the time I arrived home, Eli and our father had come in from the barn. They were helping Mother with Bartimaeus, struggling to pull a clean tunic over his head. The filthy clothes my brother had been wearing were scattered about the floor. They stank of sour wine, the contents of his stomach, and the relaxing of his bowels.

Mother gestured toward the soiled garments. "Take these out to the burn pile."

Then she turned back toward Bartimaeus and pressed a damp towel to his forehead and another behind his neck. I carried the clothes outside, concerned that my hands were covered with filth.

It was dark when Hilkiah finally came to our door, carrying a torch to light his way. He gasped for air as he mounted the outer stair, his tired old body struggling to reach the top. Upon entering our upper room, he lifted a full bottle of the brown medicine from his bag, but hesitated at the sight of Bartimaeus lying very still.

Oil lamps positioned about the upper room shed eerie shadows across my brother.

"It's too late," Hilkiah said with a shake of his head. "I regret I could not come sooner. Now, look at him. There lies a healthy man who destroyed his body with food and drink." He looked at me, like he was about to give me a lesson in life. But before he could utter another word, Bartimaeus lurched upright. He stared past us, as though remembering something, and then he began to babble.

"The angels came," he sighed. "I can see them even now, the memory is so clear. I obeyed their call and went to Bethlehem. I found the babe in the manger, as the angels predicted. The beautiful babe spoke to me. Not aloud. Through his eyes. Into my heart. I knew I had to spread the report." He looked directly at me, then shifted his gaze to Eli. "Now it's up to you. Don't stop talking about that magnificent night. Carry the message to the ends of the earth. Make it your—" He started coughing. Then his eyes rolled back and he collapsed against his pillow.

Mother shrieked. Father rushed to Bartimaeus' side. Hilkiah stepped forward with the potion. Despite his effort, Bartimaeus never opened his eyes again. He dropped into the soundless, unmoving sleep of death.

The physician stepped away from the bed. With an air of sadness, he tucked the unused vial inside his medical bag sitting on the floor. "We must prepare him for burial," he lamented. "This time it is not a trick to get Bartimaeus to listen. This time I tell the truth."

My mother crumbled to the floor, sobbing. Father wrapped an arm around her, lifted her, and guided her to my mat. She dropped onto it and continued weeping and wailing as she released a mother's anguish over the loss of her firstborn.

The rest of us—my father, Eli, and I—assisted Hilkiah with the preparations. It was difficult trying to follow the physicians orders while my own body was limp with grief. I stared through a veil of tears and tried to complete each step of the anointing. For the next hour, there was the bathing, the wrapping with strips of linen, the sprinkling of spices.

"You have a family tomb?" Hilkiah asked.

Our father gave a nod. "It sits in a grotto of tombs on the road to Bethlehem. Only my father is buried there."

Hilkiah nodded. Then he said something that would stay with me for a long time.

"It's a sad thing when a child precedes his parents in death."

This brought my father to tears. He leaned over Bartimaeus' body and poured out his sorrow. After a while, he straightened, rent his cloak, and knelt on the hard floor, his body bent with overwhelming grief. Eli and I drew close to him, but we could do nothing to ease his pain, for we also had fallen into great despair over the loss of our brother. I loved Bartimaeus. I would miss his jesting, his words of wisdom, his outspoken criticism of the Romans. But most of all, I would miss his ready ear whenever I needed someone to talk to and his willingness to bear my burden on his own shoulders. He was my big brother in more ways than physically. His death left a huge emptiness in our home. Now, with Andrew and Sophina far away from home, Bartimaeus with the angels, and Eli living his own selfish life, I felt very much alone.

Chapter Twenty-One

And they that sell them say, Blessed be the Lord; for I am rich: And their own shepherds pity them not.
~Zechariah 11:5b

As required by Jewish law, the burial took place early the next morning. The entire neighborhood came out with pipes and lyres and tambourines. Paid mourners strolled along the path before our family tomb. By late afternoon, the crowd had thinned, and we returned home to continue our grieving for many days after.

Our cottage settled into a mournful darkness—first, unimaginable quiet, then unexpected eruptions of grief, and finally soft weeping in every room. My mother cried aloud at times. Then she settled into woeful silence until the next outburst. Father went to the roof and poured out his grief in a lamentation taken from his precious scriptures.

He concluded with, "My son, my son, oh, Bartimaeus! If only I had died instead of you."

I hadn't yet known the heart of a father, could only think ahead to the day when I sheltered my own sons.

For a long time after, my brother Eli dropped into a paralyzing silence. I'd never seen him so distraught that he couldn't speak or boast or find fault in anyone else. He was like a statue, unable to express whatever was happening inside his heart.

I needed to send word to Andrew. I worried how Sophina would take the news. She had been Bartimaeus' little pet, the one who climbed onto his back and pretended he was a horse as he lumbered about Mother's kitchen knocking over stools and pottery without so much as an apology.

I retreated to the field, away from the unyielding sorrow that gripped our home. In the peacefulness of the pasture, where our sheep grazed in complete ignorance, I fell to my knees and poured out my sorrow before the Lord God, boldly rebuking Him for taking Bartimaeus. In the midst of all my weeping and wailing, the thought came to me that Eli and I had been the guilty ones. Not Yahweh. And not Bartimaeus. He never harmed a soul. He brought joy wherever he went.

When Andrew left with Sophina, it was Bartimaeus who restored laughter to our home.

"Think about it," he'd said. "In a few months, Andrew will come home dragging Sophina behind him, and begging us to take her back."

We all laughed, even Father. Eli patted Bartimaeus on the back. And mother giggled and wiped away a sudden flow of tears. The family clown had done it again. He'd eased our pain with a simple remark.

As time passed, I sometimes found myself laughing over some memory involving my brother Bartimaeus. At other times, I glanced at his empty place in the upper room and I fell to agonized weeping.

I thought about the progression of happenings. Eli and I had sinned against our neighbor. By that unlawful act, we started a wheel of misery turning. One bad thing led to another. All because we sinned. At that moment of revelation, I conceded we deserved God's righteous judgment, and our brothers and sister had been taken away. Eli and I now endured the losses.

Was there no end to the sacrifices I would have to face before my debt was paid? Wasn't it enough that I'd turned myself into a hireling to Abijah? Wasn't it enough that I'd sacrificed my favorite lamb? Now my brother was gone. How much more would the Almighty require of me?

This was a time of my life when I should have been happy. I was betrothed to a wonderful girl. Her father was building us a home. I had my own flock of sheep, cut from my father's herd, the best of our breed. I should be dancing for joy.

Instead, I felt worthless, like my debt would never be fully paid. I was in just such a downcast state one evening when Eli approached me sitting by the sheep gate, absent-mindedly twirling a piece of straw between my fingers and staring at the heavens. The star-speckled sky reminded me of the night the angels came to visit. Had they known how undeserving I was to hear their message that night would they have included me? They should have found someone more worthy to receive the good news they'd come to tell.

And the babe in the manger. He'd gazed at me with those innocent but knowing eyes. The scriptures said the Lord was all-knowing. Did he know back then that I was destined to fail?

The other shepherds ran off praising God, intent on spreading the good news that the Messiah had come. How many people had I told of his arrival? Maybe two. My brothers spread the word much farther than I had. Bartimaeus couldn't wait to go into the village and tell his drinking friends. Andrew had run off to other parts of the world and had taken the message with him. And Eli? I'd seen him talking to a gathering of his friends, their eyes round with wonder. The village girls hung on his every word. Their eyes sparkled with delight, and they gazed up at him as though captivated.

My brother never showed the remorse I held within my heart. I wondered, did he feel any guilt at all? Now he approached me, his back straight, his shoulders back, his jaw firmly set.

"Why are you sitting out here alone?" he said with impatience.

"I'm thinking."

"And what are you thinking about that is so important it keeps you from the rest of the family?"

I breathed a long sigh. "Eli, I'm thinking about the sin you and I committed. While I struggle with guilt and sorrow over it, you aren't affected at all. Tell me, how are you coping with the terrible thing we did to Jedediah's rams?"

My brother snorted. "Terrible thing? The man deserved it."

Amazed at his response, I shook my head. "No, Eli. He didn't deserve it. We sinned against God and man. I don't understand how you were able to walk away and not feel any remorse."

I flicked the straw in his direction. Eli's reaction gripped my stomach like a fist. He was grinning, and he looked about to burst out with laughter.

"It's not funny, Eli."

"I never said it was funny. I said it was deserved."

"I've been troubled by what we did, and I don't know how to make it right."

He shrugged. I despised the smug look on his face.

He sneered. "We replaced his rams, didn't we?"

"Yes, with animals of less quality. Jedediah had broad-tailed sheep. Those rams were prized animals and were able to breed more of the same."

Ignoring Eli's snicker, I went on. "Think about what happened to Abijah because of our actions. That poor young man can hardly walk. He has no life. No future."

Eli stomped his foot. "Jedediah did that. We didn't."

I studied my brother's uncaring face. "Eli, we were responsible for all of it. We did wrong. Haven't you repented? Don't you think you need to appease Almighty God who sees everything?"

He huffed. "You've been listening to too many of our father's scripture recitations. They have you thinking your every move falls under the scrutiny of an all-seeing judge."

"It's true. Think about all the things that have happened since then. We lost our sister Sophina. Andrew is gone for good. Now we've lost Bartimaeus. We're being reminded of our sin over and over again."

His grin carried no hint of remorse. "Jesse, you can go on punishing yourself for something that happened long ago. Or you can move on and make a better life for yourself. That's what I've done."

"What about the babe in the manger? What about the angel's message?"

"What about us being chosen to know and to see and to go?" he said. "We were blessed. You have to accept that blessing and think about how special you are to have received it." He patted me on the shoulder. "Stop torturing yourself. It will drive you to say things you'll regret. You don't want to open that wound again. Let it rest."

"I'm trying to move on, but there's a heavy weight on my heart, and I don't know how to remove it." I was about to start crying. I caught my breath and tried to suppress the sobs that threatened to burst forth. I didn't want to appear unmanly before my brother, who never faltered.

Still, Eli shook his head with disgust. "You have the weight because you choose to keep it. You alone can shed that burden. As for me, I've already moved on. With Bartimaeus gone I now can select a woman from the village and be married. I'm next in line. Then you can go ahead with *your* ceremony."

I sat with my mouth open. Now my brother was counting Bartimaeus' death as a blessing. I wanted nothing more to do with him. I let him walk away, knowing I had no one else to lean on, no one else to tell my troubles to, no one else to comfort me in my grief.

Then I thought about Ariel. We were soon to become one. She could be my helper, the one person, other than my father, who might understand my need to be right with God. Before we could complete plans for our wedding, I needed to pour out my heart to her and give her the right to refuse the match or share my grief.

Though night was falling, I made my way up the hill to the home of Hilkiah. I didn't hesitate, but passed through the courtyard, pounded on the door, and when their male servant opened it, I requested an audience with Ariel.

"It's late!" The nasty remark came from Ariel's mother who'd come up behind the servant. "Go away and come back tomorrow."

"I need to speak with her. Only a brief visit and then I will leave."

She began to huff out another refusal when Ariel appeared in the doorway. She pushed past her mother and joined me in the courtyard. The older woman scowled at me, then backed away and the servant shut the door.

We sat together on a stone bench beneath a sycamore tree in their garden. I began by telling her about the angels' visit and the babe in the manger. I shared my doubts about my ability to carry out the mission of telling people the Messiah had come. Then, with sadness I poured out my confession of sin. Ariel remained quiet during my entire admission of guilt. When I finished, she placed a hand on mine and gazed into my tormented face.

"My heart breaks for you, Jesse. I don't know what to say. But I know what my father would say."

I blinked against a rise of tears, expecting her to tell me Hilkiah would likely want to annul our marriage contract.

"Tell me the truth." I said, my voice trembling.

"My father would say Yahweh understands our grief, that he sees the repentant soul and forgives. Surely, your father has filled your heart with scriptures that say the same."

I nodded. "He has, but sometimes I forget what they say about mercy and forgiveness and I dwell on the verses that speak of judgment and punishment.'

"It sounds to me as though you have punished yourself enough, Jesse. Now it's time for you to accept Yahweh's mercy."

I raised my eyes to the heavens and breathed in the truth of what she'd said. Yahweh's great love. I had forgotten.

I lowered my gaze to her face, now radiant. "And you?" I said, hope filling my heart.

"I love you, Jesse. In my mind, you can do no wrong. And when you fail, I know you will do all you can to make it right. I believe in you."

There was no doubt I had chosen the right girl for me. Because of her response to my confession, our marriage plans continued, and I took comfort in knowing that, even in the absence of my three brothers, I had an advocate.

As it was, Eli rushed to the altar with Marta, the daughter of an inn keeper in Beit Sahour. I was amazed that he'd chosen a plain girl when he had half the beauties in the village vying for his attention. They spent the first months of their marriage living at the inn her father owned. Eli returned daily to the farm to help us with the sheep. In time, I was relegated to Sophina's vacant quarters, and Eli and his bride moved to the upper room of our cottage.

It turned out Marta was pregnant long before the expected time. She delivered twin girls when they hadn't been married more than six months. Out of courtesy, no one mentioned the dates or the times.

I was 22 years old when my beloved and I were married. The ceremony took place in Hilkiah's courtyard. The festivities went on for a week, with food and wine replenished whenever they ran low. Hilkiah spared no expense for his only daughter.

By tradition, I should have taken my bride to live in my father's house, but I did not want my wife to share quarters with my brother and his wife. Of course, there was the room Sophina vacated when she left with Andrew. I'd been comfortable there for a time, but the small cubicle off the kitchen did not offer enough privacy for a newly married couple.

It was no wonder Ariel's father had insisted on building us a home of our own. Whenever he visited my parents' house, he must have taken note of our situation. He could not allow his daughter to live in a place that denied her the luxuries she'd had at home.

After the week-long wedding celebration, with no end to the wine and food provided by Hilkiah, Ariel and I settled in the home he had built for us, though there was still work to be done. My father-in-law's generosity did not run dry with those four walls. Following one of his trips to Jerusalem, the physician returned with a cartful of hand-carved furnishings, many of them shipped there from across the sea. He brought us a table that stood high off the floor and seats with legs so we could sit around the table instead of reclining on cushions as we'd done in the past. Ariel swooned over a delicate set of fine pottery and fragile goblets. There were silver serving trays, iron cooking pots, and long-handled ladles for stirring. Last of all, Hilkiah provided a bed, raised off the floor on four legs and hidden beneath an assortment of colorful blankets and soft pillows. I stood with wonder as Hilkiah's servants hand-carried the gifts into our house.

"Your father's generosity is overwhelming," I told my bride.

She simply smiled. I could only assume she had become accustomed to her father's lavish displays, and I hoped she did not expect the same kind of over-indulgence from me, for I did not have the resources to provide such luxuries. Elaborate living quarters meant nothing to me, a simple shepherd who preferred the outdoors to the suffocation of a room filled with man-made furnishings.

Hilkiah didn't stop with simply sharing his material wealth. As a special gift to Ariel, he presented one of the Egyptian women who had served in his home for years. Dalia was to be Ariel's handmaid. Old enough to be Ariel's mother, she could help with the birthing of our children and other household duties.

The bony wisp of a woman with straight black hair and eyes the color of ripe olives, flitted about our home, chattering under her breath, but smiling as though she thoroughly enjoyed caring for someone else's possessions.

I had never dreamed of having an Egyptian handmaid and a well-furnished house. Such extravagance did not fit my expectations. But Hilkiah had lavished this prosperity upon us, and I could not be rude and reject his gifts. Besides, Ariel beamed with delight, so how could I refuse?

Sometimes, I thought, perhaps I was the wrong man for her. Ariel deserved a prince, and she'd gotten a shepherd. But my desire to spend my life with her overcame my feelings of insufficiency.

To ease my conscience, I turned my attention to improving my business, got to work enclosing a sheep pen, created separate barns for breeding and shearing, and added a small shelter for the birthing of new lambs. Apart from allowing my animals to feed close to home, I also had access to the broad pasture where I had encountered the angels on that starry night several years before.

Whenever I stepped foot on that sacred place, I recalled with clarity the angelic visitation, their beautiful singing, and the message announcing the birth of the awaited Messiah. To be blessed in such a way made me even more determined to live more righteously. No longer did I whine about my sin. I faced the truth, hoping to one day find a way to win the favor of Almighty God.

The problem was, sin still reigned in my flesh, and I didn't know how to move past it. Now that I had uncovered Ariel's purity on our marriage bed, I was stunned to find that I viewed other women differently. When I was in the village amidst a crowd of shoppers, my eyes often fell upon the young women, and I began to imagine what lay beneath their layers of veils. Shocked by my own vile thoughts, I quickly forced my attention on the tables of pottery, the baskets of baked bread, the coins passing from one hand to another.

The truth was, more sin dwelt within me. I was envious of people who could purchase whatever they wanted. Because of my greed, I overcharged the priests for sacrificial lambs. And worst of all, I continued to hold bitter anger against Eli for not sharing my remorse over our sin. I even imagined placing my hands around his neck and squeezing until he either admitted his crime or expired.

My sinfulness had gone far beyond killing Jedediah's rams. It had begun to permeate every part of my being.

How could I become a good husband and, one day, a father, if I couldn't control my many wicked thoughts? How could I care for my wife and guide my children properly if I didn't live a decent life before them? Surely, an all-seeing God had to know about the evil that continued to feed within me, an evil that had gone so far out of control there was no hope of restitution, unless the Almighty himself showed me the way.

Chapter Twenty-Two

And I will feed the flock of slaughter, even you, o poor of the flock.

~Zechariah 11:7a

In the first five years of our marriage, Ariel lost three babies in the early stages of pregnancy. Each time, I ran for her father, and each time he could do nothing to stop the loss. He assured us there would be other children. My mother came often to our house to comfort my wife, to fix meals, and to encourage me in my concerns.

"You must be Ariel's strength," she cautioned me. "In time, she will grow strong. Be patient, my son. Care for your wife as you do one of your ewes when a newborn is lost. With hope and prayer another child will come."

Ariel's mother reacted differently. During her visits, she hovered over my weeping bride and eyed me with contempt. Surely she didn't think the losses were *my* fault? I tolerated her disapproval, confident that one day she might admit I had been a good husband to her daughter. Still, I wondered that she had birthed only one child while most women bore a houseful. Perhaps she also knew well the pain of miscarriage. Or could it be she'd withheld her affections from her husband? That, to me, was more likely, for she was a shrew of a woman.

Despite our losses, I was confident Yahweh was able to one day bless us with a family. And so it was that, in the sixth year of our marriage, Ariel became a mother, and I became a father. We named our firstborn son young Hilkiah out of respect for Ariel's father. The old man beamed with pleasure, and true to his nature, he lavished many costly gifts on our little one.

As young Hilkiah grew, he began to take on much of the appearance of his grandfather. He was short, a little broad in the shoulders, and he had that same square jaw and wide forehead Ariel's father possessed.

Hilkiah was five years old when the voice of a baby girl filled our house. We named her Jemima. She had Ariel's reddish-brown hair and my brown eyes, a blend of the two of us. My heart throbbed with joy the day she blurted out the word I'd been waiting to hear. "Abba," she murmured, extending her little arms toward me. I knew then my life would never be the same.

Hilkiah doted on his little sister, even shared some of the toys his grandfather had given him. There were hand-carved wooden carts, jade animals of all kinds, and a top that, with a flick of the fingers, spun across the floor, drawing shrieks and giggles from Jemima.

My mother spent hours at our home, cuddling little Jemima, playing word games with Hilkiah, helping Ariel and Dalia with the household chores. She lavished our daughter with handmade dresses, delicate blankets, and soft leather sandals crafted for a child's feet. I eyed some of the more generous gifts with suspicion. My mother had most likely used a portion of her food money to purchase them.

To Mother's joy, Andrew visited twice. He came only to my house and avoided seeing our father. But during each of his visits, our mother happened to be there cradling her grandchildren and humming that familiar song she once sang to us when we were young. Her lilting voice took me back many years to a time when I sat upon her lap and rested my head against her bosom.

Andrew brought gifts each time he came, and he gave us news about Sophina and Jahzeel. They had married a couple years after moving to Alexandria. Jahzeel was working with

Andrew, now a lawyer, and was attending studies of medicine at the great library. And Sophina was about to deliver their first child.

The news of her happiness brought me great joy.

Mother appeared content with that knowledge. She continued visiting my home, day after day, allowing nothing to interfere with the time she spent with her grandchildren. Though Eli and his wife had provided her with twin girls and two young grandsons, she preferred the quiet atmosphere of my house to the screaming that prevailed in the little cottage. And so, she walked the distance daily, until one day—she didn't come.

I came in from the field regularly and asked if she'd arrived. Ariel shook her head with sadness and a hint of worry in her eyes. Later in the day, I interrupted my work and took a walk to the cottage. When I arrived, I found my father pacing the floor, his hands clasped in prayer. Mother had taken to her bed.

The old man could do nothing but recite a few verses from the Psalms, so I took it upon myself to run for the physician. On our way to the cottage, Hilkiah hurried to keep up with me, his wooden kit swinging with every step, sometimes bumping his knee and causing him to groan in pain. Upon arriving at our house, I pulled back the veil to Mother's sleeping quarters and found her writhing in agony. Perspiration had formed on her forehead, and her face was as white as the sheep's blanket that covered her. Hilkiah offered one of his medicines, but she pursed her lips and turned her face away.

Where's Eli?" I asked my father.

He shrugged. "He took his family to the inn. Eli wanted to leave our home quiet at such a time."

"Is he coming back?"

He shrugged again.

My brother had once again disappointed me. Our mother needed him, and he'd run off. Again.

I drew close to her, stared with concern at her sallow skin, and her hollow eyes. My heart quickened. She was dying. I knew it. Father saw it too. He bent close to her, his back surging with each sob that poured from his lips.

I reached for Mother's hand. Her long, cold fingers wrapped around my palm and held me fast. I didn't move, not even when Eli finally came into the house and joined us there. Time passed. I held onto Mother's hand until it slipped away and she breathed her last.

Once again, a terrible darkness fell upon the tiny cottage. Hilkiah went home and returned with the funeral wrappings. He immediately went to work applying the strips of linen to my mother's frail form. Eli sprinkled the herbs. Father stood nearby, weeping and moaning over his loss. I thought ahead to the day when I might experience the same loss. The image brought me to my knees.

The burial took place before I was ready to let go. Ariel stayed by my side, then she took my hand and led me past the mourners and the musicians and guided me home.

"My mother is gone," I wept. "Bartimaeus also died. And Sophina left home with Andrew. We ourselves lost three babies, Ariel. All of this grief may be my fault. I did not follow the will of God as I should have. I believe I have brought his judgment on myself and on our house."

Ariel stroked my arm and murmured in my ear. "Do not blame yourself for the loss of our babies. God has blessed us now. We have young Hilkiah and Jemima. And they are beautiful children." She squeezed my arm. "We've been blessed, Jesse. You were blessed long before this. Think back to the angels' visit. The Almighty must have chosen you. He does not waste a miracle."

Humbled by her confidence in me, I bowed my head. "But I haven't done what was expected of me. I haven't lived up to the miracle. Except for you and my mother and sister, I told no one of the Messiah's coming to Judea. I've failed."

Ariel drew close and wrapped her arms around my neck. "You haven't failed, Jesse. You've taken great care of me and our children. You remained faithful to your work as a shepherd.

Now you only need to trust God. As the prophet Isaiah wrote, 'The Almighty will keep in perfect peace the one who trusts in Him.'" She giggled then. "You see, Jesse? I paid attention to your father's recitations. Whenever I visited your home, it may have appeared that I was there to see you and Sophina, but I was listening the whole time."

Now Ariel was carrying on the ministry my father had started. I leaned back and stared at her, overwhelmed that my wife had committed to memory the scriptures he'd read whenever she visited our cottage. On occasion, she recited those verses to our children, teaching them the way our father had done for me and my brothers. I felt ashamed. My wife was doing the job I should have been doing.

Over the next eight years Ariel suffered two more miscarriages. When we assumed her childbearing years were over, another son joined our household. Tearfully happy, I named him Bartimaeus after my brother.

Having Dalia with us turned out to be a blessing of the greatest kind. She proved helpful in the nurturing and raising of our children, even became a second grandmother as she took charge of the three of them, cooing, guiding, feeding, and waving the hand of discipline when needed. In the absence of my mother, she filled a painful void. She was even more needed when Ariel's mother and father both passed of a horrible infection within mere weeks of each other. The physician could not save his wife or himself.

One morning, I awoke to the realization that I hadn't seen my brother Eli for several weeks. Curious about his life, I started out to his home. Marta was now the woman of the house. Their twin girls had given them seven grandchildren, and their son, Osiah, and his wife had given them three. The little cottage had beheld several generations, as Eli's offspring came to stay, then grew up and went out in the world.

Eli had inherited what was left of the original flock, and our father had settled into his final years, content to sit on the fallen log with a sacred scroll in his hands, always ready to give a recitation to anyone who might listen—adult or child, it didn't matter.

From my previous visits it was evident Eli had settled into the lifestyle our father had established for us. He'd kept the same number of sheep and sold them off as fast as he could breed their replacements. He lived a simple life in our humble cottage and appeared to be content. While I had found numerous ways to build my flock by inter-breeding with another shepherd's ewes and rams, Eli had not changed his business from what it was when Osiah ran the farm. He'd never attempted to improve his breed or increase the number of sheep beyond the number he had inherited.

I expected nothing different as I stepped onto the old familiar property. I regarded the flock, now spread out in tiny groupings throughout the pasture. It was the same field I'd walked in when I was a child. Little change had taken place over the years. Stepping inside the enclosure, I reached the separate pen where Eli's rams stood waiting for the next breeding cycle. They, too, appeared healthy enough, their long spiraling horns a sign of good breeding, their fleshy tails thick with meat. Once their years of breeding ended, they'd be butchered for the market and their horns turned into *shofars* for the temple priests.

Eli must have seen me coming along the path. He appeared at his front door and eagerly welcomed me inside the house. I entered to the same familiar odors of sheepskin pillows stuffed with chicken feathers, goat's meat sizzling on the fire, and a pot of lentil stew ready for eating. Eli's visiting grandchildren swarmed about the small cottage, hardly allowing room for me to find a place.

It occurred to me that Eli had not changed one piece of furnishing. Everything remained the same as when I lived there as a youth. The long, low table where I settled on my mat for meals. The primitive cooking corner where Mother once knelt to work her dough and chop the vegetables. Now Marta labored there, her cracked red hands wielding the chopping knife, strands of gray hair slipping from the knot behind her neck. I thought of my own wife, who was likely sitting at her loom fanning herself with a straw paddle while Dalia prepared today's supper.

We were two brothers, yet our lives had taken slightly different paths. I might have felt pity for Marta, but the girl had come from a working family. She had no reason to complain. Her life with Eli was much like what she had known while growing up at the inn. While Eli had inherited all that our father had acquired, I had fared a little better. Not only did my generous father-in-law provide both home and barns, he'd also helped me increase my flock beyond the two dozen animals I had taken with me when I left home.

The truth was, Eli should have prospered more than I had. He was wiser in the ways of the world—or so I'd thought. He'd had the pick of all the young women in town, yet he'd settled for this humble barmaid. And I had married a princess. Eli had to be aware of the differences between his life and mine. He'd visited my home often enough.

Still, with a flourish he welcomed me into the cottage as though inviting me in to see his great wealth. I was no sooner reclining on a cushion when he thrust a goblet of wine in my hand. Then he hurried over to a far wall, removed a large stone, and withdrew a bulging leather bag. His proud smile revealed a row of chalk white teeth. He cleared a place on the table and dumped the contents of the bag in the center. Out spilled an array of silver and gold coins.

"I've been saving this for the right moment," Eli announced. "I have a plan that will prosper both of us, Jesse—if you will agree."

My brows gathered in distrust, for I recalled another time when my brother had presented a plan to me, one that had brought heartache. I eyed the pile of coins with interest, but said nothing.

"Hear me," Eli persisted. "I have set my attention on the Tigris Valley. A certain sheep herder has produced the most excellent flock of flat-tailed sheep. I wish to purchase several rams and ewes, bring them home, and breed them to increase my flock. The flat-tailed rams are of excellent health. Their offspring will fill my barns."

I listened with fascination but remained silent.

"Come with me, Jesse." He leaned across the pile of coins and brought his face inches from mine. "Let's do this together," he pressed. "It's been said the man is a fool, and he settles for less than his animals are worth. I can make a fortune off of this one. I will be *rich*." He said the last word with such force, I leaned back.

He lost his smile then and narrowed his eyes at me. "You have doubts?"

I shook my head. "No doubts, Eli. I believe you will make yourself a fortune. But I once gave in to a plan of yours, and it ended in disaster."

"What?" he said, his face reddening. "That was not the same kind of undertaking. I was a foolish young man back then. This is business. And it's perfectly lawful. We won't be killing anything."

I shook my head slowly. "You said the man is a fool and will take less than his animals are worth. I prefer not to take advantage of someone who is ignorant of his own value."

Ignoring the familiar curl of Eli's upper lip, I rose to my feet and prepared to leave. He gave a loud huff and started returning the coins to the sack.

"He'll get his money," he snorted. "I'm willing to put up this entire sack of coins, everything I have. Your share will be equal. Surely, you can afford to cut away some of your fortune."

"Don't be foolish, Eli. You have a wife and family and a helpless old man to care for." I glanced at the far corner where my father sat hunched in a ball, a scroll lying by his side. "So the man has prized sheep," I continued. "How do you know there is nothing wrong with them? How do you know the buyers are not the foolish ones, and he is the wise one? Perhaps when you get the animals home, they won't produce. Or they might die."

"Your words are like daggers," he snapped. "You have been so taken with your own wife and children, with your own flock, that you have neglected your responsibility as a son and a brother. You left our father's care to me. Yet you refuse to share your wealth."

"I don't have wealth. My father-in-law had wealth, and he was generous toward me. He's gone now. I have a family and a sheep business. That is all. I work hard, Eli. I'm comfortable, and I try to be sensible in my business dealings. Unlike you, I don't have a big bag of coins to take to the Tigris Valley. Do you know how far it is? It's at least three days' journey. How do you plan to lead a flock of sheep back home with you? Some of them could wander off. What will you do then?"

Shaking his head with disgust, Eli raked the remaining coins back in the little bag. Then he returned it to its niche in the wall and replaced the stone. He turned to face me, his eyes flashing.

"I should have known you'd become selfish and self-serving," he sneered. "Perhaps you blame me for what we did many years ago." Marta raised her head from the pile of meat she was slicing. She stared at Eli, then at me. Then she went back to her slicing.

"The truth is," I said. "I no longer blame you, Eli. I blame myself. I did a foolish thing, and I continue to carry the guilt of it. I am continuously troubled. Not only because of what we did to Jedediah's rams, but because of how Abijah suffered for our misdeed. Did you know he never married? Never had children of his own? He walks a little using a staff. Most of the time, he sits at home amidst the rantings of his mother. The damage we did can never be repaired. I have forgiven you, my brother, but I have not forgiven myself."

"So your answer is no?"

"Why should I join you in this venture? You worked hard. You saved your coins. Why don't you carry out your plan and prosper? I have no desire to go to the Tigris Valley. I've already made a business arrangement with the shepherd who lives near Jericho. His well-fed sheep have bettered my flock in the past, and I am content with that. Take your hard-earned money and go with my blessing."

Shaking his head, Eli took a step closer. "What's happened to you, Jesse? We worked well together once. We labored in the field—together."

"Yes, and we sinned together. Look at what our stupidity accomplished. Our sister is gone. Our brother went to the grave. We have driven our father deeper into sadness. Look at him." I pointed at the old man, his head bowed, a steady drool seeping from the corner of his mouth.

"He grieves the loss of his daughter," I continued. "He grieves the loss of Bartimaeus. He grieves the loss of his wife. And, I'm certain he grieves the loss of Andrew, though he won't ever admit it. Has he recited any scriptures in recent weeks? Or months? I doubt he has, though the scroll lies dead at his side."

Eli's hopeful smile returned. "That's why this deal is a good thing, Jesse. It will help you forget the past and move on. As Father used to say, "If you dwell on what lies behind, you will not be able to claim what lies ahead.""

My eyes drifted to the familiar cracked water jar in the corner by the hearth. I assumed inside were the piles of scrolls our father once read to us.

I bowed my head in remorse. Then I looked my brother in the eye. "The past is who I am, Eli. I am a failure. I sinned against my neighbor. To this day, Abijah has not been able to make a good life for himself. He lives off his father's estate, trusts his hired men to care for his flock, and there wasn't a girl in the village who wanted to marry him, a cripple." I shook my head. "No, Eli, I already caused far too much heartache. Now I choose to remain in the state where God has placed me, living a humble life, content with what I can achieve from my daily labor."

I gazed at my brother, aware that my words had fallen flat. He stepped closer and placed a hand on my shoulder.

"I'm traveling the first day of the week," he said, guiding me to the door. "Go with me, Jesse. You don't have to make the purchase until you've seen the man's sheep. You may change your mind and see it as a good thing."

I didn't answer. As I departed, I thought there were tears in my brother's eyes. I had to admit, Eli was trying to restore us—as brothers, as friends, as co-laborers. But I wanted no part in his plan. To run off to the Tigris Valley, not knowing what kind of animals the man raised, was too much of a risk.

The first day of the week came and went. Eli followed his dream and went to the Tigris Valley alone. With the new additions he grew his flock into a healthy business. He prospered greatly, as he had predicted, while I continued to live a simple, comfortable life in Beit Sahour. I didn't envy my brother. I admired him. With his increase in money, he built a second, much larger house. He hired servants and allowed them to live in the cottage our father had left him. He also hired a servant girl from Beit Sahour to help Marta. I wished him well.

I visited his home several times over the next year, mostly to see my father, whose health was declining. Without reaching for a scroll, the old man recited numerous scriptures from memory, easing my concern for him.

But my heart broke one afternoon when one of Eli's servants came running to my home. "Come quickly!" he panted. "Osiah is nearing the way of the kings."

I knew exactly what he meant. My father, the keeper of the scrolls, was dying.

Chapter Twenty-Three

For, lo, I will raise up a shepherd in the land, which shall not visit those that be cut off, neither shall seek the young one, nor heal that that is broken, nor feed that that standeth still.

~Zechariah 11:16a

I dropped the rake I'd been using and raced to Eli's home where I found my father in the throes of death. I was there when he breathed his last. After he was gone, I remained for a short time at his bedside, then I returned home and slipped into sackcloth, its scratchy surface chafing my skin. I fell to my knees before Ariel and wept with deep sorrow.

My dear wife rested a hand on my shoulder and knelt on the floor beside me.

"My father has died," I told her, and she fell to weeping with me.

She leaned close and, despite the scratchy garment I was wearing, she wrapped her arms around my neck.

"Oh, Jesse, I share your pain," she sobbed. "I loved your father. He was always kind to me."

Then she lifted her head and called out to Dalia, "Please, take charge of my children while I go with my husband."

The wise older woman nodded and immediately got to work finishing the meal the two of them had begun. Jemima was at her side, her small round face lined with confusion. Rising to my feet, I helped Ariel stand. She retreated behind the veil and changed into the black garment she reserved for funerals. Then the two of us departed for Eli's home.

We arrived to find a gathering of neighbors at the cottage door. Jedediah and his wife were there, but there was no sign of Abijah. I assisted Eli with the preparation of our father for the grave, and together we stumbled over to our family tomb. Several neighbor men bore the old man's body on a pallet.

I'd been to the grotto only twice before. Once when we lost Bartimaeus, and again after my mother died. It stood like an ominous gate to the afterlife, a gaping dark opening amidst a multitude of closed tombs strewn along the hillside. Two strong men approached with wooden boards to pry the stone loose. They rolled the stone into a deep rut alongside the grave. Shuffling back and forth past the opening, paid mourners wailed and sobbed as if they'd lost one of their own. The women carried bags of spices and tossed the particles into the air. A breeze caught the scent and carried it across the garden. Men and boys I hardly knew poured out a soulful dirge on their pipes and lyres. The response was overwhelming, for I hadn't taken the time to make many friends, except for those who also were shepherds. There were a couple of shop owners from Beit Sahour, the town baker, and Marta's father, who'd closed his inn for the day.

As the bearers released my father's body into the tomb, I was instantly aware of the brevity of my own life. Imagined myself wrapped in strips of linen, sprinkled with spices, then left within the darkness of that very same tomb, unable to stop the rolling of the stone across the opening, closing me in forever. I wept, not only for my father and the great sense of loss that had befallen me, but also for the fate that awaited me, stirring up an urgency to make myself right with God.

Wiping tears from my face, I scanned the crowd of women for Marta. There she was, crumpled into a ball at the door of the cave. Eli was there too. He knelt behind her, stroked her back with one hand while wiping away his own tears with the other. Their twin daughters and two sons had fallen in with the mourners. So did all of their grandchildren, but to the littlest ones it was more like a party than the end of a life. They romped playfully amidst the bereaved.

Ariel and I walked over to my brother and his wife. Ariel clenched hands with Marta. I placed an arm around Eli. He turned his tear-stained face to look at me, then shuddered and bowed his head.

Marta gazed back at me and sobbed out her grief. "I loved your father as my own," she murmured. "He was a good man." Ariel nodded in agreement.

How blessed my brother and I were to have wives who had become so ingrained with our family there was no separation between the kind of life they had left behind and the one they now lived. We were truly one with our spouses, the way God had intended from the beginning. This moment showed me that more than ever before.

Our father had showered these two women with the scriptures, the same way he had done with his own children. Long after the stone was rolled in its place, my father's voice remained with me, echoing the verses in his precious scrolls.

"Thank you for sending your servant to summon me," I said to my brother. "And thank you for caring for him these many years."

Eli shook his head. "It was my honor," he said, and I couldn't help but think how strange it was for him to say that. My brother, the selfish one who thought only of his own happiness while growing up, had sacrificed these many years to care for our aging father.

I thought that if I had spent more time with my father in his waning years, I might have had the courage to confess my part in killing Jedediah's rams. I would never know how my father would have reacted. He'd forgiven Eli, even suppressed the truth. Now the deed was being buried with him, and there was no need for me to confess.

My father had died, and I had not made myself right with him. My father, the man who quoted the words of Isaiah to me as a child, had now left this world, and my only comfort was that he no longer suffered. Perhaps he had entered a greater pasture than the one he tended throughout his lifetime. Perhaps he'd even found our mother and Bartimaeus there.

I pulled away from Eli only to stumble upon an amazing sight. Standing behind me, his eyes trained on the tomb, stood Andrew. And beside him were Sophina and the servant boy, Jahzeel, now grown into a tall, muscular man. Sophina also had blossomed. She wasn't a little girl anymore. A beautiful woman was standing there on the path, her smile wide with recognition, her dark eyes sparkling with unshed tears.

I leaped to my feet and rushed toward them, flung my arms around Sophina, and wept into her neck. Jahzeel pressed a comforting hand against my back. Andrew wrapped both arms around me, and we stood there in a huddle, weeping and crying out with a mix of sadness and joy. In his death, our father had brought us back together again.

Drawing in a deep breath, I stepped back and looked the three of them over. First Andrew, almost a mirror image of me, but still wearing the look of the Greeks. He smiled and shook his head at me, as if to say, "You, too, have changed."

"When did you arrive?" I asked, tears of grief and joy filling my eyes.

"Four days ago, Eli sent a servant to tell me our father was failing. I arrived yesterday in time to make one last attempt to seek his forgiveness."

"Did you speak with him?" I asked.

Andrew nodded, tears welling up in his eyes.

"Did he forgive you?"

He nodded again and began to sob out his grief. "I could never have found peace without a word of forgiveness from our father. I bowed beside his bed and begged him to restore me to the family. Believe this, Jesse. He said he understood, that I had been born with a wandering spirit and I needed to fulfill my destiny." Andrew shook his head in wonder. "I didn't think he understood. But he did."

I patted his arm. "We each had to choose our own way, Andrew. For you, it meant leaving home. For me, it meant staying."

He stared at me in what looked to be wonder. "Such wisdom from my younger brother," he said.

I smiled back at him. Andrew had always thought of me as his *little* brother.

"How goes your work in the courts of law?" I asked, changing our conversation.

He beamed with pride. "I am much in demand. So many cases, I work night and day. I have no time for a life of my own, no time for a wife and family."

That was the Andrew I had grown up with, unfettered by responsibilities of home, free as a bird. I gazed at him now, in appearance almost like my twin, but I was aware of our many differences. For him, it was the call of adventure and the single life. For me it was family, wife and children, a farm of my own, and a pasture full of sheep.

I turned to Sophina. "And, are you happy, my sister?"

She turned admiring eyes up at Jahzeel, who extended an arm and drew her close.

"We have a daughter," she said. "She's with a friend. Jahzeel finished his studies at the great library, and he has became a doctor."

"A doctor?" I looked with admiration at the dark-skinned young man, amazed that he had risen from the position of servant into one of the most respected professions in the land. "And you both have made your home with a different people in a different place," I acknowledged.

Sophina nodded. "The way of the Greeks is different from ours. I do not miss my old life, but I continue to cherish the scriptures Father taught us, and I worship the God of Abraham."

Jahzeel's dark eyes glistened. "We have made a good home

for ourselves. Sophina has proven to be a wonderful wife. Andrew has shown us a new way of life. My work flourishes. I am called throughout the city to heal various illnesses. Sophina assists and has learned the work of a midwife."

"I wish you much prosperity," I said.

"And your sheep business?" Andrew said without any sign of distaste for the profession. "You also are doing well?"

"Yes, my brother. I have increased my flock. I am content. Will the three of you come to see us while you are here?" I moved my eyes from one to the other.

Andrew grinned. "We will come to your home before we return to Alexandria," he promised.

Before leaving the gravesite, we shed more tears over our father's passing. They came easily as did memories we shared about growing up with the old man and his scripture recitations. We parted there at the tomb. I walked away with a mix of joy at having seen my brother and sister, and sadness at having to say farewell to my father. I believe I left a part of myself inside that tomb. The old man had ruled my life without meaning to. The talks on the fallen log. The scripture readings. The lessons taught to me by his example as a husband and a father.

After seeing Andrew again, I had to acknowledge a piece of my youth was gone forever. I felt myself pining over former days, when Bartimaeus was alive, and Andrew and Sophina had not yet departed, when Mother was there, filling us with her special cakes, stepping in when Father's expectations became too harsh, and Father reciting the scriptures and showing us boys how to become better men.

As promised, Andrew, Sophina, and Jahzeel visited my home before they left Judea to resume their lives in Alexandria. Sophina joined Ariel in the kitchen. Another wave of nostalgia hit me as they giggled and whispered like they used to do as little girls sitting on the floor of my mother's kitchen. With Dalia helping they put out a meal fit for a king. We dined with zeal. My home was filled with happy talk, excited plans for future visits, and moments of sad reflection as we shared memories.

The time for our three visitors to leave came all too soon. Andrew promised to return one day, and he pleaded with me to visit him in Alexandria. Ariel packed them a generous supply of food for their journey. I brought out three sheepskin cloaks for the chilly nights they were sure to encounter on the way home. Andrew loaded his two donkeys with supplies, including a tent that could be folded and attached to one of the saddles. I watched them depart, three beloved shadows vanishing along the road to the north. Then I returned to the house, my mind shifting to my plans for tomorrow.

Chapter Twenty-Four

*Woe to the idle shepherd that leaves the flock! the sword
shall be upon his arm, and upon his right eye.*
                                        ~Zechariah 11:17a

Thirty years had passed since we shepherds made the trip
to the stable in Bethlehem—30 years since we witnessed the
miracle. I wanted more than anything to believe the Messiah had come to earth. But where had he been over the past
30 years? There had been no more visits by angels. No more
appearances of one called the Messiah. Where did he go? Back
to heaven? Was he still living in Bethlehem? Or somewhere
else? Why hadn't he done *something* to confirm his coming
to earth?

My firstborn son, Hilkiah, turned 21, married a girl from
the village and moved her into our home. For several years he'd
been learning the family business. I was confident he could keep
our sheep farm going when I could no longer do so.

I already had promised Jemima, now 16, to Eli's youngest
son. They were to be married in two years.

Bartimaeus was now 8. He was fascinated by stories about
my brother Andrew running off to make a different life for himself. To my dismay, those stories had sparked a spirit of adventure
in my young son. He told me that one day he planned to do the
same as his Uncle Andrew, that he wanted to leave home and
learn a different trade. I, of course, was determined not to let

that happen, but in my heart I knew I would not disown him as my father had done to my brother.

Eli had continued to grow his flock in his own way, and he'd prospered over the years. As for me, I was content with the decisions I had made. I went to Jericho once a year and bargained with my friend Simeon for ewes and lambs to add to my flock. Not only did the man breed the finest quality sheep, he grazed them on pastures close to the Jordan where the grass grew thick and moist.

It was during one of those occasions while I was visiting my shepherd friend in Jericho, that I learned about a man who was calling people to repentance. *Repentance?* It was a new concept to me.

I offered Simeon a suitable sum for two of his fertile ewes that had not yet been bred. It was time for me to grow my herd again.

Simeon offered me a cup of herbal tea, and we sat outside on a stone bench talking about how our lives had changed over the past year. We drained our cups and sat in silence for a while. His ewes formed huddles in the field. The scene was so peaceful, I relaxed for the first time in weeks. Then Simeon roused me with a most unusual question.

"Have you been down to the Jordan recently?"

I stared quizzically at him. "Why do I need to go to the Jordan?" I said, unsure of what he meant. "Will a visit benefit my sheep?"

He laughed. "No, but a visit may benefit *you.*"

I laughed with him. "How is that?"

"Jesse, have you not heard of the Baptizer?"

I shook my head. "The *Baptizer?*"

"His name is John. I encountered him a few days ago at the river, and I returned every day since. He's a fascinating man. He wears a garment of rough camel's hair and a wide leather belt. He's a big man, though he eats nothing but locusts and wild honey. His hair is terribly unkempt, as is his beard. He speaks with amazing boldness. He fears no one, not even the Pharisees and chief priests who came there from Jerusalem yesterday to question him. I tell you, Jesse, the man is like no one else."

"He may be a troublemaker," I assumed.

"Perhaps," said Simeon. "But the people love him. He draws huge crowds from Jericho and from Jerusalem and places beyond."

"What does he speak about?" I asked with suspicion.

"He stands in the Jordan and beckons people to repent and be baptized. Those who come forward he lowers beneath the water. They come up praising God. That is not the work of a troublemaker. I myself submitted to the baptism. I repented of all my sins, and I felt cleansed."

I listened with increasing interest. I couldn't imagine what sort of sins this fine man could have committed. I had never known Simeon to be anything but kind and gentle. Still, he'd grabbed my interest. Perhaps this was what had been missing in my life. Repentance and baptism. Could it be that simple? Was this how I could rid myself of the sin I committed against Jedediah and Abijah, and all the other sins of my life?

"You should not leave Jericho without first stopping to see the Baptist," Simeon said, his gaze intent upon me. "Why don't you go now? I will hold your ewes until you return."

I hesitated for only a moment and pondered this newfound opportunity to shed my guilt once and for all. I looked to the heavens. It was still early in the day.

"Yes," I said pensively. "I'll go. I admit, you've aroused my curiosity." I rose from the bench. "Go with me."

He shook his head. "I began a work this morning, a new stable, and I need to complete it."

"Then show me the way."

Grinning like he had a secret, Simeon pointed toward the path I needed to take to reach the River Jordan. I left him standing there, turned once to see him still grinning after me, and then I resumed my journey. I didn't travel far before I came upon others who appeared to be on their way to the Jordan. A great multitude went before me. I had only to follow the crowd. More travelers joined us along the way, as if drawn by some unseen force. By the time I arrived at the Jordan I found myself in the midst of a huge gathering of men, women, and children. I couldn't imagine what kind of man had the ability to draw such a great mix of people.

I moved closer to the river to get a better view of the Baptizer. He was standing in a waste-high pool of water near the edge of the Jordan. Beyond flowed a deeper, faster moving river. Simeon's description of the man was accurate. The big, burly ape of a man apparently had been living in the wilderness taking little care of his grooming and manner of dress. In appearance and mannerisms he reminded me of my brother Bartimaeus.

The Baptizer stood out boldly among the well-attired priests and rabbis. His message also was different from theirs. While those men of position pronounced man-made rules and judgment on their listeners, this man invited them to repent. From the talk at the river's edge, I discovered he was the son of a well-respected priest named Zacharias. Someone said he'd been a miracle baby, born to a woman well-past the age of childbearing.

I was startled when, in a loud voice, he called out, "Repent and be baptized!" And the people flooded toward him like the flow from a dam that had broken. He lowered each one, in turn, beneath the surface of the water. They came up sputtering exaltations. Some laughed. Some wept tears of joy. But they all had the same glow on their faces, as though they had been in the presence of Yahweh Himself.

I stood with my feet planted firmly on the riverbank. I had no intention of going into the water. But the force of the crowd swept me forward and pushed me to the river's edge. My sandaled feet squished in the mud and mire, the watery foam pulled at the hem of my cloak, and I was carried closer to the Baptizer.

He reached for my hand and repeated his call to repentance. I hesitated. Could my atonement be as simple as being dipped in the Jordan River?

"Yes," I said, my heart pounding with excitement. "I do repent."

He didn't ask me to number my sins, didn't require an explanation of any kind. He simply lowered my body beneath the surface of the water and brought me up again in one swift movement. Then he released me and moved on to the next person.

The weight of the water pulled on my cloak. Slowly, step by step, I returned to the shore. When I reached dry ground, I dropped to my knees, then I rolled onto my back, lay flat, and gazed at the clear, blue sky above.

At that moment, a hush fell over the crowd. John's booming voice drew me upright.

"Behold the Lamb of God who takes away the sins of the world! I came baptizing in water. This is the One who baptizes in the Holy Spirit. And I myself have seen, and have testified, that this is the Son of God."

I followed his gaze, turned and sought for the one he had spoken of. A lone figure broke through the crowd and stepped into the water toward John. *The Son of God?* I clambered to my feet, then stared in awe as the stranger submitted to baptism. He appeared to be about 30 years of age. I needed to see his eyes, needed to compare them with those of the babe in the manger. Could this be the same one, now grown?

Why did John refer to him as the "Lamb of God who takes away the sins of the world?" The words *Lamb of God* struck me. To a shepherd, those words carried a profound meaning. I had lambs of my own. Some would be offered in sacrifice.

I tried to get a better look at the man's face. His eyes appeared to be the same color and intensity as those of the babe. I wasn't certain. It had been a long time. Many years had passed since that encounter in the stable. I wondered, if this were the Son of God, the Messiah, why did he need to be baptized? Why did he need to repent? Wasn't he already pure? The scriptures said he was.

My head swarmed with questions. I was struck with another

profound thought. I didn't feel any different, though I, too, had been baptized and had repented. No mysterious change had come over me. I was still the same hopeless shepherd who had come to the river seeking atonement for my sins.

Discouraged, I walked away and pondered what I had witnessed there at the river's edge. The Baptizer didn't say, "Messiah." He'd said, "Lamb of God." I raised lambs for food and clothing and sacrifice. This human "Lamb" could not provide food or clothing. But sacrifice?

As I started on the road back to Simeon's place, I continued to think about what I had experienced there at the river. Yes, I had repented. But the truth was, I had been repenting for most of my life. Simply saying it aloud and then being dipped in the river had not changed anything. Others had come there and had responded to the call of the Baptizer. They rose up out of the water, their faces beaming with joy, their voices crying out praises to the Almighty.

What had I missed? I also had come up out of the water, but it was as though I'd brought my sins up with me. They clung to me now like the wetness of my cloak, and I wondered, *would I ever be truly free?*

I went back to Simeon's house, endured his smile and the gesture toward my wet clothing. I shrugged with embarrassment, claimed my two ewes, and went on my way. Though he'd looked at me with raised eyebrows and a hopeful expression, as though he wanted me to share my experience, I chose not to discuss what happened at the river. I didn't want to bare my soul and expose my sins to someone I hardly knew.

I returned to Beit Sahour and immediately prepared the two ewes for the mating pen. That night, I told my wife about my experience at the Jordan, but I gave it little credence. To me, it was one more disappointment, one more failed attempt to cleanse my soul.

My life went on as it always had, and I stopped thinking about the "Lamb of God," until one day Ariel came home from the Jerusalem market, excitedly talking about a carpenter from Nazareth who was performing miracles in the Holy City.

"He spends most of his time in Galilee but he comes to Jerusalem for the festivals," Ariel said, setting aside her bundle. "He heals the sick, Jesse, and he preaches about God's kingdom and the need for repentance."

There was that word again. *Repentance.* I lay aside the sheep-skin I'd been mending and gave her my full attention.

"Someone said he turned water into wine at a wedding in Cana," she went on excitedly. "They said it was the best wine of the celebration. He's a mere man, Jesse, but he claims to be the awaited Messiah." She smiled and her blue-green eyes sparkled with new light. "A huge crowd came to him there in the marketplace." She looked at me, her eyes wide. "Jesse, do you think he might be the babe you saw in the manger, now grown?"

I grunted with suspicion. "I don't know. He sounds like the man who came to the Jordan to be baptized. He also came there with a large crowd. We can't be certain, Ariel. Many charlatans have gone out in the world. He could be one of them."

Disappointment swept the smile from Ariel's face, and I instantly regretted my words.

"I'm sorry, my beloved," I rose to my feet and pulled her into my arms. "Listen to me. I merely sense a need for caution. But I'll go and see this man for myself. I may be able to determine if he is the Messiah or simply a trickster who is deceiving people."

"How will you find him?" she said. "Word is that he avoids the crowds and sometimes disappears into the hills to spend time alone." She thought a minute, then added, "There's a family in Bethany he is said to visit—a brother and two sisters."

I nodded. "I'll start there, in Bethany. It's not far, merely over the next rise. I'll question people who live there, and I'll try to find him."

Ariel smiled sweetly, her eyes piercing mine. "You'll tell me the truth?"

"I will," I assured her. "Look. I'll change my clothes, and

I'll wear something more appropriate, something more fitting for an encounter with the Holy One of God."

She accepted my answer and began to unpack her purchases.

I bathed at the laver in our courtyard, toweled myself dry, and donned a fresh linen shirt and a colorful cloak bearing Ariel's special hand-sewn wheat and berry pattern.

A spirit of excitement brewed within me. What had begun as a desire to please my wife had turned into my own hunger for the truth. I hurried over the rise to Bethany and immediately began making inquiries of shopkeepers and people on the street, asking everyone I met about the stranger from Galilee. Finally, a beggar sitting by the side of the road gave me an answer. "You are looking for Jesus." He lifted a gnarled finger and pointed toward a house he said was owned by someone named Lazarus. I tossed him a coin, went directly to the house and rapped on the door. A man and a young boy were sitting on a nearby rock wall. As soon as I mentioned the name Jesus, the man sprang to life.

"You are seeking Jesus of Nazareth?" he said "He's not here. Try the Holy City. He often frequents the marketplace and the temple courts. He's a teacher, a great man of God who knows the scriptures well." His smile faded. "But beware. The chief priests find fault with him. He defies their authority. And anyone who seeks Him brings judgment upon himself, as well."

"Is He truly a healer?"

The man nodded. "He healed my neighbor of a skin sore."

I thanked him and started up the hill toward the Holy City. The narrow path wove between rock walls and passed beneath the shade of cedar trees and towering pines. Along the way I encountered more strangers, some bearing bundles on their backs, some pulling donkeys, others dragging children behind them. They were all going about their own business, unaware of the mission I was on.

I sorted through the questions I wanted to ask Him, if given the chance.

Did I see you at the Jordan River the day the Baptizer was there? Why did you seek repentance? Are you the Lamb of God the Baptizer mentioned? And most important, many years ago, were you the babe in the manger, the one whose arrival the angels announced? And finally, Are you, in fact, the Messiah?

I searched the temple courts, and though many teachers sat on the steps with hoards of people before them, he was not there. I searched the marketplace, suffered the jostling of the crowd, avoided the merchants who beckoned to me, and evaded the shepherds and farmers who'd brought their sheep, goats, and bullocks into the great court. I stayed clear of the chief priests and the Pharisees, aware that, aside from purchasing my sheep, they had no interest in me. Roman soldiers stood like statues by the entrances, their plumed helmets and armored plates glittering in the midday sun. I avoided them too.

Determined to find Jesus, I spent several hours searching, without a care for the work I had left behind. My son Hilkiah and our hirelings could complete the day's labor. I needed to find the man. The sun had begun to set when I accepted defeat and started for home.

I left the temple complex and started for the Sheep Gate. Towering walls spanned both sides of the cobbled street. I passed other people, but none of them were Jesus.

Then a pair of men standing in the shadow of the wall caught my eye. They appeared to be immersed in a lively discussion. One of them wore a teacher's cloak, a simple white tunic with a blue hem. The other was dressed in the manner of the Pharisees—long, flowing robe with a fringed bottom, a striped shawl over his head, and the traditional *teffilin* strapped to his upper arm. They appeared an unlikely pair, a high official and a humble teacher.

As I drew closer, I held my breath and turned an ear in their direction. The Pharisee was speaking in a humble, inquisitive voice, as though he had assumed the position of student and was submitting to this lowly teacher. I stopped short, my eyes widening with amazement. The teacher looked exactly like the man I had seen at the Jordan, the one the Baptizer had described as the "Lamb of God," and I knew I had found Jesus.

I paused by the side of the road and listened with interest. The teacher was talking.

"Truly, truly, I say to you, except a man be born again, he cannot see the kingdom of God."

I frowned with confusion. *Born again?*

The Pharisee also appeared bewildered. "How can a man be born when he is old?" he said, asking the same question that had entered my own mind. "Can he enter the second time into his mother's womb and be born?"

Though my interest had been aroused, I said nothing. This was apparently a private conversation, and I had not been invited.

Jesus went on, "Truly, truly I say to you. Except a man be born of water and of the Spirit, he cannot enter into the kingdom of God. That which is born of the flesh is flesh; and that which is born of the Spirit is spirit. Marvel not that I said unto you, you must be born again."

I shook my head. Impossible. I had seen my children being born, had stood by my wife's bed as she writhed in labor. My children did not return to the womb and appear again a second time. Neither had I. No one had.

Jesus continued to talk in riddles, something about the wind blowing where it will and how a person who understands earthly things should be able to discern heavenly things. It sounded like he was reprimanding the Pharisee, accusing him for not already knowing what he was telling him. I thought him exceedingly bold. Then he mentioned Moses lifting up the serpent in the wilderness and other historic happenings I had learned about as a child. I didn't understand the connection with re-entering the womb. It was obvious the Pharisee also was confused. I wanted no further part in their discussion. I heaved a sigh and turned away from them.

I left them there, passed through the Sheep Gate, and started down the hill toward home. I needed to get home while

I could still see the path in the growing darkness. *Born again.* Those two words kept running through my head, but I was left with no explanation.

By the time I reached home I wanted nothing more than a hardy meal and a place to lay my head for the night. I wanted to forget the conversation of the two men on the hill.

Ariel ladled stew into a bowl and placed it before me at the table.

"Did you meet the healer?" she asked, her eyebrows raised in hopefulness.

"No. I couldn't find him," I lied.

Chapter Twenty-Five

*He is brought as a lamb to the slaughter, and as a sheep
before her shearers is dumb, so he opened not his mouth.*
~Isaiah 53:8

I slept fitfully that night. Thoughts of wayward winds and babies being born anew tumbled around in my dreams. I awoke several times, troubled by the discussion I had overheard near the city wall. Once during the night, Ariel sat upright and asked me what was wrong. The glow of moonlight pouring through our window lit up her puzzled face.

"You've been flailing about for the last two hours."

"Nothing is wrong. Sorry if I woke you."

"Something happened last night, didn't it?"

"What do you suspect happened?"

"I don't know, Jesse. You told me you didn't find Jesus, but something must have happened."

It was time for a confession. "All right, Ariel," I said, sitting up. "I did come upon someone as I was leaving the city, but I'm not certain it was him. He was engaged in an unusual conversation with a Pharisee."

I sat very still, pondering again what I had seen in the city.

"And?" Ariel said, straightening.

"Perhaps this Jesus, this miracle worker, simply has tricked people into believing he can do wonderful things. Or maybe he does those works, but not under the power of God."

She frowned at me, as though my words offended her.

"How can you say that when you visited the Messiah yourself, as a babe in a manger? How can you deny that the angels called you to a wonderful experience that should have set you off on a mission of your own?"

I kept shaking my head as though the movement might rid me of all the trouble swirling around inside my mind.

"I can't make sense of it all," I admitted. "Though I've tried for years, every encounter, every unforeseen happening only makes the confusion greater."

Ariel sighed and patted my shoulder. "Go to sleep, husband. Tomorrow everything will be clear."

Content with her response, she lay back, rolled away from me, and pulled her covering up to her neck. Moments later, she settled into a deep sleep, while I laid back and stared at the ceiling. Sleep continued to escape me. I was still troubled by the rabbi's words to the Pharisee, still trying to understand the idea of rebirth, spirit winds, and Moses' serpent raised up in the wilderness. I couldn't connect them, no matter how hard I tried.

Days passed, and that experience in Jerusalem drifted to the back of my mind. Before long it was forgotten, and I assumed it was gone forever. But additional stories came to Beit Sahour, many of them through Hannah the Hawker. Interest in the man from Galilee grew in the little village, and many people began to speak the name of Jesus openly.

"He works miracles," Hannah insisted one day as she stood on our doorstep. "He heals people. He speaks of a kingdom we cannot see."

As usual, Ariel handed her a basket of sweet breads and sent her on her way.

Excitement continued to grow. Some of my neighbors left town in search of the miracle worker from Galilee. The insanity went on for months. Whenever a fresh rumor surfaced, more people rose up and hurried off to the place where the healer had been seen. I chose to ignore the chatter and set my mind on what needed to be done on my sheep farm. I had taught my son, Hilkiah, to take over the business with an agreement that one day all three of my children would benefit from the inheritance.

Almost a year after my search for Jesus in Jerusalem, Hannah the Hawker, now close to 90 years old, appeared again at our doorstep. Her visit was no surprise, for she'd come there often these days, her hands open to receive whatever reward might come in return for her stories. To my dismay, Ariel didn't hold back. She had been showering the woman with baskets of food and warm clothing from the first day we married. She'd always regretted that her mother had not been as generous to the old woman. From what I could see, she had more than made up for her mother's negligence. She continued pouring good will upon Hannah at every turn.

On this particular morning, I was in the enclosure, tending to an injured ewe, when I caught sight of the wrinkled old woman shuffling along the path to our door. There was Ariel, graciously welcoming her inside. I set aside the cruse of olive oil and hurried from the sheep pen to put a stop to the intrusion. Upon entering the house I found the old woman sitting at *my* place at the table, a horrible stench rising from her filthy robe.

I cast a frown at Ariel, but she shook her head in my direction and placed a bowl of vegetable stew in front of Hannah. Then she set my bowl at another place and urged me with a smile to accept the new arrangement.

Defeated, I settled in the chair she'd chosen for me and set my attention on the steaming bowl of vegetables. I watched with irritation as Ariel sat in a chair beside Hannah. At the moment, I had no desire to address the old woman sitting mere inches away from me. I reached for a piece of bread, took a bite, then, with Ariel eying me impatiently, I reluctantly passed the basket to Hannah.

The old woman spread her lips in a toothless grin and grabbed for a piece of bread, her gnarled fingers digging deeper into the pile. As I should have expected, Hannah spit out the latest gossip between bites of food. There was the marriage between the rabbi's grandson and the daughter of a local merchant, an announcement of newborn twins produced by the baker's wife in Beit Sahour, and the failed business of a local potter. Then she leaned toward me and widened her eyes like she had saved the best for last.

"The man Jesus has returned to Galilee," she said, assuming I knew who she was talking about. "They say he heals everyone who comes to him." She tipped the bowl of vegetables to her mouth, swallowed loudly, then returned the bowl to the table. Her eyes sparkling, she continued to spout praises for the man named Jesus.

"Multitudes follow him," she said. "They find out where he is going and they rush ahead to greet him there. He most often travels the western road through Samaria. By the time he gets to the sea of Tiberias, a huge crowd is already there awaiting his arrival. Twelve men—most of them fishermen—journey with him. He calls them his apostles. Others—some of them men of means—tax collectors, merchants, Roman soldiers, even Pharisees—join the crowds at different places. He calls them his disciples."

A memory flashed in my mind of the Pharisee I had seen conversing with the teacher in Jerusalem, and I regretted that I didn't stay to listen to the rest of their conversation. There was no crowd at that time. I could have drawn closer, perhaps asked questions of my own, questions that now remained unanswered.

If what Hannah was telling us was true, Jesus was likely in Galilee at that very moment. If he truly was a healer—whether the Messiah or simply a man with great powers—then perhaps I should go there. I thought about Abijah who had suffered many years with both legs shattered. Was it too late to seek healing for him? Abijah was now 46 years old, exactly one year older than I was. Most people would laugh us to scorn if we sought healing at our age. But I had a wife and three children. Abijah had no one. It was time I put off my feelings of embarrassment and helped another person.

The man's pain went beyond his physical wounds. Inside he was hurting too. With the Healer more of a possibility, I wanted to help my friend. I could take him to Galilee to find Jesus. But I couldn't do it alone. I could ask Eli to help. Though we had never again talked about joining our hands in business, and Eli had cared for both of our parents until they died, I was certain there existed no ill will between us. After all, Eli had inherited all of what our father left behind, and he'd prospered. Now, with my daughter, Jemima, pledged to his son, Adam, I believed we had renewed the bond that broke the day I refused to go to the Tigris Valley with him. I determined to talk to Eli and perhaps make a plan to help Abijah. How could he refuse? This could also alleviate any guilt we might be suppressing over Jedediah's slain rams.

After finishing my day's work, I left the remaining chores in the care of Hilkiah, and I went to Eli's home to seek his help. I approached the property and stopped short of the massive house my brother had built with the money he'd earned after his journey to the Tigris Valley. Eli's flock had grown to more than 200 ewes, plus a dozen flat-tailed rams, and enough lambs to start a whole other flock. With the help of his hired men, he'd put in fencing around three large enclosures, and he'd planted a lush field that far excelled the plain where we once grazed our father's sheep.

I wasn't envious of my brother. In truth, I admired him. Nor did I covet anything he had, for I was content with my smaller herd and the pasture on my property. I didn't wish for more. I'd found contentment as a humble shepherd living a simple but comfortable life.

The truth was, I had acquired everything I'd ever wanted. Ariel had proven to be a fine wife. She'd given me three healthy children. My income provided all we needed, and I had enough extra to generously pay my hired workers. Yet, for the moment,

I stood there, looking at the large stone house with its massive courtyard and rows of balconies, and I experienced a twinge of concern. Eli had gone his own way and had never regretted the past. I needed to find out if he could care enough to help Abijah.

There I was, still punishing myself for the sin that brought so much heartache to my neighbor, and Eli was living the good life, without a concern in the world. I wouldn't call it envy or even resentment. I'd call it injustice.

"How long are you going to stand there?"

Eli's voice drew my attention to the enclosure on my right. Behind him was a wooly gathering of his sheep. He shut the gate on them and strode toward me, a staff in one hand, a sheepskin bottle in the other.

I stared at the bottle and wondered if this brother had gone the way of Bartimaeus. If he had, then how long before strong drink also took *his* life?

I set aside the thought. "Peace, my brother. I come in friendship with a request."

Eli's face brightened with interest. I stared at his full head of hair, now gone gray, his neatly trimmed beard, his broad shoulders, and his back straight as a fencepost. He hadn't aged like the rest of us had.

Though I shrank before his intense gaze, I announced my plan with confidence.

"I came here to ask you to travel with me to Galilee," I said.

His brow wrinkled in puzzlement. "Why do I need to travel so far? I have everything I could ever want right here." He spread both arms and gathered in his entire property, the house, the field, and the many enclosures and barns.

"Let me explain," I said. "Word has come to me that the Healer has been seen near the Lake of Tiberias. They say he works miracles."

"What does that mean to me? I'm in good health." He tapped his chest in a display of strength.

"I'm happy you are well," I told him. "I'm not concerned

with *your* health. I'm concerned about Abijah. I want to take him to Galilee and ask the miracle worker to heal him."

Eli took a step back. His lip curled in warning. "Haven't you moved past trying to make amends for what we did? Abijah's father inflicted those injuries, not us. Let Jedediah take his son to Galilee."

"Jedediah is old. He can't make such a journey. But I can. I want to do this, Eli, and I need your help. Abijah can hardly walk. We might have to carry him part of the way, or perhaps we can use your dray and one of your fine donkeys." I nodded toward his barn. "Yours are younger and far stronger than mine."

He snorted. "So you need my help."

I nodded, a little sheepishly at first, then with more boldness. "Yes, Eli. I need your help. If you truly have put all hurts behind us then you will agree to come with me."

He stepped around me, his eyes sweeping over my form from head to toe. I was instantly aware of my clothes, far less costly than his. My shoes, caked with sheep dung, while his sandals looked new and clean. My pockets, empty compared to the riches that likely filled his belt.

"Forgive me for asking," I said. "I assumed you might feel a little sympathy for Abijah."

Eli grunted. "Why do you think I'd care? And why should *you* care? Wasn't he your greatest rival for many years?"

I searched his stone-like face, troubled by his lack of compassion.

"We did wrong, Eli, and someone else suffered because of our actions. Abijah and I have been friends for a long time. I want to help him."

He shrugged. "It's no concern of mine if you choose to carry this burden."

"Then we have nothing more to discuss," I said, and I began to turn away.

But Eli wasn't finished. "Stay, my brother. We must discuss this a little more. We are more than brothers. Our children are promised in marriage. Come into my home. Dine with me, and allow me to share my good fortune."

"Good fortune?"

He nodded. "I am selling my entire herd," he boasted.

Shocked, I planted my feet on the path and didn't move. He waved a hand at me, again inviting me inside. Still, I didn't follow him.

"Everything?" I said, frowning. "Who wants to buy your entire flock?"

His chuckle sent a shiver down my spine. "Do you recall the rich shepherd in the Tigris Valley, the one who sold me my flat-tailed sheep, the one you refused to trust with a bargain?"

The memory came rushing back. One of the sore moments from our past. "I do. Is he your buyer?"

"Every last animal." His proud smile sent me reeling.

"But, Eli, how will you survive without your sheep?"

"I'll tell you." My brother grabbed my arm and guided me into his house. Once inside, he directed me to a seat at the table. Dumbfounded, I quietly sat with my hands folded on my lap.

Marta rose from her stool by the hearth, and without a word from her husband, she summoned her servants and began to prepare a meal for us. I sat in silence as Eli tipped the sheepskin bottle over two cups, filling them with a bright red liquid. The scent of fermented grapes wafted from my cup and confirmed my suspicion. I released a sigh and lifted the cup to my lips.

We sipped in silence. I stared at my brother, unsure if I should press him any further, for he obviously had something else on his mind. Marta delivered a tray of food, and one of her servants placed another beside it. Without saying a word, Eli's wife returned to her stool in the corner of the kitchen. She was the wife of a successful sheep herder, and yet she appeared over-worked and haggard. Her black hair fell in sweaty curls around her face, and she struggled to smooth the wrinkles from her dress. She'd been pleasant to look at once, but now her youthful skin was hidden behind the harsh labors of a scullery maid. Being the daughter of an inn keeper and well-trained in the labors of serving, Marta had never shed her life of toil, for now she worked day and night caring for a quiver full of children and grandchildren.

"My poor ignorant brother," Eli said, breaking into my thoughts. What had he called me? Ignorant? I immediately took offence. But he continued to rant. "I have fared better with that one transaction than you could ever dream to accomplish," he went on. "My coffers are full. I can live the rest of my years in comfort. No work. No hirelings to steal from me." His comment drew hurtful glances from the two servant girls. "No responsibilities," he went on. "No need to work in this tiring, dirty job, caring for a bunch of filthy, ungrateful animals."

He plunged into the cakes and cheese Marta had provided and followed every bite with a long drink from his cup. Disgust flooded over me. This was not how our father had raised us, to be lazy and self-serving. I ignored the food and looked my brother in the eye.

"What's happened to you, Eli? Father left you everything and now you want to throw it all away. You speak of a good life?" I tipped my head toward Marta. "Your wife labors endlessly and all you want to do is rest."

He laughed with disdain. "My poor brother," he snorted. "You see only what you want to see." He wasn't the least bit repentant. "I'm happy, Jesse. So is Marta."

I looked at the poor woman but did not see one sign of happiness. She had endured a houseful of ungrateful children and grandchildren, and a husband who cared little for her well-being. How could I have thought a man like that could care enough to help Abijah?

Eli finished his cup and poured another. "I tried to include you in my transaction with the shepherd in the Tigris Valley," he went on with his accusation. "You refused. Now look at us. I'm wealthy enough to sell all I have and sit back in luxury. And you're destined to spend the rest of your life laboring over your flock of worthless sheep."

I shook my head. "You're wrong, Eli. I am happy with my life. The difference between us is what makes us happy. I'm content with my work, my wife, my children, and my humble home. You were never satisfied. You always did what you wanted without concern for the consequences."

I plunged ahead, intent on reminding my brother of our terrible deed. "If not for you, Eli, I would never have slain those rams. The truth was, I worshiped you back then. You were my hero, my older brother who could do no wrong." I rose from the table. "Forget that I came here today. I will go to Galilee myself and find the Healer. I will take Abijah with me, and I'll do it without your help."

Eli lurched to his feet, but before he could respond, I strode out of the house and marched toward home, relieved to be away from that sorrowful place. My brother was a disappointment. Once again he'd chosen a path I didn't want to take. Without his help I'd have to use one of my own feeble donkeys to carry Abijah to Galilee. I wanted to find the Healer and plead with him to restore Abijah's legs to good health. Perhaps after my friend walked away healed, I finally might feel that my debt had been paid.

Chapter Twenty-Six

I will give you shepherds after my own heart, who will feed you knowledge and understanding.

~Jeremiah 3:15

My visit with Abijah and his parents did not go as well as I'd hoped. Jedediah's flock had dwindled to a sparse scattering of ewes and lambs. It had been years since I helped Abijah with his chores. Once my children started coming along, I was overwhelmed with my own work, and he willingly had let me go. It saddened me that his herd had declined while mine prospered.

I entered the home and found Jedediah, now old and feeble, sitting by the window, staring out at a neglected pasture. He turned to see who had entered, scowled, then upon recognizing me, he allowed a weak smile to cross his lips.

I presented my plan to take Abijah to Galilee to find the Healer. Jedediah struggled to stand, the scowl returning to his tired face.

"Healer?" he sneered. "Such talk is blasphemy. The man is a devil. He leads people away from the truth, not toward it. He makes promises no human can keep, and he claims to be the Son of God. Listen to me, Jesse. Stay away from him."

Though I wilted under Jedediah's angry glare, I couldn't give up my plan, not if there was the slightest chance I might help Abijah. The poor man had suffered for far too many years, and I had carried the responsibility for his pain on my shoulders. Now that I had conceived of a plan, I had to carry it through.

"I'm going to find him," I insisted, keeping my voice low but firm. "They say He has compassion on the suffering. He speaks about a kingdom beyond what we can see. He expects no payment. Only that people trust Him and believe."

Abijah was listening from his bed in the corner. Light streamed through an open window and cast a beam across his troubled eyes. I had offered him a chance he'd been wanting for a long time—to be completely whole again. He might be able to walk without assistance, to work his father's farm again, possibly marry, and most of all, be free of the pain he'd endured for many years.

Jedediah stomped his foot and advanced toward me, raising his fist. I caught my breath and waited for the blow.

"You will *not* take my son to Galilee. You will go home and tend to your own business." The blow never came, but he continued to keep his fist raised.

I glanced at Abijah. His eyes flashed with a silent plea for help. I steeled myself and stepped boldly toward the old man. He lowered his fist and backed away.

"Why don't you let Abijah speak for himself?" I challenged him.

Jedediah sucked in his breath and straightened his back. Then, setting his jaw, he rushed to the entrance and grabbed a rod that was leaning against the doorpost. He spun toward me and raised the rod above his head like he was about to strike me. My body tensed. The man had used a rod before, many years ago, and had crippled his son's legs. I prepared myself, ready to fight back if I must.

But the attack never came. We were distracted by a movement in the kitchen. I turned to look as Ischa stepped out of the shadows and approached her husband. Her face was like stone, her black eyes penetrating. Gone was the weak, submissive female who had remained in her husband's shadow during the meeting with my parents, many years ago. In her place stood a crouching lioness, ready to protect her cub.

"Let him go," was all she said. I froze. Ischa had broken the age-old law of submission, but she'd done it with such courage she silenced both of us. I stepped back from Jedediah, amazed when the angry lines slipped from his face. Instead of rebuking his wife, as I expected he'd do, he nodded slowly and released a sigh.

"My wife has spoken," he acknowledged. Lowering the rod, he stepped back from me. "As you have requested, I will leave the decision to Abijah. He's a grown man. If he wants to go, I will not oppose him."

The harshness had left Jedediah's voice. He appeared defeated. His back bent and his step faltering, he returned the rod to the doorpost, then he joined his wife at the foot of Abijah's bed.

I gazed into my friend's eyes, now sparkling with optimism.

"I can't promise you instant healing," I told him. "Only a willingness to take you to Galilee to find the Healer. What do you say, my friend?"

Abijah moaned and unfolded the broken sticks that had been his legs those many years. He raised up on his elbows, set his jaw, and nodded.

"I want to go," he said. Then, with a rush of courage, he gazed hard at his father. "I *need* to go." Sighing, he lowered himself back on his pillow. Tears spilled from his eyes. "I want to find the Healer. I want to walk again, Father, like every other man. I want to tend our farm and bring it back to life. I will go with Jesse to Galilee and find the Healer."

Jedediah approached me, the sharpness gone from his countenance. "You will do this for my son?" His entire demeanor had changed. He sounded like a concerned father, pleading for help.

"I will," I promised. "I can take him there, but I can't promise what will happen."

"Then let me help," Jedediah said. I couldn't believe the transformation in him. Only moments ago he'd been adamantly opposed and now he wanted to help.

"You have always been kind to us, Jesse. I trust you."

Kind? Trust? If the man only knew.

"Do you want to go with us?" I offered. "The journey will be long and arduous, but you can ride."

He shook his head. "No. I am unfit for travel. But I can provide two strong donkeys. One for Abijah to ride, and the other for you and whatever supplies you might need. The journey could take as many as four days. Then you'll face an equally long way home."

"We won't be alone, Jedediah. We will join a caravan and will travel along the western road through Samaria. By doing so, we will have protection along the way. The caravan will have a host of well-armed guards. Your son will be safe."

A faraway look had settled in Jedediah's eyes. I waited for him to respond. He blinked away the thought and returned his attention to our journey.

"What supplies will you need? A tent, perhaps, for sleeping on cold or rainy nights. Enough food for four days and money to buy provisions for the journey home." He kept offering whatever he could spare, astounding me with every word of kindness.

He vowed to have everything ready for our journey the next morning. And I promised to be there early.

I left Jedediah's home still thinking about the amazing change that had taken place in that disgruntled old man. With his blessing, I was going on a mission to help his son find healing. But I had to admit that, while seeking healing for Abijah's physical injuries, I had another purpose. I also wanted to seek healing for myself. The difference was, my wounds could not be seen, for they'd been festering within my soul for far too long.

Before retiring for the night, I shared my plan with my family. Hilkiah promised to tend to the work on our farm in my absence. Jemimah eyed me with such admiration I thought my heart was about to burst. And Bartimaeus begged to go with me.

"Not this time," I said, temporarily quenching his desire for adventure.

Then there was Ariel. As expected, she wrapped her arms around my neck and promised her full support. "That is a kind thing you are doing," she praised me. "Promise me you will return safely."

Early the next morning, Ariel and Jemima packed a supply of food for my journey.

My daughter flung her arms around my waist and lifted her sweet face. "Abba," was all she said, and that was enough for me.

Hilkiah's wife, Onah, came close and handed me a ram's horn filled with goat's milk. "Go with God, my father," she said.

Then they all circled around me and placed their hands on my shoulders. Hilkiah gave a blessing. Then, slinging the pack of food over my back, I tore myself away from my family and stumbled out the door. I could hardly see the path for the flood of tears that filled my eyes. Never before had I been away from my family for more than a single day.

The departure at Jedediah's house was no less emotional. Ischa held onto her son until the last minute. Jedediah was true to his promise. He brought out two of his strongest donkeys, piled on some bedding and a folded tent for sleeping at night, and handed me a pouch of coins for our return trip home. Then he placed his hand of blessing on us, and weeping, he said something that gripped my heart.

"May the Almighty preserve and care for my two sons."

My two sons? Jedediah had bestowed on me the greatest honor a man could give another. This was not the fierce neighbor I had known as a boy. That one had a cruel nature. This one was kind and humble. What could have changed him? Could it be that he now wanted to believe the Messiah had come and that He could heal his son? Perhaps then he'd also find forgiveness for the guilt he must have carried for so long.

I added my pack of food to the pile on my donkey's back, growing more anxious as the time neared for our departure. We shepherds rarely traveled more than a day's walk from one field to the next to graze our sheep. The journey to Galilee was supposed to take three or four days. Then there was the return trip home. My mind reeled with doubts about my own ability to complete such a task. I had slipped on my strongest pair of sandals, though I had little faith in the fragile bindings. I shrugged it off as the least of my worries.

With the donkeys saddled, I stepped forward to say farewell to Jedediah and his wife. Ischa's eyes fastened on mine, and I caught a glimmer of admiration in their depths. This was the woman who once had set her heart on my father, but lost. A surge of compassion swept through me. I smiled at her and she responded with a smile that bore a hint of longing. Gone was the bitterness. The woman held no ill will for me, the son of the man who rejected her.

Then I turned toward Jedediah. This man, who never knew what my brother and I had done to his rams, now extended a hand of kindness to me. The guilt resurfaced. Perhaps, if I admitted my transgression I might find that long-awaited freedom. I could take responsibility for my part in that terrible act. But such an admission would definitely put an end to our journey, so I chose to bury it once again.

My father's words rose from the depths of my heart. *If we bury our sins alive, they will rise from the grave one day.*

How true that was, for my past mistakes truly *had* kept rising up over the years, and I had yet to find a way to absolve my guilt. All of my efforts had fallen short. Even what I was about to do was not enough. Still, I intended to go on.

Abijah pulled away from his mother's embrace. Jedediah and I helped him onto one of the donkeys. Ischa handed him a woolen cloak, aware that the nights on the desert could turn bitterly cold. Smiling, she handed me a similar garment, which I accepted with gratitude. I flung it over my donkey's back, hung a sheepskin water bag from my saddle, and grabbed the reins.

Jedediah's demeanor turned even more mournful as he mumbled something to Abijah. Then he turned to look at me and delivered a silent appeal. I nodded with understanding.

I suppressed a chuckle. Abijah and I were no longer little boys. We were grown men now. Still, I understood a father's heart, and so I gave Jedediah another nod of assurance as we departed.

The truth was, I didn't know what kind of obstacles we could expect to meet along the way. Nor was I certain we could find the Healer. Strangely, my apprehensions began to fade beneath the thrill of adventure. I never had left the comfort of Beit Sahour before. Feeling a little of the excitement Andrew must have experienced when he left home, I straightened my shoulders and set my eyes on the road ahead.

As I had planned, we connected with a caravan that had left Jerusalem and was traveling north along the western road. The caravan leaders accepted us into their mix and demanded a small fee, which I released from Jedediah's pouch of money.

As we expected, the heat of the day gave way to bitter cold in the evening, but we had come prepared. After laying out a bed of palm branches, I unrolled our mats and raised the tent for a shelter. I first got Abijah settled inside, then I tossed Iscah's wool blanket over him and grabbed the other one for myself.

While Abijah and I found shelter inside the tent, most of the caravan workers slept outside under the stars. The awareness humbled me. So, during the next two nights, I set aside our shelter, and we did the same. It turned out to be a heavenly experience. Lying on a blanket under the stars, I recalled the night the angels came. I whispered a prayer for the Almighty's protection, and, exhausted from the day's journey, I easily closed my eyes in slumber.

Early the next morning, while the sun lay somewhere beyond the eastern foothills and only a thread of light appeared on the horizon, the caravan leaders roused us from sleep, their shrill voices piercing the morning air. Within seconds I was on my feet and helping Abijah onto his donkey. We began moving toward Galilee once again. Most of the time I rode in comfort, but occasionally I took the journey on foot and allowed my beast a little less of a burden. Abijah, of course, remained on his donkey for the entire distance.

"I wish I could walk on my own two feet," he grumbled more than once.

"You may be able to do that on the journey home," I said to encourage him, though I couldn't be certain. I could only hope.

As expected, we reached Galilee on the morning of the fourth day. Our journey had been uneventful. No quarrels among the other travelers over food and water. No wild animals threatening to attack. No thieves, for we were traveling with well-armed guards. And we didn't starve, as Jedediah had feared. In addition to the pack of fruit, cheese, and bread Ariel had sent with us, we plucked ripe dates from the palm trees along the way.

We approached the south end of Galilee, a lush spread of wheat fields that gave way to low-lying, grassy hills. The sun beat down on spreads of wild flowers and golden stalks of grain. It was like entering a well-watered paradise. The rock-crusted edge of Tiberias released the pungent odor of fresh-caught fish. We continued along the western rim of the lake where patches of sand blended with large rocks, and the water lapped against the shore in an almost musical rhythm. Fishing boats were everywhere on the lake. The men aboard them appeared to be hauling in nets filled to breaking with flapping fish.

Eager to find the Healer, I broke away from the caravan and began my search. I talked to merchants and people walking along the road and asked if they knew where the man named Jesus might be found. The answers were always the same—a raised shoulder and an apologetic shaking of the head.

"Jesus moves around Galilee from town to town," one man said. "He goes where he wishes. His friends? They are mostly fishermen who live in the surrounding villages—Capernaum, Bethsaida, Nazareth, and Cana. They are most likely out there on one of those fishing boats." The last bit of information he offered with a tilt of his head in the direction of the sea.

Then someone else offered us a ray of hope. "I know the man. Multitudes follow him. He performs miracles almost daily. Simply go after the crowd. He'll be walking in their midst."

As the man had predicted, a large group of people drew my attention to the north end of the lake. They were following a few men who had come off the fishing boats. Like a flood, they moved toward the hill country. They reminded me of the eager people who rushed to the Jordan to see the Baptizer.

Abijah and I followed on our donkeys. We reached a remote place at the bottom of the largest hill and could proceed no farther. My stomach began to churn, and I was suddenly aware that we had eaten all of our provisions during our journey in the wilderness. I thought about going to a nearby village to buy food, but the crowd was surging up one of the hillsides. Fearing we might miss the Healer, I chose to stay with the crowd.

I tied our beasts within a copse of myrtle trees, standing like soldiers with their thick, woven trunks and lacy green and red leaves. I helped Abijah off his donkey and pondered how I might get him up the hillside. An idea came to my mind. I retreated into the copse and with a flash of my knife, I cut free a long, straight branch, scraped off the foliage, and created a sturdy walking stick for my friend.

With Abijah leaning on the stick and me straining to support him on his other side, we mounted the hill, painfully slow, step by step, blending in with the crowd. Halfway to the top, I found a grassy shelf where we could sit comfortably in the shade of an olive tree.

I didn't have to wait long for the Healer to appear. I recognized him the moment he stepped into view. Again, he wore a simple teacher's robe, white with a blue trim around the hem, and thick sandals that looked like they could endure a great deal of walking. He remained close to the bottom of the hill. The entire slope resembled a giant amphitheater with the central place for the speaker down at the bottom and the rest of us seated in rows up its sides.

It was past noon, and again I thought about running to a nearby town to buy food. But, the tension in the air told me something was about to happen.

The next thing, someone shoved a basket in front of us. My jaw dropped. It was filled to the brim with seared fish. I removed two crisp pieces. Someone else offered another basket piled high with unleavened bread. I accepted two portions, nodding my gratitude. The salty flavor of the fish was the best I'd ever tasted. I suspected being this close to the lake they were fresh-caught, perhaps brought in on one of the boats I had seen from the shore and immediately roasted over a hot fire. The bread also was better than anything I'd ever eaten. Oddly, I thought about the manna the Israelites received long ago during their time in the wilderness. Such delicious food could only have come from the hand of God Himself.

Amazed that the two of us had been well fed without having to go and buy anything, I looked around. Others were tearing off pieces of bread and savoring bites of the seared fish. Thousands of people had gathered there, but not one went away hungry.

Close by, a man began to clap his hands. "As always, he's done the impossible," the man shouted.

"What do you mean?" I asked him.

"Jesus' companions wanted to leave to buy food. But he insisted they stay. Then one of them found a boy who had brought five loaves of bread and two fish to the gathering. I wondered how they expected to feed so many people with such a small amount of food."

I listened in awe as the man continued. "It was not a problem for Jesus. Look around you. The same one who turned water into wine at the wedding in Cana has now turned two small baskets of fish and bread into a meal for thousands."

The next moment, several more shouts of exaltation went up. Now it was no longer food they shouted about. People cried out that they had been healed of one disease or another. An elderly man walked for the first time in years. A blind man claimed to have received his sight. A woman wept tears of joy over the disappearance of stomach pains.

I looked at Abijah and tried to suppress my concern. He

looked no different. His legs remained crippled. What if we'd come all this way merely to learn such miracles happened to only a chosen few? What if there was no hope for Abijah? He'd been lame for more than 20 years. This was his last chance for healing.

A hush fell over the crowd. All eyes were on the one who had provided enough food to feed thousands.

"It's a miracle," said a man kneeling on the grass, his face turned toward the heavens.

"What do you mean, a miracle?" I asked him.

"Look," he said, a triumphant lilt in his voice. He rose to his feet and tossed aside the walking stick he'd been carrying. "When I came here, my legs did not work for me. Now I'm standing on two legs I have not used since my childhood." He shook his head and gazed again at the heavens. "Praise God," he sang out. "Praise the Almighty, who has healed me through Jesus. I must go and tell my sisters."

With that, he stumbled down the hillside and started off toward one of the nearby villages.

I turned my attention to Abijah, saddened to see there'd been no change. My friend had not been healed. Were we to go home in defeat?

Abijah looked about to collapse in tears. I needed to encourage him, but I didn't know how. A passage of scripture came to mind, one that my father spoke whenever the task before me appeared insurmountable. I offered it now to Abijah.

"Listen to me," I said, drawing from the words of my father. "He who waits on the Lord will renew his strength; he will run and not grow weary, he will walk and not faint."

Abijah turned sad eyes on me. Then he brightened with understanding, nodded his head, and smiled. He shifted his attention to the man at the bottom of the hill, shut his eyes, and moved his lips soundlessly, as though in prayer.

Suddenly, Abijah reached for my hand. "Look, Jesse," he said, excitement in his voice. "Look at my ankles." The bones that moments ago had protruded now appeared to be straight and firm. "My scars have disappeared. It's as if they never were."

Abijah shifted his legs beneath him and rose to his knees, then, resting a hand on my shoulder, he struggled to his feet. I reached out to steady him.

"Abijah!" I cried out. "You're standing under your own power. You're legs are straight. I can't believe this. There is no sign of injury, none at all."

People looked in our direction, clapped their hands, and sang out for joy. I could not contain my excitement. I spun around, looking at this person, then at that person, wanting everyone to see the miracle I'd witnessed. They also were excited about their own miracles.

One claimed to be free of headaches. Another boasted about renewed abilities in his hands. Still another pounded his chest and declared a strengthening of his lungs.

As for Abijah, he was dancing around on the knoll, unconcerned that he might look foolish. He was so happy, he wanted the whole world to see the miraculous change in him. I laughed and allowed him to carry on as long as he wanted to.

"Enjoy your new legs, Abijah," I exalted. "You deserve to walk and dance. You came here for healing, and your prayer was answered.

I hadn't seen Abijah smile for a long time. Now he couldn't stop smiling. He spun around, then stopped dancing, and his gaze landed on Jesus, who stood near the base of the hill, teaching and blessing the people around him. He rushed down the hillside and fell to his face before the Healer, praising him in gratitude.

I recalled the babe in the manger, the man being baptized in the Jordan, and the teacher in the shadows, talking to the Pharisee. And I knew without a doubt. They were all three one and the same, and now he was standing right there in front of me, and he had healed my friend. What if I ran to Him and pleaded with him to free me from my affliction? Did I have to confess my sins in front of everyone? The thought frightened me.

I held back. Saddened and having no confidence, I turned away and stumbled down the hill toward the place where we had tied our donkeys. Abijah soon followed, his face lined with concern.

"Didn't you want to speak to the Healer?" he said, sympathy showing in his eyes.

I shook my head. "There is no need," I said with sadness. "We came here for you, Abijah." I patted his arm and gave him the biggest grin I could produce. "Let's go home."

Chapter Twenty-Seven

He heals the brokenhearted and binds up their wounds.
~Psalm 147:3

During our journey back to Beit Sahour I fell quiet. Abijah was trying out his new legs, dancing and skipping along ahead of me, while I labored to keep control of the two donkeys. Though I was happy for him, I continued to mourn over my own sense of loss.

Here I was, a humble shepherd who once threw a staff farther than any of the boys in the village, including Abijah. He, in turn, could outrun me to the next town and back. We competed evenly in almost every challenge. Until the day Jedediah attacked his son with a rod. Abijah had been bedridden for more than 20 years. Now he'd found renewed strength in his legs. While I grew tired after the first day of our journey and rode the donkey much of the time, Abijah declared he never wanted to ride again.

I should have been dancing with him. But the meeting with Jesus had not brought me the healing I'd been seeking. My injury could not be seen, for it remained inside me, eating away at my heart. I had hoped I'd be able to shed my guilt on that hill. Many people were healed. They fell at Jesus' feet in gratitude. He smiled down at them and said, "Go and sin no more," over and over again. "Go and sin no more."

I should have fallen at Jesus' feet, should have begged

His forgiveness, should have listened for the words, "Go and sin no more."

I wanted His blessing. Longed for it. Yet I didn't ask. Was it because my faith was weak? Did I travel all that way only to discover I didn't have it within me to be free? Had the purpose for our journey been for Abijah and only for him?

As I trudged along toward home, my back was bent beneath the weight of my disappointment. The great sin Eli and I had committed against Jedediah and his son was as clear as if we had done it yesterday. I thought about the hatred I had held onto for so many years, my guilt multiplied by lust, envy, and lack of faith. Then there was the fight I had with Andrew over Ariel. I wanted to kill my brother. At that moment I had murder in my heart.

The truth was, I would have to go back many years and confront many more sins. If I wanted forgiveness for every sin I ever committed, I'd have to go back to the womb and start over.

"I'd have to be born again," I whispered to the donkey I was riding—and the reality struck me like a bolt of lightning.

Born again. Those were the words spoken by Jesus during his conversation with the Pharisee. He said a man had to be born again. *Born of the Spirit*, he said. I didn't understand it back then, hadn't stayed to hear the rest of His message.

Now I wished I *had* stayed. What had I missed? Something that would have made a difference in my life, for certain.

I continued along the trail, still pondering the little I already knew. Andrew didn't stop dancing before me. He rested only when we camped on the trail for the night. I sat hunched beside the fire we started. I pulled the warm cloak around my shoulders, and mentally thanked Ischa for the warm garment.

Abijah stared at me, his eyes questioning. "Are you all right?" he said.

I responded with a weak smile and a nod of my head. "Just thinking," I told him.

I couldn't say I was annoyed by his high-spirited reveling.

Couldn't tell him I also needed healing, but of a different kind. I eyed him with envy. My friend was healed, and I was not.

We spent each night in silence, simply went through the motions of setting up our camp, sharing a meal, and falling asleep, without a word passing between us. Abijah must have sensed my need to be alone. He did not press me further. And I? I had allowed bitterness to creep into my heart. I couldn't speak. I was jealous, one more sin to add to the others, and I wondered if I would ever be free.

Thankfully, the caravan leaders were eager to reach Jerusalem. They roused us early and kept us moving past watering holes with few stops to rest. We reached home on the evening of the third day instead of the expected morning of the fourth. Jedediah hobbled out to meet us. Ischa was right behind him. They must have been sitting by the window anxiously watching the road for our return. The old man paused on the path, astounded to see his son skipping along the road toward him. Then he stumbled forward, flung his arms around Abijah, and screamed with joy.

"My son, my son," Jedediah shouted, tears streaming from his eyes. "Thank the Lord Almighty. My son is healed. I no longer must bear the guilt of my sin. Forgive me, Abijah. Forgive me."

"I never faulted you, Father," Abijah assured him. "I was a wayward son, always doing whatever I wanted. My own actions brought me down."

Tears wove down the wrinkles on the old man's face. I stood aside with pleasure as father and son embraced. Jedediah had been carrying the pain of guilt much like my own. Now he was free.

Then the old man did an amazing thing. He let go of Abijah and rushed toward me. He enfolded me in a father's embrace, thanking me over and over for helping his son.

"Jesus healed him," I said in honesty. "I did nothing but get him there. Jesus healed many people on the hill, including Abijah. I witnessed the miracles, myself. And I believed Jesus must be the Messiah. There can be no other answer."

Jedediah nodded, his face aglow. "I also believe, though I have not seen as you did. But I trust your account, Jesse. I know in my heart, the Messiah has come."

As the old man and his wife shuffled into the house, arm-in-arm with their son, I tied their donkeys by the watering trough, turned away, and started for home. I longed to feel only a small part of the joy they must have been experiencing. After all those years, Abijah was healed. He could follow his dream to take over his father's sheep farm. He could live the life he'd been missing, perhaps marry and have children.

By the time I reached my cottage, I had fallen into a terrible pit of despair. It appeared my search for atonement required many more sacrifices, many more trips to the temple. I'd brought Abijah to the Healer, but I was the one who needed healing. I'd been close enough to touch the hem of Jesus' cloak, close enough to plead for his help, but I never asked.

Perhaps Jesus would come to Judea one day. During the next Passover I could look for him. If the opportunity arose I could approach him, fall at His feet, and beg for healing. I needed to keep listening to Hannah's reports. She somehow knew when Jesus was in Judea. I'd pay attention, wait for her to announce his presence. Then I could go and look for him in the marketplace or perhaps find him seated on the temple steps speaking to yet another crowd. If I confessed my sins, perhaps he might have compassion on me. If he truly was the Messiah, as I now believed he was, he might offer mercy and healing. All I had to do was believe, like the others on the hill. Simply believe, they'd said.

The odd thing was, I was punishing myself. Instead of submitting to public stoning, I had condemned myself. I wondered if God's hand could have possibly been heavier than my own.

Now I stood in front of my house, grateful for all the Almighty had given me. The barns, the fenced enclosures, the broad stretch of grazing land, a cottage filled with happy faces. Instead of giving me the chastening I deserved, he'd blessed me beyond anything I could hope or imagine. I'd married the girl I wanted, and we'd had three beautiful children. My quiver was full.

My blessings abounded. Ariel's father had poured much wealth upon us. Young Hilkiah and his wife were about to deliver my first grandchild. My offspring had been healthy, full of energy. They had filled our home with joy these many years. My sheep business had prospered beyond my wildest dreams.

Our house was one of the finer constructions in Beit Sahour. It contained the latest furnishings from the coast. My barns and pens were built of the sturdiest materials. My animals thrived. I was respected in the village, no longer looked upon as a poor, struggling shepherd. I had hired men to do my bidding. I directed them in their work, and I reaped the benefits through my sales. People favored the lambs I brought to the marketplace. The priests knew I bred the purest of sacrifices. I had risen to a favorable position and was no longer ashamed of my occupation. I had acquired everything a man could want. Except peace.

More than 30 years had passed since I witnessed the miracle of the angels. At times I still wondered if it might have been a dream. The message had grown vague. Had the angel said "babe?" Had he said, "Messiah?" Had he directed us to go to Bethlehem, or was it my father's idea? I was 15 at the time, not yet a man, and unable to fully comprehend what was happening.

For years after, I tried to convince myself it was a dream, though the other shepherds claimed to have seen the angels too. How was it possible we all had the same dream? We agreed something had happened on that spring night in the field. But we didn't agree on the details. Angels? My brother Eli insisted they were other shepherds who wanted to get us out of there so they could attach our grazing land for themselves. My brother Bartimaeus, however, had insisted they were angels. Our father also took a firm stand and often recited scriptures in support of the miraculous event.

"The prophet Micah said the Messiah was to come to Bethlehem," he declared. Then he quoted portions from the writings of Isaiah and Zechariah. All of those prophecies pointed to what we experienced in the field that night.

How could I argue with the scriptures? I knew we had experienced something wonderful. I wanted to believe we'd received a message from God. But when I reflected on my frail life, I doubted that such a proclamation should come to a mere shepherd boy. A king maybe. Yes, the Messiah would want to appear to a king. Or one of the nobles of the Holy City. The priests perhaps. The Pharisees who already claimed an intimacy with Yahweh. God's chosen had to come to someone far more worthy than a simple shepherd boy.

I recalled how, from his deathbed my brother Bartimaeus rambled on about that night on the plain. While our mother hovered over him with herbs and poultices, trying to ease his distress, Bartimaeus mumbled about angels and the babe in the manger. I stood nearby, amazed at how someone could recall so many details while he was fighting for his life.

By his final words, Bartimaeus declared what he believed. He knew the Messiah had come. Over the years, he'd spread the word, like so many of the other shepherds who'd been there that night. Eli also had told others about the miracle, though in the telling of it, he glorified himself.

I, on the other hand, merely described that night to my mother and sister, and then to Ariel, but to no one else. I didn't think anyone would listen to a simple shepherd boy. But when our children came along, Ariel insisted I tell each one the story about the night the angels came. It was like reciting a children's tale, over and over again. Ariel stood apart from us with a smile on her lips, encouraging me with her loving gaze.

Here I was, about to enter my home, and I was going to tell my wife and children about another miracle. Abijah was healed. I entered to their exultant cries of welcome. Jemima rushed to my side and flung her arms around my neck. "Abba. You're home."

Ariel drew close to kiss me. Then she asked the question that was on everyone's mind. "How is Abijah?"

While I told the story, she kept nodding and smiling. When I finished she clapped her hands. The rest of the family joined her exaltation. Jemima jumped up and down, clapping and singing, a gentle reminder of the way Sophina behaved when something wonderful happened.

"Hannah wasn't lying," Ariel said. "She claimed the Messiah had come to deliver us, and she was right."

Young Hilkiah came up beside me and rested his hand on my shoulder. His wife, Onah, pressed her hand against her abdomen.

"I will tell your story to my own child," she said. "My children will grow up knowing their grandfather witnessed the Messiah's birth and the healing of a friend."

"You saw a miracle," Jemima proclaimed. "I want to know more about the people who were healed. Were there many, Abba? Tell us everything."

"Yes, my daughter," I said. "There were many miracles on that hillside."

I listed the healings, drawing more gasps and utters of wonder from my family. What harm was it if my children believe in miracles? Abijah was healed. He didn't ride the donkey on our way home. The man walked. No, he *danced* along the road home.

Young Bartimaeus approached me, his face aglow. "Can we go to Galilee, Abba, so I can see the Healer too?"

I shook my head and smiled at his innocence. "Jesus doesn't stay in one place for long. Abijah and I were fortunate to have found him in Galilee. But the people said he moves quickly and sometimes cannot be found."

I gazed at my son's innocent face, a small pout forming on his lips, and my heart melted with love for him.

"Listen, Bartimaeus. We cannot go to Galilee, but I promise, the next time Jesus comes to Jerusalem, we will go and find Him together. Will that be agreeable to you?"

He bobbed his head. The pout was gone. A broad smile lit up his face.

I would soon have to fulfill that promise, for within the year, the Passover celebration was again upon us. Hannah came and delivered the news. The Messiah had come to Jerusalem.

Be thou diligent to know the state of thy flocks; and look well to thy herds.

~Proverbs 27:23

Early in the day, my sons and I readied our lambs for the journey to the temple. Now that Abijah had taken over his father's farm, he'd reignited a challenge that left me striving to get to the Holy City ahead of him. This time, however, there was no animosity between us, only a friendly competition, sometimes resulting in applause over the other one's success.

Hilkiah remained behind with three hired servants to manage our flock, while I took Bartimaeus along to help deliver the lambs. Instead of using the old dray, we wove ropes out of strands of hemp, and we strung the lambs together. Then we started off toward Jerusalem—a father and his young son, leading a line of sheep to be sold in the marketplace or to be offered in sacrifice.

Bartimaeus played his flute along the way, and I began to recite a portion of one of my father's favorite Psalms.

"He who dwells in the secret place of the most high shall abide under the shadow of the Almighty," I sang out. Then raising my voice, "I will say of the Lord, He is my refuge and my fortress: my God; in Him will I trust."

I repeated those verses several times before we reached the Holy City. The strength of that Psalm had me believing that whatever I did and wherever I went the Lord God was looking down on me, guiding me, protecting me. I kept hoping that my next sacrificial offering might free me from the guilt I had carried for most of my life.

Then another teaching of my father's came rushing back to me. "Yahweh wants mercy, not sacrifice," he'd said, and now those words had me wondering if the lambs I was about to offer were enough. By this time in my life, I had sacrificed hundreds of lambs, never to be truly free of my transgressions.

Tucking his flute inside his robe, Bartimaeus grew silent for a while. Then he turned to me. "Is it true what Hannah says about the man named Jesus? Did He come from heaven?"

I gazed at my son. Was he ready for the rest of the story, the part I kept trying to believe was a dream?

"I told you about the babe in the manger, did I not?"

Bartimaeus nodded, his innocent face aglow with interest. "I'd like to see him for myself. Are you certain the Holy One came to earth as a real person?"

"My son, I have no doubt he is a real person. He may have been born into poverty, a babe in a manger, but today he walks the streets and speaks about a better world. And, like Hannah said, he works miracles."

"Tell me again about the times you've seen him, Father."

I nodded as memories flooded into my mind. "Besides that time in Bethlehem, I encountered him three more times," I said. "Once, at the River Jordan while people were being baptized. He also came there to be baptized. Again, when I was leaving Jerusalem, I came upon Jesus and another man—a Pharisee— talking. I chose not to interrupt them, listened for a while, then kept to my own business and walked away. And the third time was in Galilee, when I took Abijah there to be healed."

"Hannah said he comes to Jerusalem for the feasts," Barti- maeus said, his face aglow. "The Passover is upon us, Abba. He must have traveled here. Couldn't we try to find him while we are delivering our lambs?"

I shrugged and gave him a sad shake of my head. "You ask the impossible, my son. It's said he visits friends in Bethany. But he doesn't stay long, sometimes one night, and then he goes off somewhere else. I don't expect to be able to find him."

Bartimaeus wrinkled his brow. "Perhaps you don't *want* to find him, Father. Perhaps you don't believe."

"No, my son. No. No. No. He *is* the Messiah. I am convinced he is the babe I visited in the manger many years ago. And he has great powers beyond anything we have ever seen."

"Then the Almighty sent him?"

I nodded with confidence.

"What else can you tell me about him?"

I released a sigh. "Only that he stirs up the authorities with every visit he makes to the Holy City. Though he draws huge crowds of faithful followers, he angers the chief priests and the Pharisees. It's been said they try to entrap him and end his power over the people. Word is, they have even plotted to kill him."

Bartimaeus grew sullen. Then brightening, he lifted his face and stared at me, his expression thoughtful.

"We should protect him," he said.

"No, my son. We could put ourselves in danger."

"But he works miracles. You said he does."

"It's true, no one else can claim to do the things Jesus has done. I saw Him feed thousands with only a few pieces of fish and bread. He heals lepers and cripples. Even raises the dead. Or so I've heard."

"When did he raise the dead, Father?" Bartimaeus pressed.

I shrugged. "He supposedly visited the tomb of a friend who had died and called him from the grave. The man's name was Lazarus."

"Father, please." Bartimaeus' hopeful smile pricked my heart. "I want to see this man. Couldn't we try to find him?"

I heaved a long sigh. I'd been arguing with myself about what was true and what wasn't. I had seen the miracles with my own eyes, had tasted the bread and fish he provided for thousands, had rejoiced as Abijah walked away healed along with so many others. I couldn't explain why I continued to doubt, except that I had not experienced my own healing. It was easier for me to doubt than to admit that I, myself, had failed.

Now my son was looking up to me, his eyes hopeful, his face aglow with expectation, and I had to concede to the truth.

"I don't know why the Almighty has chosen this time to bring deliverance, but I do believe Jesus is who Hannah said he is. A healer, a miracle worker, Savior of the world, perhaps Almighty God Himself."

I was taken back by my own admission. I knew Jesus was the babe in the manger, now a grown man. He was the right age—about 33 years old. So much time had passed since I followed the angel's call to Bethlehem. Now I was a grown man, too, with a family of my own. And I was again having to admit the truth of what I'd seen so many years ago.

Tears streamed unexpectedly from my eyes. Bartimaeus stared at me, confusion written on his young face. I didn't feel shame. Like my son, I wanted to see Jesus again, this time to plead for the healing of my soul.

We passed through the Sheep Gate, and I whispered a prayer of my own making. "Yahweh, I have strived all these years to earn your forgiveness. Show me what more I can do."

It was our first delivery of the day. We had started out while it was still dark, and we'd reached the Sheep Gate at sunrise and the blowing of the shofar from the temple. We went straight to the Pool of Siloam and cleansed our lambs free of the dust and dirt of the road. I checked each lamb for imperfections, separated the flawed for customers in the marketplace, and reserved the purest for sacrifice. We completed our sales in the market, then started off toward the temple with the lambs following and Bartimaeus nudging them on with a tap of his rod. We located the priests who'd been charged with receiving the sacrificial animals, and we departed with a pouch full of temple coins.

With Pesach upon us and the seven-day Feast of Unleavened

Bread to follow, I expected to make many more trips with lambs for the sacrificial altar. With heavy heart, I imagined the fate that awaited each of my lambs. I had witnessed their births, had assisted with their weaning at the appropriate times. Now I was surrendering them for sacrifice. How could I end this constant sacrificing of lambs? By offering my own life on the altar? Is that what it would take? A human sacrifice for human transgressions?

A *shofar* sounded again from the pinnacle of the Temple, this time signaling the beginning of the sacrifices. I pondered the ritual that had continued over the years—one life after another sacrificed for the sins of man.

As we departed the temple court, a large crowd swarmed around us like a big flowing river sweeping me and my son onto the main road leading out of the city. I was about to break from the crowd and follow the downhill path toward home. But something about the people's shouting and the flinging of their arms drew my interest. Then the revelry ceased, and the people paused on the hill commonly known as Golgotha, *the Place of a Skull.* To the Romans, it was Calvary, a place they reserved for the punishment of criminals who had broken Caesar's laws. Positioned on the main road as it was, the hill was open to the sight of all who entered or left the Holy City.

Two wooden crosses had been raised on the top of the mound. Two men were bound there with ropes tied around their wrists and ankles. They turned their anguished faces on the crowd, but no one offered to relieve their pain.

A third man who'd been beaten beyond recognition lay on the ground on top of a third wooden cross. Unlike the other two, this one was not bound with ropes. Instead, one of the soldiers raised a hammer and pierced the man's wrist with an iron spike. The sharp *ping!* of metal against metal shattered the morning air. With each blow came the splintering of bone and the agonized cry of the one restrained there. The soldier repeated the attack on the man's other wrist and then his feet. Then several soldiers moved in to lift the cross. They deposited it in a hole between the other two. In the end, three crosses stood there together, mere shadows against the stark light of morning.

I turned to look at Bartimaeus, saddened by the horror on his young face. His attention was on the cross in the middle. The man who hung there hardly resembled a human anymore. He had been stripped of his clothes, and his bloodied flesh hung in pieces from the bone. Deep marks left by a whipping encircled his waist. A wreath of sharp brambles dug into his brow, releasing streams of blood into his eyes and down his face to his beard.

Bartimaeus started weeping, and I immediately regretted exposing him to such brutality. I placed a protective arm around him. In the past I'd been able to shelter my children from the Romans' acts of cruelty. But now those barbarians had introduced one of the worst forms of punishment to our people, and the Jewish authorities had given their approval. There was no more sheltering of the truth. My children were growing up in a brutal world, and it was time Bartimaeus also understood this, painful as it was.

According to custom, each cross bore an inscription naming the offense of the man who hung there. The writing on the two outside crosses indicated the men were thieves. But, the inscription on the center cross declared, "Jesus of Nazareth, King of the Jews." Like many notices, it was written in three languages—Greek, Latin, and Hebrew.

I pondered the inscription. *King of the Jews?* He didn't look like a king. There was no purple robe, no scepter in his hand, and his crown did not consist of gold and jewels, but of sharp thorns. *Jesus of Nazareth?* I shifted my attention to the tortured face of the man who hung there. His eyes brought back a host of memories. The babe in the manger had that same penetrating gaze, innocent but bearing a depth of wisdom beyond human ability. The Baptizer then came to mind. He'd referred to Jesus as "The Lamb of God." *Lamb of God?* Like a sacrificial lamb? I recalled one of my father's recitations from the scroll of Isaiah.

He is brought as a lamb to the slaughter, and as a sheep before her shearers is silent, so he did not open his mouth.... For he bore the sin of many, and made intercession for the transgressors."

My father had read that passage to me so many times I could recite it from memory. Now I wondered, had this been Jesus' destiny from the beginning? I stepped closer to the cross. Apart from his torn flesh, the man who hung there could have been the Healer I'd seen on the hill in Galilee. A troubled thought gave me pause. If this was the Healer, why didn't he save himself? I stared at him, confused that anyone purposely submitted his body to such torture.

More verses rushed to me from my father's collection.

All we like sheep have gone astray; we have turned every one to his own way; and the Lord has lain on him the iniquity of us all.

The truth struck me like the soldier's hammer against the nail. *I* was that sheep that had gone astray. *I* had turned to my own way—the sinner who needed a Savior. I struggled with the reality that now swirled inside my head. I recalled the name of the child in the manger. Jesus. *Savior.*

What did the Baptizer call him? *The Lamb of God.*

What did Hannah say? *He works miracles. He heals people. He speaks of a kingdom beyond what we see.*

"It's Him," I acknowledged aloud.

"It's who, Father?" Bartimaeus turned innocent eyes on me, his brow raised with interest.

"It's Jesus, my son, the one I told you about. The babe in the manger. The one who was at the Jordan with the Baptizer. The one who healed Abijah. We've found him."

"That's him? Are you certain?"

"You've heard my stories, Bartimaeus. You've listened to Hannah talk about the miracle worker. Did you think she was lying? Did you think *I* was?"

Bartimaeus shook his head. "No, Father. I believed Hannah was telling the truth. I believed you encountered him those many times. I believe Jesus is the Messiah. But why—?"

I frowned in puzzlement. "Why what?"

"Why did it take you so long to see it too?"

Humbled by my son's profound declaration, I raised my head to look again into Jesus' face. Instantly, I was back in Bethlehem, standing before the manger and the newborn babe. Now he was hanging on a cross, dying. I was with him on the first day of his life, and I was with him on the last.

The truth struck me cold. After sacrificing lamb after lamb, year after year, the reality was, this was the one sacrifice that was able to rescue me from my sins. I was brought to my knees, humbled beyond belief, finally aware of the truth. This man didn't only come to preach and heal. He came to save.

The crowd grew more active, more riotous. Someone challenged Jesus to call down angels to rescue him. Some waved their fists at him and shouted accusations and blasphemies. It struck me that only a few women were grieving for him, but a great multitude displayed hatred.

But Jesus looked down on them with pity. "Father, forgive them, for they know not what they do."

The men hanging on either side of him began to argue. One of them added his own words of condemnation to the curses from the angry crowd. The other spoke in Jesus' defense, saying he had done nothing wrong. Then he pled with him for mercy.

"Remember me when you come into your kingdom," he cried.

"Today you will be with me in Paradise," Jesus promised him.

I couldn't help but compare myself with the thief on the cross. For years I'd carried the burden of my guilt. I'd made hundreds of sacrifices, unblemished lambs paying for my transgressions, including my favorite, Reuben. I'd done one good deed after another, sacrificing my own good pleasure for others, giving until I had nothing left to give. Each time I came away feeling empty, with my sins still weighing heavily upon my soul.

And here this criminal had found mercy with one simple statement. Moving only my lips, I silently repeated the man's heartfelt plea. *"Remember me when you come into your kingdom,"* I whispered.

Did Jesus shift his gaze in my direction? I wasn't sure.

A thick cloud descended, and the hill was plunged into utter darkness. It was the sixth hour, the middle of the day. Bartimaeus started and grabbed my hand. I pulled him close and held onto him. I could no longer see the path down the hill to Beit Sahour. I could only stand still and wait for the darkness to lift.

A terrified hush fell over the crowd. The eerie silence brought with it a fearful anticipation.

With the hill illuminated only by the light of torches people carried, I led Bartimaeus to a separate place where we sat on the grass and waited for the darkness to dispel. Time passed. Shadows continued to move about on the hill, people coming and going, their torches lighting the path before them. The beams swept quickly past, then the darkness swallowed up the hill again.

Jesus' agonized voice pierced the stillness. "My God, my God, why have you forsaken me?"

Someone close by said, "He's calling on Elijah."

I pondered this, but found no reasoning in it. What could Elijah do? The man was dying.

Sometime later, Jesus said, "I thirst."

A soldier brushed past us. A pungent odor rose from the sponge he carried. I recognized the aroma—vinegar mixed with gall, an elixir Ariel's father once sent to ease the stomach pains my brother Bartimaeus suffered. The soldier offered it to Jesus. He tasted it and refused the rest.

My son lay back against the grass, and before long he had fallen asleep. Time passed. My own eyelids started to droop, my head bowed toward slumber. I shook myself awake, determined to keep an eye on the man on the cross as more shadows passed between us.

Then, at the ninth hour, the darkness lifted. I shook my son awake. Then I rose to my feet, and, taking Bartimaeus by the hand, I helped him up and stepped closer to the cross. My heart pounding, I stood before the cross of Jesus, and I believed I was looking at my final sacrifice, the only one that truly mattered.

"Thank you," I mumbled, my heart surging with overwhelming warmth.

Jesus lifted his face toward heaven and uttered, "It is finished."

Finished? What was finished? His life? His mission? What?

Then, He made one last statement. "Into your hands, I commit my spirit." And Jesus bowed his head and breathed his last.

At that moment, the ground began to shake. I held tight to Bartimaeus. Men shouted curses. A woman screamed. Rocks tumbled from the hill. The trembling of the ground lasted for several minutes. Then it stopped as suddenly as it had started.

A soldier, clothed in all the regalia of a servant of Rome, stepped up beside me, his face aglow as he viewed the body of Jesus now slumped in death. "Surely this man was the Son of God," he said, speaking the same words I believed in my heart.

Though daylight had resumed, the sun was drifting toward the western horizon. The Sabbath hour was drawing near.

A soldier swung a hammer at the legs of the two men on the outside crosses. The sound of shattering bone broke the silence. The blow prevented them from holding themselves erect. They died gasping for air.

A soldier approached the cross in the center and was about to swing his hammer at Jesus' legs when one of his companions grabbed his arm. "This man is already dead." To prove it, he plunged a spear into Jesus' side, releasing a flow of blood mixed with water. Bartimaeus shuddered and buried his face in my cloak.

Suddenly, the crowd became more active. Priests swarmed onto the rise, demanding the Sabbath be observed. I shook my head in wonder that the Romans agreed to honor our Jewish law and hurriedly took the deceased off the crosses.

Mourners flooded onto the hillside. They rushed toward the crosses and claimed the bodies of the men who had died there. Three women fell to the ground near Jesus' broken body.

Then two Pharisees broke through the crowd and approached the body of Jesus. People stepped back and allowed the two figures to pass. One of them carried jars that sent off an aroma of spices. I recognized him as the one I had seen at the city wall speaking with Jesus. The other spoke with authority to the soldiers and claimed he had received permission from Pilate to receive the body of Jesus. The two Pharisees were out of place there in the midst of soldiers, railers, and mourners. Beneath their royal robes, their striped shawls and well-trimmed beards were two humble men, grief-stricken over the one who had died there.

Bartimaeus shook my arm. "The Sabbath," he reminded me. Our day of rest was about to begin. We needed to hurry home.

Acknowledging his plea, I turned my back on the activity on the hill and started down the path toward Beit Sahour. Even as my feet moved closer to home, my mind and my heart remained on Golgotha and the broken body of the Messiah. Then the prophet's words revived as clearly as the day my father last read them to me.

Surely he took up our infirmities and carried our sorrows.... He was pierced for our transgressions, he was crushed for our iniquities; the punishment that brought us peace was upon him, and by his wounds we are healed.

By his wounds we are healed, I repeated. Then I rethought it. "By his wounds *I* am healed," I acknowledged aloud.

I picked up my step, eager to get home and share my newfound understanding with Ariel and my children. This time, I didn't expect to hide the truth of what I'd seen, as I did more than 30 years ago after visiting the manger. I wanted to do as the other shepherds had done, spread the news that salvation had come to Israel. I wanted to profess my faith to everyone I met, starting with those who lived in my own household, then to my brother, Eli. After that, I could tell anyone who would listen, maybe cross the Great Sea and talk to Andrew and Sophina and Jahzeel. A fire had been kindled within my heart, and I did not want to extinguish it. Not this time.

Chapter Twenty-Nine

*And if his offering be of the flocks, namely, of the sheep,
or of the goats, for a burnt sacrifice; he shall bring it a male
without blemish.*

~Leviticus 1:10

That evening, as the family gathered around me, I held them captive with the account of what I had witnessed on Golgotha. Ariel was thrilled that I had found the man Jesus, but she was saddened by what had happened to him. She asked the same question people had shouted at the foot of the cross, the same question that discomfited me.

"If He really was the healer, why did He not heal himself?"

Though I couldn't have answered that question before my revelation, I knew what to say now.

"It was the Almighty's plan," I told her. "He sent His only Son to earth to rescue us from our sins. The Messiah came here with the intention of dying. He became our last sacrifice, the only one we need."

Ariel raised a finger to her lips and thought about what I had said, and then she gave a nod of understanding.

"All these years, we have been waiting for the Messiah to come as a deliverer, a warrior who could rescue us from the oppression of the Romans," she mused. "But the Almighty had a different plan. Like your father said, Yahweh's ways are not man's ways."

I nodded in agreement. "We will never fully under-stand," I admitted. "But we can find comfort in the promise of everlasting life."

I slept better that night than I had in a very long time. The next morning I arose with the cock's crow, my heart beating with excitement. I grabbed my cloak and ran to Eli's property, passed the large home he had built for his family, and went directly to the cottage where I'd grown up. The servants who now resided there opened the door to my anxious knocking.

"I came to see my brother," I said. "Will you summon him?"

"He's in the big house," said the man. "Why don't you go there?"

"I have business here." I nodded toward the interior of their home.

The man's wife stood beside him. She shouted for their youngest child, a boy of about seven, to run for Eli. Then she gathered her two other children into the kitchen where they huddled together, their round eyes on me.

I entered cautiously. The man didn't raise a hand to stop me. I went to sit on the bench by the wall, the place where my father spent much of his time in his waning years.

A simmering pot sent a tantalizing aroma into the air and took me back to my youth when Mother stood by the hearth tending her vegetable stew. The entire room erupted with visions from my past. My brothers and myself seated around the low table, taunting each other. My sister, Sophina, assisting Mother with the serving. And Father, reclining on his favorite cushion, in his hands a weathered scroll spread open to the place where he was about to read.

I set my attention on the water jars standing in a row, like three soldiers, beside the hearth. A fourth jar stood off by itself, a long crack running down its side. This one held no water. It was the one where my father had stored his precious scrolls.

I rose from the bench, walked over to that lonely jar, and ran my hand along the crack. It scraped my skin, but not enough to draw blood, and the feel of it evoked another memory, this one of my father reciting the words of the prophet Isaiah.

I leaned over the rim of the jar and peered at its contents. There they were, a dozen or more ragged parchments, standing on end and obviously unread for many years. They were covered with dust.

A rustle from outside got me turning to see my brother Eli entering the doorway. Upon seeing me, he narrowed his eyes.

"Why did you come here?" he said, his voice gruff. "Why did you not come to my house?"

I took a breath and fully faced him. "I'd like to take some of Father's scrolls," I said, aware of the tremor in my voice.

He shook his head emphatically. "You can't have them, Jesse. They're mine."

"They belong to all of us."

He stepped closer to me. "I took care of Father. He left everything to me. The farm. This house and everything in it, including the scrolls."

I straightened my shoulders. "He was my father too."

"You left. I stayed," he snorted. "You and Andrew. Two ungrateful sons who left their father's care to me. You can't have the scrolls, Jesse. Go and purchase your own."

"Father didn't purchase these scrolls," I reminded him. "He got them from the rabbi when they rebuilt the synagogue." I tried to calm myself. "Listen, Eli. It appears you have not read the scrolls. They've been sleeping inside that jar, collecting dust. It's obvious you've had no interest in them. Allow me to borrow some for a time. I want to read them to my children and my grandchildren. I want to listen to what the prophets said about the coming Messiah. Father found comfort in those scrolls. I want to do the same."

Eli curled his upper lip and glared at me. "You walked away years ago. Now, suddenly, you want the scrolls?" He stomped his foot. "I will defend my ownership of Father's scrolls—to the death, if necessary."

Eli's servants huddled together with their children in a corner of the kitchen. The discord between us had created an uneasy tension in that little cottage.

I lowered my voice and spread my arms in supplication. "Eli, you're my brother. While growing up we spent much time together in the upper room. We shared secrets, laughed together. worked together, tended our father's sheep, and built up this farm you now own—with my blessing. Don't let a few parchments come between us. I only want to take two or three and I will leave the rest in your care. Then, sometime in the future, I will bring them back and take two more. What do you say?"

The frown on Eli's brow began to relax. I waited. If I pushed my brother too hard, he'd want to fight back. Eli had never had any interest in those scrolls. But, because *I* wanted them, *he* wanted them. It was brother-against-brother. He obviously resented me for leaving home and taking my share of the sheep. Apparently, Eli thought I had treated him unfairly, leaving him to care for our parents and the remaining animals in our father's flock. But, as I could remind him, he'd benefited a great deal from the exchange, for he was the sole owner of everything. Including the scrolls.

He backed away from me, paced to the window and back. He appeared to be deep in thought. I kept silent. He had said he would fight me to the death for those scrolls. I hoped he might remember we were blood brothers.

"Jesse," he said at last. "I have never understood you. After going to the manger in Bethlehem and witnessing the miracle of the angels, I went on with my life with confidence, but you acted like a scared rabbit, afraid of your own shadow."

"What are you saying, Eli?"

"The Messiah had come. We were chosen to witness his birth. Do you know what that means? It means we can do no wrong. We can go on with our lives and never have to suffer the consequences for our mistakes."

I recoiled in shock. Was that what my brother had

understood from that night in Bethlehem? Did Eli think the call to the manger meant the Almighty was allowing him to live his life as he pleased? No regrets? No rules? No guilt? That would explain his lack of remorse for killing Jedediah's rams. My brother thought he had the right to carry out vengeance. After all, he was chosen by Yahweh.

"Eli, you're wrong," I said shaking my head at him. "The Messiah didn't come here to tell us we could sin and not face judgment. You came away thinking you could do anything you wanted, without punishment. But I believed we'd been given a greater responsibility. You believed our sin against Jedediah was just. I bore the guilt of it."

Lines of anger reappeared on his forehead. His nostrils flared and his eyes flamed with rage. "My actions were righteous, Jesse. Jedediah and his son deserved what we did."

I nearly crumbled to the floor. My brother was no different from the Pharisees who passed unfair judgment at will. He'd done it with Jedediah and Abijah. And now he was passing judgment on me. Somehow, I had to wake him up to the truth.

"When I left our home, I took nothing but my clothes and the cut of sheep Father had allowed me. You received everything our father owned. I never wished you harm, Eli, never thought ill of you. Now I ask one favor of you, to let me borrow a few scrolls."

A stark silence fell between us. A shuffling of nervousness came from the corner. Eli's servant and his wife appeared stunned by the discourse that was passing between us. Two brothers at war. Unheard of. But there we were, feuding over some worn, old parchments.

I was about to turn away and leave when Eli grabbed my arm.

"You refused to go with me to the Tigris Valley. You've been avoiding me for years. Now you ask a favor of me. What am I supposed to do? Bow to your demands? Become your slave?"

I shook my head with sadness. "We're two different people, Eli. I love you as a brother, but I don't understand you as a person."

He released a sigh. "Take what you want," he said, his

face hard as stone. "Take whatever you desire, and return them when you will."

I studied him for a moment. His voice said one thing but his manner said another.

I hesitated for only a moment. Then I walked to the water jar and removed three scrolls.

"Thank you, Eli," I said. "I promise, I'll return them soon and exchange them for a few more." Then, cradling the delicate scrolls in my arms, I took to the street.

I flew home, eager to put distance between myself and the cottage. I burst through the door of my house, and scattered the scrolls across the table. Ariel set aside her spindle, left her stool, and stepped up beside me. She stared at the scrolls, then lovingly ran her fingers over them.

"These belonged to your father, didn't they?" She looked at me expectantly.

"Yes, Ariel. They contain the scriptures my father used to recite to us. Their words carry promises about the Messiah. I want to restore them to my memory. I want our children and grandchildren to hear them too."

Jemima looked at me, wide-eyed, from her stool in the corner. She smiled like she understood and approved.

Onah had been tending a pot on the hearth. She hung the ladle on a hook and turned away from her labor.

"Father Jesse," she said, her eyes lighting with eagerness. "I want you to read the words of the prophets to my child when he or she is born, the way your father did for you. I want my children to grow up knowing Yahweh and living according to His commandments."

At that moment, Hilkiah and Bartimaeus burst in from the field, breathless. They must have seen me running home with the scrolls in my arms. They rushed over to the table, their eyes wide.

Hilkiah lifted one of the scrolls, tilted his head, and grinned at me. "Your selfish brother allowed you to take them? I can't believe it."

I nodded. "He resisted at first, but then he agreed. My brother is not such a horrible person. Somewhere inside lies the man my father wanted him to become. One day, I hope to help him understand the truth. But how can I tell a proud man he has sinned against Almighty God? How can I tell him he needs a Savior?

I turned to Ariel. "Eli was right about one thing. The Messiah appeared to us for a reason. We were chosen—along with the other shepherds—not because we were special. We were chosen for a purpose. It's time we lived up to that calling."

Ariel's quiet nod was all the encouragement I needed. I lifted one of the scrolls, and, taking care to protect its brittle edges, I unfurled it and selected a verse.

"He was wounded for our transgressions, He was bruised for our iniquities: the chastisement of our peace was upon Him; and with His stripes we are healed."

Why hadn't I seen it before? I'd grown up learning the scriptures in the local synagogue. I had a father who taught me daily from the word of God. They were not vain repetitions. They carried a message straight from the mouth of God. The truth finally came to me that afternoon on Golgotha. The Messiah truly *had* come to earth, not to rescue us from the Romans, but to rescue us from ourselves, from the enticements of the world, and from the pit of hell itself. Now it was up to me to pass the good news to others, starting with my children and my brother.

I rolled up the parchment, content that I was able to read them to my children and—and, glancing at Onah's round belly—to my grandchildren. Gathering up the scrolls, I carried them to an old empty water jar, much like the one my father had used to house them. In the coming days, I planned to remove one of the scrolls and read more passages to my family. I wanted to challenge them to think about ways those messages can help them to live a better life. And the truth was, as my children learned, so also would I.

"There's something else," I said directly to my sons. "No longer will we raise sheep for sacrifice."

Bartimaeus grinned with interest. "We won't be shepherds anymore?"

I laughed. "Yes, my son. We will still be shepherds. But we will raise our animals only for food and clothing and precious oils." I lowered my gaze at him. "Do you recall what we witnessed on Golgotha yesterday? The man on the cross in the center?"

He blinked his eyes and his innocent smile returned. "You said He was the Messiah."

"That's right," I said. "Instead of a lamb on the altar, the Messiah offered Himself as a sacrifice. That means, no more sacrifices are necessary. His is the last and only sacrifice we need."

How I wished I had understood that truth before I sacrificed my dear Reuben. My sins and my guilt had been washed away by the blood of Jesus. I wanted to carry the message of good news I first learned from the angels. The message that made complete sense to me now.

✝✝✝

Three days later, Hannah the Hawker came to our door all in a flurry over some new report. Instead of Ariel opening the door to her, I was the one who welcomed the old woman into our house. I was the one who helped her into my chair at the head of the table. I was the one who scooped a portion of stew into a bowl and set it before her.

Ariel stood nearby, her eyes wide. Her gaping mouth then eased into a broad smile, and she gazed at me with such admiration, I thought I might faint. Smiling with satisfaction, I sat beside Hannah and turned a willing ear in her direction. Ariel joined us on Hannah's other side.

"The most amazing thing," the wrinkled old woman said, and she paused to lift the bowl to her lips. I held my breath and leaned expectantly toward her.

"The Messiah has risen from the grave," Hannah sang out, drippings of beans and gravy running down her chin.

I sat back in astonishment.

She laughed at me. "That's right. The man Jesus, the Healer, the Messiah, has defied death. His tomb is empty. Once again, he walks among us, alive and well."

Ariel leaned close to the old woman and placed a hand on her arm. "You've seen Him?"

Hannah shook her head. "I regret I have not. But others have seen Him and are spreading the word that He lives. The authorities, of course, have denied the truth. But the tomb lies open, and no one is inside."

The house had grown so quiet, I could hear the ewes bleating in the field a great distance away. Another verse from the prophet Isaiah came to mind, one that my father had me memorize as a young boy. Now it had meaning like never before.

"All we like sheep have gone astray; we have turned every one to his own way; and the Lord hath lain on him the iniquity of us all."

All my life I'd been on a journey of sorts. From the manger to the cross—from Bethlehem to Jerusalem—a Sabbath day's journey for some, but it had taken me 33 years to make it.

At last, I was able to trust in the only one who could remove my sins, the only one who could free me from the burden of guilt I'd been carrying for most of my life. I'd witnessed the arrival of the Messiah as a baby and I'd witnessed his death on the cross. Now Hannah had mentioned the empty tomb. I pondered this for a moment. My heart nearly burst with joy. I turned to the old woman and smiled. She smiled back at me.

"The empty tomb," I said, my heart in my throat. "Was that the end?"

"No, not the end," said Hannah. "The beginning."

Worthy is the Lamb that was slain to receive power, and riches, and wisdom, and strength, and honor, and glory, and blessing.

~Revelation 5:12

No book comes together without the help of readers, editors, family, and friends. I thank my Beta Readers, Pastor Wayne King and my daughter Joanna Jones, for their comments and critiques, making the text so much better.

Much appreciation for *Back to the Bible* speaker, Woodrow Kroll, who one Christmas mentioned he would like it if someone would write a story about a shepherd who visits the manger and later visits the cross. That comment became the seed for *The Shepherd's Walk, from the manger to the cross and beyond.*

I also want to acknowledge W. Phillip Keller, author of *A Shepherd Looks at the 23rd Psalm,* a wonderful book filled with insights from his experiences as a shepherd. Keller's book was invaluable in my research.

Also helpful was my visit to Fairmeadow Sheep Farm, where owner, Carol Postley, and farm manager, Cherokee Vadala, gave me a hands-on experience with those gentle, wooly creatures, and clued me in on the ins and outs of sheep farming, now and back in biblical times.

Many thanks to WordCrafts Press editor, Mike Parker, whose patience and experience play a huge role in the crafting of my books. I am so grateful he took a chance on me, and I consider him a dear friend as well.

And, of course, the highest honors go to my Lord and Savior Jesus Christ, the Great Shepherd, and the one who inspires me daily to keep on writing.

APulitzer Prize nominee in the field of journalism and an award-winning novelist, Marian Rizzo earned a bachelor's degree in Bible education, trained for jungle missions with New Tribes (now Ethnos 360) and served at a Youth With A Mission training center in Southern Spain. She also was a field and telephone counselor for the Billy Graham Organization.

A personal tour of the Holy Land provided much of the backdrop for Marian's biblical era novels, along with virtual tours, study books, and online research. Marian lives in Ocala, Florida, with two daughters, three grandchildren, and a dog named Buddy.